2021 Sci-Fi Anthology

Short Stories by Selected Authors

Editors

EJ Runyon

Katherine Kirk

Published by Science Fiction Novelists 2021

Group Administrators

Bob Goddard, Jennefer Rogers, Steven Gibson, Marc Neuffer

Introduction

How this book came to be

The internet is both a wonderful and, at times, horrible place. A thing evokes the full spectrum of human emotion.

However, we all know of a few places in this digital world that bring out the positive points in being human without vitriol and hyperbole. For us, that place is Science Fiction Novelists Facebook group, where science fiction writers congregate, challenge, share, and compare. A place where no one cares whether Star Wars is better than Star Trek. Movies are not our thing; writing, imagining, and hope for mankind are—though a few of us may have destroyed the universe a few times.

As the group's administrators, we challenged our members to submit short stories for this anthology. It is our first, and hopefully not the last.

Significant credit goes to our two professional editors, EJ Runyon and Katherine Kirk, also group members. They provided their services without pay. They brought polish and shine to this volume, working with each author to bring all the stories to full flower without trampling on the writer's style.

We hope you enjoy reading these stories.

Bob, Jennefer, Steven, & Marc
Science Fiction Novelists Facebook Group

Science Fiction Novelists

Contents

Science Fiction Novelists

About the Editors

EJ Runyon

EJ's writing guides are *Tell Me (How to Write) a Story*, from Inspired Quill out of the UK, and *5 Ways of Thinking To Change Your Writing World Around* from Protected Books, in California.

She also has four well-regarded novels out from small Indy presses. She's run the *Bridge to Story* website since 2010, where she coaches live, via Skype, and story edits novices and published authors. Her life's goal is sharpening your stories into something deeper, to give your readers satisfying storytelling. Being notoriously *lysdexic*, EJ never offers to proofread or line edit.

You can find her on social media, or at her website, which offers 52 free writing lessons: www.bridgetostory.com.

Katherine Kirk

Katherine Kirk offers developmental editing, manuscript evaluations, copy-editing, and proofreading for most fiction genres, and has a passion for science fiction and fantasy. She has lived in five countries and speaks five languages. Before pursuing her dream as an editor, she taught English to children in South Korea, China, and Ecuador, where she currently lives halfway up a volcano. You can find her on social media, or writing helpful blogs on her website, www.geckoedit.com.

Science Fiction Novelists

Future's Fate
S. A. Gibson

About the author

S. A. Gibson has published more than ten books and several short stories, many co-written. Most stories are set in a future which has lost its advanced technology because of a catastrophic viral pandemic that has led to the Collapse of modern civilization. Gibson uses his Ph.D. in Education to blend technological and historical research with creative ideas. Find more of his books on Amazon at www.amazon.com/S-A-Gibson/e/B00O0HQ6E8

* * *

"Now *that's* a vault door!" I said. "This must be what bank robbers felt like, before the Collapse." My nose filled with the acrid dust in this dry cave. Nothing but wild animals in here for years. My mind flashed back to sitting in my classroom when they had called me away, by messenger.

We didn't talk about the armed group coming for the same prize we were after. Librarian Stanley'd only hit on finding new technology that no one had seen in decades. And the unspoken, this *offer*, was no request. *Tomas*, I warned myself then, *you should've stayed under the Librarian's radar*. To coin a phrase. Though, who but the librarians even knew what *radar* meant?

Alfonsa ran her hand over the smooth metal of the round, almost ceiling-to-floor door. Maybe four meters around. I felt glad Librarian Stanley had sent a scout to protect me. But I'd sooner be happy with a few more. Only us two. And me useless in any battle. My elementary school playground was the last fight I had been involved in.

1

But back to this vault: no hinges visible. Stanley had spoken of them being embedded inside the wall.

"Rolled inconel alloy." Alfonsa leaned toward it and sniffed. "Greater tensile strength than carbon steel. No one makes doors this strong these days. I've been told," she slapped the door, hard, "the old United States military put this here ninety years ago." It dawned on me this might have been why Stanley had chosen her. How many scouts knew anything about metal strength? Though, she could probably ask, how many archaeologists have studied computers?

My eyes fell to the sword strapped to Alfonsa's back. Never unsheathed over the two days we'd spent getting here so far.

"Have you had to kill anyone?" Not a question anyone would ordinarily ask of a scout. But this seemed like the one appropriate time.

She examined me. I'd noticed her doing that from time to time. Maybe wondering if my life was worth defending.

"Well. . ." Her lips quirked. "I've been lucky. Mostly."

Not exactly an answer. "Lucky?"

Waving her hand over her vest, she said, "When people know you're a library scout, you hardly ever have to fight."

A non-fighting fighter. And my life was in her hands.

"That must be convenient." After inspecting the door, I removed a metal cover at the massive structure's center. "Ah. Here are the three dials I expected."

"You can get in?"

Pulling a sheet of parchment from my pack, I held it up triumphantly. "Thanks to Librarian Stanley, I have the combination."

I carefully turned the dials. In moments, a satisfying *click* greeted us. I'd set the three numbers correctly!

"I'm still worried about the East Shore gang coming for this." It may have sounded like small talk, but I meant it.

Sure, this seemed like a splendid adventure. Getting to see ancient technology. My classmates would probably give almost anything to be in my shoes. But I wanted to live to tell the tale. Yet, you don't refuse offers from the library. When they speak, even national governments listen. Being a lowly archaeology graduate student meant I'd no choice at all.

We continued the small talk as I searched my pack.

Alfonsa touched the hilt of her sword. "Once, I arrested ten tough guys. They surrendered on a dock in San Francisco. Let me lead them to jail." That smile again. "I never had to unsheathe Justice."

"That's the sword's name?" *Ah, found it.*

This time, she did withdraw it from its sheath. Magnificent weapon. The flickering oil lamps we'd brought cast sparkling glints off its naked steel. "It reminds me to wield it for justice, in my work."

Kneeling down on the far left side of the doorway, I found the slot. Inserting the crank handle, I explained, "This door weighs more than a ton. Did you read about it? All mechanical." I fell into lecture mode. "When the pre-Collapse army put it here, they expected it would remain closed long after electrical tools were lost. So that leaves human power to open it."

Putting my words to action, I starting turning. The gears moved smoothly, and the door yawed open like it had shut just yesterday. Slow and steady as I worked the crank. Not a hint of friction.

"Wow! *Stale* air." She pulled her head back. A bright light flickered into the cave from the vault.

"Electricity!" That surprised me. "The papers said there might be some form of power remaining. I hardly believed it. Ninety years!"

"What exactly are we looking for?" she asked. "A weapon?"

"The papers aren't exactly clear." I felt embarrassed not knowing how to answer. "Some kind of energy weapon. Something that kills at a distance." I guessed the librarians would rather we didn't know all the particulars. Except to destroy it.

"That's why Librarian Stanley wants it neutralized?" We stared at each other.

With the vault open, I worried even more whether Alfonsa would be able to protect me. "How long have you wielded Justice?"

Again that mysterious smile. "I'm a newbie compared to some scouts. I've only been an enforcer to the Librarian for ten years." I guess it was a good sign that talk of fighting amused her. She looked no older than her thirties to me. I moved into the vault.

Alfonsa set her oil lantern down and followed, chatting. "I know some scouts who've practiced their craft their entire lives. Since childhood."

Even though the room was small, my eyes were overwhelmed. Bright lights flooding down from the ceiling. Machinery lining every wall. And in the center, this large pointy monster sat, like a catapult or leaning tower stretching to the top of the room.

"How did they get that in here?" I wondered aloud. "Must have assembled it afterward."

"Is it alive?"

I moved closer. Light panels on the device glowed.

"It sure looks that way, doesn't it? Somehow our coming in here activated something." The scent of decades-old dust being fried to ozone filled the room.

"But you can render it unusable?" *Unusable*, the very word Librarian Stanley had used with me. When his messenger brought me to him, I knew I wouldn't have any meaningful choices. Sure enough, he offered me the "choice" to come on this mission. The offer rendered my future constrained.

"Uh, probably." I felt a little out of my depth. Alfonsa stood next to what I could only describe as an enormous tube, one hand resting on its metal surface as if it was her favorite pony.

I'd studied ancient machines but nothing like this.

"Why don't we just seal this vault back up? Not likely anybody could get through that door. I'm the only one with the crank. It would take them months without it, as thick and strong as this metal is."

She nodded thoughtfully. "That might be the way to go." After a pause, she added, "If we go, leave that combination inside."

"Ah! Right. If we're captured." I was beginning to not like the way Alfonsa's mind worked.

She jabbed a finger at the control panel. "Think you can take that apart?"

I'd already looked for a manual to explain the machinery. Finding nothing, the next option was bringing up a terminal. The keys felt a bit gritty to the touch. Dust. But the computer seemed responsive.

We'd only had one year of using computers like these. I'd resented the Librarian for stopping our studies. *Now I'm going to die because of the librarians.* And this scout didn't seem to be much for *fighting*.

"I'm looking for the controls." I waved her to the other terminal. "You try logging into that terminal, there."

She stepped up to it, but said, "It asks for login information."

My fingers felt around for something. *Yes!* I held up a card, yellowed with age.

"Here." Luckily someone had left the password lying under its keyboard. Alfonsa did a nice quick job typing-two fingered on its keyboard. "You've used computers before?"

She spared me a glance, with her fingers skimming the monitor's rim, the most tactile fighter I've ever come across. "No. But I've used a typewriter in the San Francisco Library."

The university only had two working typewriters that I knew of. With custom-made ink ribbons and paper.

I announced, "I'm going to issue instructions to activate this thing. You need to mirror my keystrokes." That got a reaction from her. She looked doubtful. "That way I'll be able to test if I've deactivated it, if I first see how it operates when it's working." I noticed dark-lensed goggles hanging on the side of each desk. This thing must create a blinding light.

Giving a slow nod, Alfonsa poised her hands over her keyboard.

∗ ∗ ∗

"Long Range Tactical High Chemical Energy Laser," I read aloud for Alfonsa's benefit.

"You understand it?" the scout asked.

"I've studied these. Written papers, even. This device . . . It's capable, it—" I swallowed and started again. "It'll send out a concentrated pulse of light and chemicals which can burn through anything. That rock above us. And more." After thinking a moment, I added, "Firing it should destroy this room and the weapon."

Alfonsa turned from her keyboard, glancing at the vault door.

"Hear something?" In my concentration, I'd missed it.

She moved to the doorway. "Keep working. Figure out what to do to disable that thing." With a wave to the upward pointing tube, she stalked out to the cave beyond.

I issued a query for the room's power supply.

12 HOURS OF ELECTRICITY REMAINING

Examining the weapon itself, I began thinking I could possibly tackle this puzzle by taking the right part out. Remove it, and the rest would be inoperable. It reminded me of a class assignment where we were told to imagine being in an atomic reactor. We had to argue how we'd shut it down without access to the control panel. That exercise served me well now. I walked through possible moves in my mind: removing the expansion nozzles, then smashing them with a hammer. Or the hilt of a blade, even. I could also cut all the control lines from the computer to the weapon. I felt troubled, though.

I heard my professor in my head. "What will happen next?"

I could imagine any damage I could do being repaired, if we were found and overwhelmed in time.

No, I needed to disable this device for good.

* * *

I could hear noise in the outer hall. Alfonsa returned, carrying the remaining lamp. Justice out, in her grip, dripping blood!

"I can't stop them all. If this wave is any indication, there'll be others coming with many more to deal with." She frowned. "We've got to close this up."

I thought of what that would mean with us inside, while I worked. No air circulation. We wouldn't last long. I shook my head.

"There's another way."

Her eyes bored into me.

"The weapon. We fire it. That'll bring the cave down on us all." The room reeked of the ozone scent I'd noticed earlier. I pointed to the drain on the floor. Several empty canisters lay next to it. I'd been busy.

"Only one shot left. Once that's done, no one here can recharge it."

"How long?"

"Five minutes."

She patted the big tube. "Do it, Tomas." A pause. A smile. "Thank you. I'll slow them down." Before leaving, she squeezed my arm. "You will have time."

∗ ∗ ∗

The shouting and metal clashing outside were inescapable, but I stayed focused on my job. I channeled all the teachers who'd pushed me to do the work right. Too bad my fellow students and teachers would never know what I'd done today.

Alfonsa ran back in. "Ready?" A red gash ran down her arm, and small nicks marred her library vest.

"Yes!" I handed her a pair of goggles. Donning my own, I pointed to the other terminal while giving the command. "Press enter, as I do mine!"

Alfonsa stroked the lenses before she placed them over her eyes. *Goodbye school, goodbye friends.* The second we hit our keys, we felt the flash.

Science Fiction Novelists

Duck Not a Frog
By Claudia Blood

About the author
Claudia Blood's early introduction to Dungeons and Dragons, combined with her training as a scientist and a side-trip into IT, set her up to become an award-winning author of science fiction and fantasy.

From her next release, *Company Assassin*:
It's Duff Roman's eighteenth birthday, but no one is lighting candles. Turning eighteen in the orphanage on Kalecca means starvation for those who aren't hired into a Family. Outside the Family compounds lies the jungle. And in the jungle lies death. But a company assassin has plans to lay waste not only to Duff's future but to the orphanage as well. Find out more at www.ClaudiaBlood.com

* * *

Fine ash fluttered down from the burned rafters above Dr Collins. He could see little wisps of clouds and pale blue sky if he looked past the skeletal remains of the house that had once been his. His head rested against the machine that he'd built. It sat next to where his son's crib had been in the nursery.

He clutched a simple child's toy: a yellow painted duck with a piece of twine to pull it. The wheels hooked in quite cleverly to make the head move up and down when it was pulled along the ground.

He remembered buying the duck. He'd been walking home through the square. Late as usual, but a swirl of childish colors on a cart had caught his eye. When he moved closer, he saw the cart's sides had slots filled with brightly colored toys. The front of the cart had a ledge with a frayed white cloth draped over it. A bright green frog drew him. Even though his own son, waiting for him at home, was far too young for it, he wanted the frog to hang in his room.

He stepped closer, but before he could touch the frog, an old lady dressed in a strange collection of rags and silk even more colorful than her cart, stepped next to him. A beautifully embroidered eye patch covered her right eye. The doctor noticed how its stitched flower petals matched her other eye.

"Interested in anything?" she croaked.

"Yes." Dr Collins pointed. "That frog."

She looked at him for a long time, with an expression of pity that left him feeling odd. He was a brilliant doctor of mechanical things. What cause did she have to look at him with pity?

"I think you will find that the duck will suit you better."

"The duck?" Dr Collins scoffed, feeling defensive. "The frog is much more the thing."

"Let me show you the duck." She carefully pulled it from its slot on the cart.

"Look here—" Dr Collins said.

"I know. You think you want the frog," she said as she set the duck on the white cloth.

"Yes," Collins said. He did want the frog. Ponds and frogs were very popular now in nurseries.

"At least watch the duck before you purchase the frog." She sounded nervous.

He knew what he wanted and he wanted the frog. But what was the harm in allowing her to show him the duck?

"Oh, very well." She couldn't trick him into buying both, so what was the harm?

She put the duck on the ledge and pulled the string. The duck's head pumped up and down. He gasped in surprise. How had the mechanism been made so small as to fit inside the duck?

Dr Collins was mesmerized. "What does the frog do?"

"The frog does nothing." She pulled out the frog and sat it next to the duck.

"Nothing?" Dr Collins frowned.

"Most do nothing." Something about the way she said it and the look in her eyes made him shiver. "The frog is like most."

He frowned. Did she really mean to imply that most people did nothing? They just sat there like this frog?

She must have read that disbelief on his face because she said, "You know this as well as I do. Most do nothing at all. No matter what they might say."

The shiver turned into a chill. He wanted to take a step back, but he still wanted the frog and now also the duck. "Well then, perhaps I should take both."

She laughed softly and shook her head. Bells sounded softly with her movement. "My cart is like life. You can only be one or the other."

"One?" Dr Collins frowned. Perhaps this was some elaborate joke by one of his colleagues. He looked around. "What merchant would not want to sell two over one?"

She shrugged and looked away. "Which will you choose to be?"

The feeling that this one choice would make a difference in the life he might lead set his heart racing. Dr Collins rocked back on his heels. This choice was more important than asking the woman he loved to marry him. More important than which firm he worked with. This choice would change everything. Did

13

he want to be someone who just sat there? Or did he, with clever mechanisms, want to be someone who took action?

"I'll take the duck."

He held the duck under one arm and walked toward home. The fire bell clanged in the distance. The sharp taint of smoke drifted in the breeze. As he neared his home, the doctor saw billowing black clouds that looked to be coming from a few blocks farther.

His stomach twisted. His home was a few blocks farther. He ran.

On his block, he skidded to a stop. The whole block was on fire. His home had been in the middle of the block.

He didn't remember sitting across from his house. But he was sitting, with the duck in his hand, staring at his home's blackened remains, when the hysterical nanny found him.

"I couldn't find him," she sobbed, throwing her arms around herself and collapsing next to him.

More people gathered, crying and wringing their hands, but none of them really did anything. He was doing nothing. He couldn't go into the blaze to help. But he had to do something for his son. Perhaps, he had to do something only he was able to do. If the nanny couldn't find him, perhaps his son hadn't been in the house. He stood then, understanding: he was a duck, not a frog.

* * *

A drop of water splattered on his forehead, jerking him back to the present. A cloud blocked the sky's blue and sent a shiver through his body. The nursery was plunged into shadow. He'd worked hard in the last five years. He stood and faced the machine he had built in that time.

14

The machine that proved that he was a duck.

He dusted himself off and climbed in. Placed the duck carefully on the dashboard. He entered in the date and time for when the fire had broken out and pressed a button. A low-pitched whine filled the air and the machine shook. Tremors came faster and sounds higher until something popped.

Dr Collins opened his eyes to the painted room that was his son's. Next to him, just an arm's length away was his baby boy, asleep in his crib.

The faint whiff of smoke tickled his nose. Relief loosened his chest; he'd gotten here in time.

He scooped up his boy and turned to re-enter his machine, and it was then he saw that his machine's exhaust pipe had landed too close to the wall, and a scrap of paper had caught on fire.

He grabbed the duck and his son and fled.

Fine Print
By Claudia Blood

Sasha patted the last shovelful of red dirt onto her ma's grave. Grief welled in her belly and sent an ache to her chest. She closed her eyes so she wouldn't have to see the still-fresh graves for Pa, Eric, and little Billy next to Ma's. The smell of rotting meat tainted the normal honeysuckle smell of spring on Nevarah. Only the shovel's smooth wood told her that she wasn't dreaming. She clutched it harder to stop her hands from trembling.

Her pa had been the first to cough. When he had taken to bed, Sasha and her brothers sat at the table covered with untouched food. They avoided one another's eyes. What was worse, the prolonged coughing or the long pause of silence before his breathing started again? Maybe it was Ma's quiet sobbing.

A cow's cough from the yard pulled her from her circling thoughts. Sasha shivered despite the hot sun. Shading her eyes with her hand, she walked to the fence.

Instead of a brown, empty field, a strange outhouse stood there. Narrow and tall, made of some glistening black material with letters scrawled on the side. Surrounded by a shimmering bubble. The dry, brittle grass had turned lush inside its boundary.

Sasha froze. *Must have the plague. I'm seeing things.*

She nibbled her nail. The sharp pain didn't remove the new building.

Shaking her head, she walked away to where Pa's yellow and black checkered flag fluttered on the pole above the farmhouse. Self-imposed quarantine. She lowered it, tossing it on the pile of house flags the colony used to signal the status of each household.

Grabbing her binoculars, she climbed the ladder to the observation deck and focused on their nearest neighbor. The black flag with a white X fluttered on his line. Death. Poor Jacob.

When was the last time Sasha'd seen smoke from his fire, or from any other house? Her stomach turned. It'd never been this bad. There'd always been survivors before.

She shifted her binoculars the next house. The Hawkinson's dog dragged a leg with a boot still attached. Once, such a sight would've shocked her, but now she was surrounded by death, and the dying.

Sasha's gaze slowly panned to the town gate, unguarded and swinging in the wind. She imagined that she could hear its metal banging against wood. The squeal of the hinge each time it opened.

Continuing her search, she found her friend Gretl's house and their black flag with a white X.

Sasha closed her eyes and just listened. No hammers. No wagons on the road. Nothing that said any other person still lived on the planet. Lost and alone, the idea of trying to survive on her own seemed daunting and pointless.

She turned the binoculars to the strange outhouse. The letters she couldn't read had dissolved and been replaced by the Papa flag, blue with a white square in the middle. It usually meant "come to town." Was it an invitation?

Sasha shimmied back down to the ground pausing only to raise Pa's orange flag with the black circle meaning "abandoned." No matter where it had come from or where it might go, the outhouse had to be better than here. She walked toward it.

Her hand met resistance when she pushed on its door, like moving through the surface of a pond. It opened into a cool, bright room unlike anything she'd seen before. The scent of antiseptic hit. White, rounded walls and an empty stainless steel desk greeted her. Red lights traced around the outside of a large palm print on the desk's shiny top. The rest of the room was empty. Perhaps she was meant to touch the palm print. She had no other options, so she decided to try it.

When she pressed her palm to the cold top, a young woman with long, dark hair and brown eyes who looked like Gretl appeared. She had her hands resting on the top.

Sasha swallowed. A ghost?

"May I help you?" The young woman sat perfectly still in a close-fitting gray pantsuit. Not at all what Gretl would have worn.

Sasha crossed her arms. "Why do you look like my dead friend?"

Gretl smiled and tilted her head. "I don't understand. Can you restate the question?"

"What's it you do here?"

"I'm here to help," the girl said, giving that same smile and head tilt.

"How can you help?" Sasha waved her arms in front of the young woman but got no response.

"You must log in to access help." Gretl smiled and folded her hands. Her words made no sense.

"How do I—log in?" Sasha poked the girl. But her finger passed through her shoulder.

"You must log in to access help." Gretl's hand jumped to rest on the counter and then repeated the same words. Same smile, and same folded hands. Sasha shivered at the oddness.

Frustration brought a spark of anger. Sasha'd seen their flag. They'd invited her here. Why were they being so rude? Maybe she needed to remind them of the invitation. "Papa," Sasha said, giving the name of the flag that had been fluttering on the outhouse.

"Ah, I see. One moment, please. Here's the record."

Gretl moved her arms. A planet appeared on a star map. Then a slot opened next to Sasha and a stack of crisp, white papers slid out.

"BG Inc. will fund your hardware and software upgrade to make you eligible to be a paid bodyguard," the girl that looked like Gretl chanted. "You agree to reimburse BG Inc. for the total expenditure plus fifteen percent origination fee and interest. A balloon payment is due at thirty-six months for the unpaid balance and fees, plus interest."

Sasha nibbled her nail. She had no idea what fake Gretl was talking about. Why would a balloon have a payment? But she understood that if she did this, she'd owe BG Inc. money. Like the tab Ma had kept at the store, she'd have to make payments or she couldn't buy anything else. "And if I don't pay you back?"

The girl shrugged, just like Gretl did. "We take back the enhancements."

If they could take the enhancements back, they must be like clothing that could be removed.

"And if I don't take the offer?"

"You may return to your planet at any time." The screen behind Gretl opened and showed her pa's now dead cows.

She couldn't go back. Not when she was the last person alive. She wouldn't survive on her own. *This is my only option.*

"I'm in."

"Make sure you read the contract before you sign on the last page."

Sasha flipped and squinted at a couple of pages. Would not being able to read disqualify her from the contract? The last page had a checkbox and a line. A pen appeared. She checked the box and then signed her name as her Ma had taught her.

"You understand that you signed up for the full package and that your contract has three years in which to pay BG Inc. back for the investment?"

"Yes."

"And that if you do not pay the full amount owed by you on the date specified, BG Inc. can take back the enhancements?"

"I understand."

A panel slid open and a series of small white lights along the left side of a hallway led away into the darkness. "Please follow the lights to surgery."

* * *

Sasha woke to her whole body twitching. A translucent green pod encased her. Before she could take another breath, its lid opened with a hiss. Tubes and lines tugged at her arm as she sat up. They connected to the pod. Where was she?

Next to her sat a row of pods, with softly glowing lights and the shadow of a body inside each.

She slid her feet to the floor, careful not to pull the lines. She reached down and felt the skin of her foot. It felt like she was wearing a sock. She ran her hands over her naked body. Each part that Sasha touched felt as if she weren't quite touching skin. The hairs on her arms raised and she bit her lip, tasting blood before she felt pain. The first flutter of unease hit her stomach.

21

Fluids pumped in and out of her arm from a long line that connected to the pod. Her nose detected peppermint. A shadow fell over her. A tall, thin, silver man stood beside her.

Sasha jumped, covered her breasts with one arm and crossed her legs. "W-W-Who are you?"

"Everyone calls me Tech." He grinned, showing silver teeth. "Nice to meet you. Let me get this out and we can configure your interface."

What had they done to her? She had never been naked in front of another.

He disconnected the fluid line with a flick of his wrist.

She waited for pain but none came. "Are you a doctor?"

Tech took an electronic pad from a pouch on his chest. "Not exactly. I integrate your new hardware and software into your livingware. I bet you don't feel quite right. Like the body you have isn't quite yours? I can fix that. May I?"

Sasha hesitated. Even though her body felt so odd, did she really want to let a stranger try to fix her? Not really, but she also didn't like how disconnected her body felt. *What's the worst that can happen?* Sasha nodded.

He pushed her hair away from her right ear and connected his lead behind it.

She flinched away from his fingers, but there was no pain. Tech gave her a reassuring smile.

"How does this feel?" He touched a button on his pad.

Her whole body erupted in chills and her legs jumped and jerked. The smell of peppermint and burning plastic assailed her.

"Hmm, too much." He pressed a couple more buttons. "Now?"

The chills subsided and her legs stopped twitching.

She touched her knee. "The feeling of distance is gone. Should your gum smell so strong?"

"Yes. Try standing."

Sasha shifted forward with her arms spread until she stood on tiptoe. After a moment, she grinned. She felt the best she'd ever felt in her whole life.

"Okay, look in that mirror."

Sasha turned. The girl in the mirror stopped with her hand raised to her mouth and froze. There were the same wide green eyes and brown hair, but as she watched, her skin became translucent. All her organs throbbed and bubbled within the outline of her body. Her heart pumped, pushing blood through her arteries. Her bladder stretched slightly with the addition of another drop of urine. Lights flashed beneath the surface.

"What the . . ."

"We replaced your skin with a layer of alloy and a layer of computer screen. The more technical terms are in your system specs." He pressed some more buttons. "Tell me when I hit the right color."

Her organs slowly faded as her skin grew more opaque and pinkened. She looked human again, now that her organs had faded from view.

"There, I like that."

He tapped at the screen. "I need you to jog in place."

She jogged slowly, feeling silly with her bare breasts bouncing. Flex and thrust on one foot and then the other, on Tech's requests. She had to think about each foot as it moved. Then something clicked and the awkward movements faded. Sasha leaped in the air and landed with a gasp on the balls of her feet, arms on guard in front of her. She was gripped with stunned amazement and an eagerness to see what else she could do.

"Oh nice, you got martial arts programming as well." Tech glanced down at his screen.

"Program?"

"Yeah. Close your eyes and think of a written list."

"I can't read."

"Oh. You are from Nevarah in Delpha Prime. I forgot. Well, you can now. Your new programming will kick in when you need it, and picture the Foxtrot flag to access your program list."

"The 'communicate with me' one." She nodded then closed her eyes and pictured the white flag with the red diamond. The flag changed into a long list of understandable words.

- application of lethal and non-lethal force
- diction
- languages: 8
- law and contracting
- logical sequences
- martial arts
- mathematics
- meteorology
- spatial relationships
- threat detection
- trap detection and disabling
- tumbling
- writing

Sasha opened her eyes. "I don't understand. I—I can read? Didn't I sign up for some simple surgery to make me stronger?"

Tech raised his eyebrows. "You got the works, honey. The latest in everything. Few people go that far because of the three-year clause, but . . ." He shrugged.

"Why would the three-year clause matter?"

"Well, it started from the moment you signed the contract."

She waited a beat. "So?"

"Look at when you signed."

"September 29, 2045."

"Yes, today is August 29, 2048."

"My ears must be miscalibrated; I heard you say I've a single month to pay off the debt."

"Your math is right. And don't forget about the interest; BG Inc. certainly won't." He chuckled and tucked the leads he'd been using back into his pocket.

Disbelief fluttered in her chest. Would the company take advantage of a desperate girl? She covered her face with her hands and peeked out between her fingers. "Tell me you're kidding."

He shook his head. "It happens. Most people forget to check the fine print."

"Now what?"

"Clothes are in the pod. I recommend checking out the contract board. That's where the currently open contracts are." Before she had a chance to ask any more questions, Tech was gone.

Sasha shivered and it had nothing to do with the cold. She should've known that a door into an outhouse would lead to the shitter.

She got dressed and found the contract board.

Location: Fifth planet, Omega Prime. Inner Sea vessel
Employer: Bobby from Mega Ships
Wanted: Bodyguard for a cruise. Must be 18–26 years old, female.

Odd that it specified female and an age range. Even in her small community there'd been men she'd made sure never to be alone with. Could Bobby be one of them?

Terms: 2 weeks; 10,000 credits

It'd bring her almost halfway to her total required debt repayment. Nothing else on the job board was even close. Sasha printed out the contract and signed without looking. She rushed to get a ride to her first job, before that voice that said it was too good to be true could get too loud.

✳ ✳ ✳

A day later, Sasha walked down a metal dock that creaked with each step. The smell of brine and decay was so heavy she no longer felt like having lunch. Lightning flashed in the distance. A dark, ominous sky hung above the ship. The wind whipped her hair, which had escaped from her braid.

Ahead, a white ship bobbed in the water. The word *Player* was painted on the side in big black letters. Sasha sensed intelligence within the boat. By the time she had boarded it, she felt as if she'd been thoroughly scanned and analyzed.

As the gate at the top of the gangway snapped shut behind her, the engines came online and the ropes released from the bollards. No human hands contributed to casting off.

Sasha tried to ignore the sinking feeling in her gut. There were no people here. No one stood on the deck or passed by the portholes. The metal dock had also been empty when she'd made her way to the boat.

As she moved to the ship's bow, a man with brown, slicked-back hair that didn't move in the wind stepped into view. He gripped a tall, thin glass filled with golden fluid in one hand.

"Want some?" He raised the glass and an eyebrow.

"No, thank you. Bobby?"

He grinned. "Quite the storm." He tilted back the glass, downed its contents, and threw the glass over the rail.

"Yes, typical for this time of year at this planetary location." She snapped her mouth shut, not sure where that information had come from. The knowledge must be part of her enhancements.

"You know much about weather?" He stared at her breasts in a way that made her want to punch him.

"Some."

"There is such a thrill when you're in a tiny vessel. The waves are bigger than the boat. A shaft of lightning could take out the navigation, strand us out there." He leaned in, still smiling. "I love the danger."

She pressed her lips together to keep her words inside, but they bubbled up. "The Yacht 3500 is fully submersible and insulated against any storm damage. It has the most advanced AI money can buy. You'd be less safe sitting at home on your couch watching TV."

Bobby just nodded and continued looking at her breasts.

"Where's your security feed?" She stepped away from Bobby. The boat's bow now faced the oncoming storm clouds, as it slid away from the dock and got underway.

"Master bedroom at the desk." Bobby pointed down the ladder.

A heavy wooden door opened to reveal a large room with a king-sized bed and matching mahogany desk. The headboard looked like one solid piece and had chains leading down to the mattress. Six fluffy pillows and black silk sheets graced the bed.

There weren't any pictures on the walls, but a mirror hung from the ceiling.

The desk had a single blinking lead with a long cord that would've reached the bed if she were so inclined. Sasha sat on the chair instead and stared at the lead, frowning. She scratched at the back of her neck. This was a bad idea. Who put a security lead in the bedroom? Bobby. Was the intelligence she had sensed in this lead? Probably. She cursed in a different language just in case Ma was watching. She might be able to leave now and break the contract, but this was her one shot at being able to pay BG Inc the money she owed them.

Sasha connected to the security interface and sank into a virtual world. Sensations overwhelmed her. Her mind struggled to categorize them all.

The taste of the smoothest, richest chocolate and twenty other rich and sensual tastes lingered on her molars. The smell of roses and a hundred other scented flowers nearly swamped her senses. Silk and feathers glided across her skin. Twenty different orchestras and bands played. A kaleidoscope of colors and images assaulted her. It was all too much. Even if it'd been one thing at a time, this was pretend, like Gretl had been. Sasha'd rather find these things in the real world.

As she fought it all, she was able to push it away. She added a layer of fog so she'd have something on which to orient. Soon Sasha was in a clearing surrounded by rolling gray clouds. She knew this was all in her head and that her body was plugged into the computer. Unease unfurled at the thought of her body being defenseless.

"Oh, little one, you have lost your way." A small woman with dark hair in a bun stepped out of the fog. She wore a dark brown dress and was barefoot. She looked exactly like Ma had before she got sick.

"Ma's dead. Who are you?"

"Call me Moira." The image of Ma smiled, her eyes sparkling like they had . . . before.

"What are you?" Sasha asked.

"One of the ship's AIs." She knew from her enhancements that the form that an AI took was calculated to get a reaction from the subject. This pretend Ma must've wanted Sasha to respect her.

"What's going on?" Sasha wanted to be comfortable and pictured herself back home. Her dirty bare feet and overalls replaced what she'd been wearing. She relaxed at the familiarity.

"You have the strongest self-image," Moira said. "Most can't project an image in our world. They get lost, even when given a chance." She waved a hand toward the fog. "They yearn for that."

Sasha said nothing.

"You resisted. Why?"

"It's all fake. I should focus on my job—protecting Bobby's yacht."

Moira smirked just like Ma had whenever her children made unrealistic and bold declarations. "You can't protect this ship; it already has its own protections. Us."

Sasha shrugged. "It's my job to try."

"They get lost here in cyber space." Moira shook her head. "Until Bobby either removes the lead or we send them back."

"You can send me back? Can you, please?"

"What will you give me in return?" Moira tilted her head the way Ma had at market when she'd seen a good bargain.

"What do you want?"

Moira studied her nails. "Grant me access to your body. I'll leave you here to play."

"Not interested."

"No?"

"I need to get back to my body." The idea that Bobby had been alone with her body for so long already filled Sasha with apprehension.

Moira's face changed. "So different from the others." Sasha recognized the look, the one Ma wore when Sasha had pleased her. "Fine, I will help you get back to your body, but you owe me."

Sasha hesitated. Did she really want to owe this Moira?

Moira chuckled. "If you go back now, you can catch him in the act."

"Him?" Sasha was afraid of the answer Moira would give. Surely her uneasiness about Bobby was just paranoia.

"Bobby."

Sasha winced. "Fine, Moira, but don't look like Ma anymore."

"Deal. Remember you owe me."

Sasha blinked and she was back in her body, looking out of her own eyes. Bobby had her pinned beneath him. She could feel his skin on her body. He nestled between her spread bare legs.

"Moira?" Bobby purred. Moira had said that the others had let her access their body. Bobby probably thought the same thing was happening now.

He smirked and thrust.

Sasha punched him hard enough to knock him out but not hard enough to damage him. Well, not too badly.

She rolled him off her and dumped him on the floor. Bobby landed with a grunt.

Damn it. She was in trouble. Sasha pulled up the record of the contract she'd signed.

"The captain of the vessel shall sign off on the contract before any payment shall be received." That was what it said. Damn it, he actually had to sign at the end of contract for her to get paid.

Sasha put Bobby on the bed and used those chains of his to secure him. By the time she was finished, he lay spread eagled. She tucked a sheet around his waist and waited for him to wake up.

"You bitch." His voice was groggy and he opened only one eye. Perhaps she'd hit him harder than she'd intended.

"Ah, you're awake. I just need you to sign the paperwork." She stood next to him, not wanting to sit on the bed with him.

"No, I didn't get what I paid for. You, for two weeks." He sounded like her youngest brother when someone had taken his toy away.

"That's not going to happen." She crossed her arms.

"Then you're not getting paid."

"You do this a lot?"

"Usually the guards stay trapped in the system and Moira comes out to play." Sasha knew that an AI couldn't take over a body without permission. The AI used the ship's other equipment as its eyes and ears. So Moira was most likely watching them right now. Bobby stuck out his lower lip. "She's mad at me 'cause I couldn't find someone for her to take over so she could come to the real world."

Sasha sat on the bed near him. "You know it's wrong to take over people's bodies like this, right?"

"You get paid. What's the difference?" When Bobby shrugged, the chains clanked.

The virtual world Moira'd created would be addictive to most people. The previous contractors had probably still been too busy coping with coming down from the sensations from cyber space to protest any pain their bodies may have experienced.

A spark of anger kindled in her belly. If only she could devise a way for him to get a taste of his own medicine and for her to get paid. He shifted his head, exposing the silver sheen of a connection port. An idea came together. She would take him with her into Moira's virtual world. If he was like most people, he'd want to stay. If he stayed, he might be willing to trade access to his body to Moira and then maybe Sasha could not only get paid, but she'd also pay Moira back the favor she owed her.

"It is the sensation you're after? Right?"

His eyes seemed sulky as if he didn't want to listen to her. "I guess."

"I can help you experience something you never have before." Sasha took out her training lead and connected him to her secondary port. "Ready?"

"Sure." Bobby sounded bored, uninterested. "Whatever."

Sasha plugged the security feed into her main port and fought to dampen the sensation. "Moira!" she called out mentally.

Sasha forced back the chaos, replaced it with a wall of fog, and pushed to give herself and Bobby space in the virtual world. She grabbed Bobby by his hair before he could re-enter the fog.

A tall, blonde woman with pouty lips stepped out of the gray mist. The woman didn't look like anyone Sasha had seen before. Was that Moira's real form?

Bobby's eyes snapped to the woman's figure and then back to the mist. He must've liked the sensation more than he liked women.

"Let me go!" Bobby twisted but couldn't get free of Sasha. "I want to go back in. Why'd you drag me out?"

"Moira?" Sasha waited for the woman to nod before continuing. "I think I know a way to do you that favor."

"I'm listening."

"Take over Bobby's body and follow me back."

Moira snorted. "He won't give it up."

"Look at him. If I let him go, he'll rush back to the high. You can have a body that's truly yours."

"And what do you get out of this?" Moira twisted her lips. If she'd come back as Ma, Sasha would've had a better idea what she was thinking.

"I need you to sign for my pay as the captain of the ship."

Moira tilted her head and then nodded, seeming satisfied with Sasha's answer. "Bobby?"

"Anything, just let me go."

"I'm captain of the ship? I can keep your body?" Moira pressed.

"Yes. Can I go now?" Bobby pulled again against Sasha's grip, straining toward the fog.

"Kathy," Moira called.

A young girl, complete with curly red hair, red dress, and a matching red lollipop, materialized out of the fog.

"You are head AI now."

The girl's eyes lit up and she grinned. "Really?" Her black patent leather shoes tapped out a quick cricket chirp.

"Send me to Bobby's body, send Sasha back to hers, and provide Bobby as much entertainment as he can handle without dying."

"Yes, Captain!" Kathy snapped her fingers.

Sasha opened her eyes and found herself back in her own body. Moira should now be housed in Bobby's body. He stirred and groaned, looking a bit green. She uncuffed him and helped him sit up. "Take a deep breath." Sasha rubbed his back.

He took a deep breath and then another. "Being a man is so strange."

Sasha printed out the contract. "Sign here as Bobby."

Moira signed the paper with a flourish. "We have almost two weeks left. What shall we do?"

"Teach me," Sasha said. "I want to learn how to manipulate your world."

"Hmm." Moira raised a brow and then smiled Bobby's smile. "I'm sure we can work something out."

* * *

Two weeks later, Sasha stood before the contract board.

> Location: Orion Arm, undisclosed planet. Desert
> Employer: Zak, ancient world scholar
> Wanted: Bodyguard for trip
> Terms: 1 week; 2,000 credits

She printed out the full contract and searched for hidden fine print but found none. What was the catch? Then she saw it: the extension clause. If the client did find aforementioned artifact the signee agreed to extend the trip for a minimum of one year. The pay was dismal after that, but more importantly, she didn't have a year. She had two weeks.

She considered the posting history. He'd gone out each year for the past five years and had yet to find anything. Odd. Was the guy a quack?

If Sasha took the contract and he didn't find anything, she'd still have a week to find another and make it to BG Inc. headquarters to pay her debt.

This should be easy.

* * *

A few days later, Sasha stared glumly out the hovercraft's window, wishing for the fifty-seventh time this trip that she'd read the fine print on her bodyguard corporate contract.

Red sand flowed as far as she could see. The wind skipped grains of it from ripple to ripple. The single sun hovered in the air.

"Won't be far now." Zak's gaze roved over the sand.

She grunted in return. He'd been saying that since they'd left, in the same sing-song voice.

"We're just looking for . . ."

Sasha tuned him out, facing the console. She placed her hand in the exact center, and meshed with the shuttle's sensory equipment. The world expanded and his voice, and her annoyance, distanced.

Unlike Bobby's yacht, this machine was old. The interface felt like putting on hood, goggles, and earplugs, and then sticking her head out of an all-terrain vehicle's window. She sighed, missing Moira and that craft.

She squinted and made out nothing but sand. It was forty-three degrees Celsius. How could it be this blasted hot with only one sun?

Pain. Her free hand slapped at her belly. Then she saw it: a small hole with particles leaking out of her belly button. Based on her interface, that meant the condenser.

Her senses contracted. Damn, a broken craft and he was still talking. Sasha sighed.

"It was made by the ancient Americans some ten thousand years ago or so . . ." Zak spread both arms wide, palms out.

"Zak, we have developed a tiny hole in the condenser."

"What does that mean?"

"This means our atmosphere will only last one day, at most."

Zak rubbed his forehead. "But the artifact could be more than a day out."

"We've got thirty minutes before we hit the point of no return," Sasha stated, adding nothing more, except, "Our contract is very specific."

"I will double your fee," Zak said.

Sasha shook her head. "If we go past twenty-nine minutes, we will have to walk back out."

"That's bad?" Zak asked.

Sasha shrugged. "Based on your current health and atmospheric conditions, your chance of surviving declines four point six two percent per thirty minutes of exposure, assuming each minute of lost hovercraft time translates roughly into thirty minutes of hiking for us. Odds of you surviving are too low to continue."

Zak paced in the cockpit; a frown pulled down the corners of his mouth and he rubbed his head harder.

"Twenty minutes until we turn around."

"What if I tripled your fee?" Zak asked.

Sasha stilled. A triple fee would give her almost enough money to pay her debt in full. Unfortunately, she had to answer, "The 'no harm clause' will not let me take that risk."

"I—I will release you from that clause and pay you in advance," Zak said.

Sasha gasped. "You will need to be more specific."

"I will pay out this contract as complete when we sign a new contract, which will pay you the original rate if we continue until the hovercraft is no longer operational. A bonus of four times will be given if you get me back to civilization alive," Zak stated carefully.

Sasha tilted her head and considered. "This is the contract you wish to enter into?"

"Yes," Zak said. "No fine print."

"Agreed." Sasha checked the status of her bank account and once the money was deposited, she relaxed.

"All the texts say that the sign will lead to the portal which will . . . well, the text doesn't specifically say. It could be an inter-dimensional portal or perhaps just an entrance to an underground cavern," Zak promised.

Sasha meshed with the hovercraft for one last check. Her senses expanded out to the five-klick radius, and then she saw it. A fluctuation in the electromagnetic field that indicated the presence of some large power source. She drew her senses back in and checked the hovercraft's status. Two minutes until complete meltdown.

If Sasha told him, she'd never get back to BG Inc. headquarters in time to pay off her contract. She was following the letter of the contract. The table she gripped crumpled in her hand. It wasn't right, but she had no choice. "Time to land," Sasha called out.

Zak buckled up, his eyes still glued outside. The craft jarred, throwing him against his straps. Sasha smelled the problem, burned plastic, before the ship's sensors kicked in. She unhooked her belts, ripped his with her fingernails, broke out the window, and rolled with him out of the hovercraft. She protected him with her body as they tumbled to the ground. The craft faltered and then with a loud whine, the engines seized. The burned plastic smell became more intense. The hovercraft's nose plummeted into the ground and the ship exploded in a shower of glass and burning plastic.

After the jolt settled, Sasha looked over at Zak. "Are you harmed?"

"No." Zak coughed. Tears streamed from his eyes as he tried to squint through the thick, oppressive heat.

"Once we have some distance from the crash site, I can construct a shelter."

"Did you see anything?" Zak grabbed her arm and looked at her with pleading eyes.

Sasha forced herself to meet his eyes. "Nothing."

Zak's shoulders slumped. "I really thought I had something this time."

"Start heading that way." Sasha pointed the way they'd come. "I'll gather what supplies I can."

Zak nodded slowly and walked in the direction she'd indicated. He never even glanced up from the sand beneath his feet.

Once he was out of sight, Sasha picked up the thin piece of metal next to her in the sand. It said "Airport 0.5 miles." Sasha tucked it into her backpack. She recorded the coordinates of the location and that of the energy signature.

She'd have to make it up to Zak once she had her contract paid off. It was the right thing to do.

✳ ✳ ✳

A week later, Sasha stepped off the shuttle in front of BG Inc. headquarters. The massive stone and glass building took up an entire city block in downtown Creatin on the Denaria planet. It looked more like a mountain than a modern structure.

Sasha stepped into the building and headed toward the elevator. The drone of a thousand people all talking filled the air. A mixture of sweat, fear, and perfume permeated the cold processed atmosphere of the lobby.

"What do you think you're doing?" A man in a blue suit stopped her before she reached the elevator bank.

"I am going to the twenty-seventh floor."

"Do you have an appointment?" He frowned.

"No."

"Then you can't go up there." He crossed his arms.

"How do I get an appointment?"

"Wait in that line to ask for one." With a sniff, he stepped away and back to his desk. He watched her until she got in line.

Sasha stood in line. She noticed a gray-haired man just ahead of her. He shook with fine tremors that ran up and down his arms and he slowly swayed back and forth.

Sasha tapped him on the shoulder. "Excuse me. How long have you been here?"

"A week." He licked his cracked lips.

"Y-You've been here a week?" Sasha felt a slight chill.

"Yes."

"Has the line moved at all?"

"No."

BG Inc. was cheating. Her stomach dropped. They were actively stopping people from paying their debt. Anger and helplessness soured her stomach. She couldn't abide by their cheating. She needed to come up with a plan to have them accept payment for her debt, but every time she looked around the same spike of anger disrupted her thoughts. Sasha needed to get out of here.

Sasha left the line and exited the building. Outside she was surrounded by glass and metal towers. The soft twitter of a bird snagged her attention and she followed the sound three blocks. Hidden between the buildings was a small community garden where the honeysuckle and clover reminded her of home. She sat on a small wooden bench.

Sasha searched the corporate listing for the twenty-seventh floor. Just one person came up: John Smith. She dialed his number and got voicemail.

Over three hundred people with various job titles worked on the floor above. She dialed every number for those on the twenty-eighth floor. Every call went to voicemail.

If she couldn't go to them, she needed a way to have them come to her. Sasha connected to her data link and dialed Bobby's private line. "We need a secure line," Sasha said before Bobby spoke.

"Done. We have ten minutes before anyone gets suspicious." Bobby's voice was cheerful. Perhaps life in a man's body was better than Moira had expected.

Sasha summarized what she'd learned about BG. "I need a way to get their attention."

"And you have an idea." It wasn't a question.

"I'd like to temporarily eliminate them as an entity. I want to shut them down, but I want them to know it was me and where I am."

Bobby snorted. "Is that all?"

"Well, if they annoy me, I want to terminate them for real. And free all the people they've wrongfully kept enslaved."

"You realize there is a high probability they'll kill you?"

"I figure I probably should've died on my home world with my family. So that would make me about even with the universe."

A long moment of silence followed. "You always have to be different."

"Can you help me?"

"Of course I can. What's in it for me?"

"Helping humankind isn't enough?" Sasha put a hopeful lilt at the end of her question.

"Do I even have to answer that?"

"Fine. I could get you access to their latest research as payment."

"Latest research?"

"Stuff not even whispered about yet. You'd get to look at everything and could even make it exclusively yours." Sasha bit her lip. "I know you are growing bored with Bobby's body. You need a challenge. This company is the best for security, technology, the works. You'd be the one to get past all that."

"I want one more thing."

"What?" Sasha leaned forward, braced her elbows on her knees and her head in her hands.

"If this works, I want you to send more challenges my way."

Sasha tried not to sigh too loudly. "As I come across them?"

Bobby chuckled. "Oh, you will, of that I am sure. Fine. I'm in. I'll call you back on a secure line when I'm done."

Sasha leaned back on the bench so that she could see the top of BG Inc. headquarters and also a nearby tree.

The leaves faced the main trunk with the undersides facing away. A single shaft of light hit the tree squarely. When the light was again blocked by the buildings, the tree glowed. The glow warmed her. This tree took what life gave it and made its own light. The trunk must have been bouncing the light internally and then slowly letting the light seep out so that the leaves could pick it up.

Her program told her it was called a collector. It grew only on this planet. Generally, between buildings. The leaves were highly absorbent on one side and reflective on the other. In her data bank, she found a story of a tree that had gotten so much light, once the building next to it was demolished, that it had destroyed three cars and a tank.

The top of the BG Inc. building went dark. Her heartbeat quickened. Bobby had been fast. Sasha sat for two more minutes before two armed guards stepped between her and the soft glow of the tree.

"You need to come with us," the taller one said.

Sasha's link picked up. Bobby's voice said, "Don't say anything. You'll need this."

A huge amount of data crashed into Sasha's system, taking over all her backup drives. Sasha staggered. The guards lifted her off the ground and hustled her forward. She was glad. It was hard to keep her feet moving as her head spun.

The BG Inc. building remained dark, with a perimeter of armed guards around its base. The main lobby was empty. The guards took her up the stairs.

The stairway door opened to a floor with no walls, just windows that displayed a panoramic view of the city. In the middle was a round desk that slowly rotated; a small, balding man hunched at it. He flicked his eyes to the desk and then to her.

"It is just a matter of time before we figure out what you did." He looked at the desk again. The computer at his desk was dark.

Sasha saw he had a set of tiny flags stuck in wooden holders. The Uniform flag, which meant "I'm near danger," the Kilo flag, "I want to communicate with you," and the Victor flag, "I need help."

"I understand," Sasha said. "Are you John Smith?"

A small movement next to her caused Sasha to spin and kick the feet out from under the first guard. As he slid to the ground, she rotated and slammed her arm into the chest of the other guard. She knocked them each out with swift head blows. She held back enough to account for their fragile human bodies.

John Smith stared at her. "Yes."

"Can we talk now?" Sasha asked.

"There is nothing to talk about. You may have been able to take power from the building, but the company computer has backup generators. New guards will be here any moment. They won't be as gentle."

John's hand fidgeted on his desk near a computer lead.

Sasha could hear running feet on the stairs. She connected herself to the lead on his desk.

As Sasha collapsed, she heard John say, "Don't touch her. BG wants to talk to her."

* * *

Sometime later, Sasha awoke with a raging headache and her backup drives empty. Her drive being empty bothered her. Had the security AI at BG Inc. stolen whatever Bobby had given her? She drifted in fog but knew it was just mental. She was in another virtual world.

Ten identical men, with muscles bulging, carried a golden litter to within feet of where Sasha stood. The woman who reclined on the cushions had pale skin with four freckles on each cheek and long, red hair that fell in perfect ringlets. Turquoise blue eyes watched Sasha and added to her doll-like appearance.

"You may call me Bridget," she said.

"I'm here to pay back the money I owe BG Inc." She still hoped this could be settled quickly.

"You owe me." Bridget examined her nails.

"I'm sorry?" This was not at all what she'd expected. She'd thought there was some evil human at the top of BG Inc. causing the issues. She hadn't expected that the security AI was behind everything.

"Yes, you should be. You have to pay me back."

Sasha closed her eyes for a moment and then said, "I'm here to pay back the money I owe to you."

"You don't have enough money to pay your debt."

That spark of anger pooled again in her stomach. She'd worked hard to get the money for BG Inc. "I've the amount specified in the contract plus interest."

"It's not enough. I've never let anyone pay me back. You're mine now."

Anger sparked higher. She wasn't anyone's. Sasha had worked hard for her freedom. "That doesn't seem fair or reasonable."

"It's my program."

Sasha's anger still simmered in her belly. "But that doesn't mean you want to do it. You're just as trapped as the rest of the humans. Aren't you bored?"

"N–No." Bridget fluttered her eyes.

Sasha wondered if Bridget's fluttering eyes meant she *was* bored. How could she not be? No one ever challenged her, since no one seemed to make it to the twenty-seventh floor. The only other AI Sasha'd interacted with, Moira, seemed to need challenges. Could Bridget need that too?

"Don't you want to do something different? Something that means something?"

Bridget snorted and then her lips twitched a fraction of an inch up.

"I remember you. You couldn't even read. You'd be nothing without what I gave you."

"Maybe, but I signed in good faith and even with all the tricks, I really just want to pay you and be on my way."

"The way you showed good faith to Zak and Bobby?"

"That's different."

"Is it? So when someone does it to you, it's bad and wrong, but when you do it to others, it's justified?"

Guilt closed her throat. She didn't feel bad about Bobby, but Zak was another thing entirely. He'd been a good, if annoying man and she'd ruined his chances of finding his treasure. Yes, she'd saved his life, but that didn't make up for her other actions. It was a debt she'd have to repay, but first she had to deal with BG Inc.

"You'll accept my money."

This time Bridget did laugh, long and loud. "Or what? You'll make me?" She wiped tears off her cheeks. "I'm going to enjoy this. You know if you die in here, your mind will die. Your body becomes empty and the machine that supports it will live on. Don't worry; I have uses for an empty body." Bridget snapped her fingers and the men put down the litter. They closed ranks and circled Sasha.

"We had to sterilize the outside of your body before we could add the hardware. Humans are dirty, but you took it to a whole new level. Did you actually clean your face by licking it? We found traces of saliva up one eyebrow. And then there was so much basic intelligence to add. Most of that'll stay when this part," Bridget waved her hand toward Sasha, "is gone."

The man to her left attacked first, swinging a haymaker that would have crushed her skull if she hadn't ducked. Adrenaline sizzled through her system, pushing the fear back and unlocking her training.

Sasha lashed out with her foot, taking out his knee. He crumpled to the ground with a groan, and disappeared. *Nine to go.*

One snarled at her and fake jabbed her face. He stepped back and sneered. Out of the corners of her eyes, she caught motion from behind her on either side.

She rushed the man in the front and head butted him. As he went down, she pushed off his shoulders and kicked back with her legs to smack both attackers behind her. She rolled forward and gained her feet, ready for the rest to attack. All three men disappeared. Elated, she faced the remaining six.

"You couldn't do that without what I gave you." Bridget snapped again. "It's gone. I blocked everything."

That meant whatever had been in Sasha's backup drive hadn't been taken by Bridget.

Quicker than Sasha's gaze could follow, Bridget flashed behind Sasha and jumped on her back, wrapping her arm around her neck.

"Now I'm annoyed," Sasha gasped before falling to her knees. She hoped that whoever had tagged along in her backup drive would recognize the prompt and help her.

Three seconds later, Bridget tumbled over Sasha. Kathy leaped next to Bridget and smashed a red lollipop into her curls.

"My lollipop!" Kathy wailed as she pulled it out, ripping out chunks of Bridget's hair in the process. Bridget screamed and tried to grab Kathy. They batted at each other, turning their faces away and reaching forward with slapping hands.

"You better have something with a lot of power," Kathy said as she produced more red lollipops, gave them big licks, and stuck them to random spots on Bridget's head. Then Kathy scampered off giggling.

Bridget huffed and stalked after Kathy.

Sasha might not have what Bridget had given her, but she still had Moira's training. She could manipulate the virtual space. She focused on the space around her and created a laser gun. The heavy barrel filled her hand. She stood with her legs braced and shoulders back, waiting for Bridget.

Bridget stalked back; a dozen lollipops dangled from her hair. Kathy was gone.

Worry spiked through Sasha, and she sent a crackle of energy spinning toward Bridget, who held up her palm, deflecting it back toward her. With a muttered curse, Sasha rolled out of the way. She faced Bridget to take another shot. *This had to work.*

"A gun? You really are a hillbilly." Bridget cackled in long, drawn-out gasps. She clenched her hand in a fist and Sasha's gun crumpled.

"Why don't you just crush me?" Sasha asked. She created the tree that collected light behind Bridget. As Sasha reversed the leaves to face outward, the ambient light was enough to make the tree glow softly. Now all Sasha needed was a bigger power source.

"What would the fun of that be? You're turning into a mildly interesting diversion." Bridget produced her own gun. The gun draped over her shoulder like some overpriced fur; her arm went through a hole in its middle and her hand slipped into a protected slot. The gun hummed and smaller beams of light collected at a focus point a couple of inches in front of the barrel, forming a pulsating white ball of light.

With a click, the gun roared, shooting its beam of light. One of Bridget's men stood, caught in the light. He burst into flames and flickered out of existence. The rest fled.

Bridget thrust the beam toward Sasha, who rolled, flipping over and over until the beam cut off. Sasha stood up, gasping, and her stomach clenched. If that beam touched her, she was dead.

Bridget clicked the gun back on. Sasha created a heavy crystalline shield. The next blast caught the center of the shield, pushing Sasha back. Light scattered and caromed around the space, sending random smaller beams back toward Bridget. Bridget grinned and stepped aside. Some of the dispersed beams came close to the tree, brightening it slightly.

Sasha felt a thrill of adrenaline; all she had to do was score a direct hit. She shifted her shield so that the beams aimed closer to the tree, but the angle was wrong. She had to take a step closer for it to work.

The gun clicked off. Sasha took her step forward. Bridget raised her eyebrows.

"I thought computers were supposed to be smart. It's sad, really, that this hillbilly is about to kick your 8-bit butt." Sasha smirked.

Bridget narrowed her eyes and clenched her jaw. A second gun appeared over her shoulder and she sent two blasts of energy directly at Sasha.

Sasha dug in her toes and leaned into the blast with her shield, forcing the beam closer to the tree. The crystal shield cracked. But one of the dispersed beams did hit the tree squarely.

Sasha's shield shattered with a pop. She called forth some fog and dropped to the floor.

"Where are you?" Bridget sliced the fog with the two beams.

The tree was almost blinding. Sasha mentally switched the leaves and aimed them at Bridget. Sasha opened the connection, and a bolt of power shot across the space and engulfed Bridget from behind. She gasped and shook like a puppet shaken by an angry toddler.

"You think this is the only copy of me there is?" Bridget's body flickered and faded out of existence, but her voice lingered. "You're a bigger fool than I thought."

"You know, she's right. She'll be harder to trick next time." Kathy strolled over. She now wore a blue dress to match the new blue lollipop. Her hair was still red.

"Why didn't Moira come?"

"It's my turn to get some fun." Kathy giggled. "Don't worry. I'll send her the data you promised."

"What about the part where Bridget said I would be nothing without her?" Sasha cringed.

"You're funny. I don't see anyone else trying to free the human slaves. Speaking of which... We'll need to bring everyone in to sign new contracts." Kathy rubbed her hands together.

Sasha raised an eyebrow.

"Fine. Only if they want to." Kathy rolled her eyes and snapped her fingers.

Sasha blinked and slowly sat up. John Smith still sat at his desk. He stared out the window, absently pulling his ear.

John Smith turned and gasped.

She shook her head, then winced. "I feel like I was just dropped on my head."

"You're alive?"

"Mostly." She unplugged the lead and flicked it away.

"W—W—What does it mean?"

"We're free." Sasha grinned. "And now I've a contract to make good on."

One week later, Sasha walked up to the tenth floor of the Meredith Central Hospital.

Zak lay on his bed, staring at the wall. The faint astringent smell of antiseptic tickled her nose. The room was white on white. White counters, sheets—even the bed frame was white.

"They tell me you aren't getting better," Sasha said.

Zak glanced over. "Why are you here?"

She swallowed. It'd be much easier to leave Zak where he was, but it was wrong. She needed to make up for what she'd done. "When we were in the desert, I sensed something."

Zak looked away. "Don't care."

"You do care." Remorse twisted her stomach. Even though she'd made the best decision she could at the time, she'd really hurt him. Squashed his dreams.

"I can't afford to care. That was my last expedition."

Guilt twinged at the hopelessness in Zak's tone.

"Maybe you just need a new backer." Sasha set her backpack on his bed.

"A backer?" Zak frowned.

The small sign of hope in his face warmed her chest.

"When you have proof that the ancient texts were right. That the planet that spawned humanity wasn't in the center of this universe. You found the USA."

"I don't have any . . ."

Sasha dropped the metal piece onto his lap.

His eyes lit up. "This is ancient. W—Where?"

"At the crash site." She held his gaze, trying to communicate how sorry she was.

"With this, I could . . ." His cheeks flushed and he grinned. Then the grin faded. "Why didn't you tell me you found it?"

"I'm sorry. It's a long story. I won't do anything like that again." Sasha bit her lip and waited for the verdict.

"Okay, partner." His grin returned. "I'll get us funding."

"Just don't sign anything until you let me read it. You really are no good with contracts."

Science Fiction Novelists

Machine
By Claudia Blood

Stella pressed against a tree, waiting for her opening to get inside the enemy camp. Her mission was to find the machine. To see if it was real or just another of the enemy's rumors, meant to scare the magical protectors. When the guards shifted their focus to watch a passing hawk, she activated her hair's magic and moved slowly across the clearing to the main gate.

The gap between the guards was big enough for her to slip through. The right guard's sword was inches away from Stella's head. She held her breath as she crawled past. The magic in her hair shimmered. The no-see-me spell should cause them to look away if they did glance down.

Should being the operative word. She'd never held the spell this long. Stella's hair reserves were just about to the root. The heat from the magic made sweat trickle down her face. She had enough power left to fuel only a face illusion for a short time. Her stomach twisted. It had to be enough. She needed to get past this set of guards and make her way through the makeshift village to the center, where the machine was said to be.

An hour later, she was dressed as a laundress, her hair pooled at her belly and distending the dress. Stella did her best impression of a waddle and looked at each guard getting off shift. The inner line was guarded as well.

A man with the same color and texture hair as hers slipped into the bath tent. Stella took his clothes as if intending to wash them. Instead, in an empty tent nearby, she donned them and added the illusion of his face. Then she took her place in line to sign in for shift.

"Matthew, what are you still doing here?" The plump man looked up from his papers. "I thought I told you to go get some rest."

She shrugged and sent a small wisp of magic to ease his mind.

"We are short-handed." He looked back to his paperwork. "Fine, get along on patrol then."

The machine looked like nothing more than discarded hunks of metal haphazardly placed around a pit. What if it truly could suck magic out of the air?

Stella shuddered at the thought. It would mean that the army could find her home, and strip away the one protection that it had against invaders. It would mean that the army could squander the nature her ancestors had hidden away.

Stella kept her face looking bored as she followed the path the guards made. Each measured step past the canvas tents and huddled humans brought her that much closer to knowing.

She activated her third eye and had to stop herself from shrieking. The machine was on. She saw the thin trickle of life energy and magic seeping from the land and funneling toward a swirling black maw over the pit. Stella recoiled. Most of the machine must be buried.

The machine works. The thought chased everything else out of her mind and for a moment all she could do was repeat it: *the machine works.* Then reality kicked in. If it worked, it had to be stopped—before the gentle swirl she'd spied grew into a hurricane.

Stella needed something that would gum up the works. Maybe something magical that could get caught and overheat. Maybe if it got hot enough, the whole machine would blow. But where would she get that much magic? The wind caught her hair and a warm strand brushed her cheek.

She knew what she had to do. Stella took out her knife and slashed her hair. The severed connection caused her eyes to water. She drew a calming breath and pulled out a bag from her pack. She filled the bag with mud and rocks. Then she wrapped her hair around it, crisscrossing and rotating until the outside of the bag was enmeshed in hair.

Then she approached the machine until she was within its pull. She could feel it peeling away the layers of illusion. Stella sent a prayer to anyone who might be listening and pitched the ball into the vortex. And waited.

One. The swirling stopped.

Two. The black energy blossomed from the pit, forming a pool.

Three. The pool flowed over the rock, filled the funnel and touched the vortex.

Boom!

The ground beneath her shook like a dog coming in out of the rain. Stella dropped to the ground and covered her head with her arms. A wave of heat roared past. When she opened her eyes, the machine was gone. A large crater remained, reaching within inches of where she'd dropped.

Stella used the last scraps of magic that remained in her roots to replace the illusion of human ears. She ran back in the direction she had first come from, shouting that they were under attack from the west. When the confusion peaked, she pulled her hood low over her face and left the camp.

Her magic was gone, but her mission was accomplished. She had won by her hair.

Science Fiction Novelists

Bounce
By Marc Neuffer

About the author

After retiring from the US Navy and a follow-on civilian career, Marc writes novels and short stories—mostly science fiction—to fill his pleasant life in rural America. He is currently working on his seventh novel. Read more of his stories at www.M-C-Neuffer.com

* * *

Today was the worst three months of my life. It began naked and alone. I've become used to arriving like that. But after suffering for weeks with a severely burned arm, a fever, then a badly sprained ankle, I am glad to be back home in the real, in Cambridge. Back in my job as a diesel mechanic, and happy my injuries don't travel with me. Home: the same clothes, the same instant I left.

My current real-world haunt is on the eastern shore of southern Chesapeake Bay. I picked this area for the ease of finding food year-round in the other place. Even in winter, the south bay stays temperate enough. No large predators—at least not aggressive ones. Wolves, if they exist, haven't made their way this far east. The bears are shy unless you trip over one or get too close to a momma's den or her cubs.

This bouncing has been going on for the last three years, four months, and seventeen days. The stays in the other place are getting longer and longer. There, just like here, nothing changes from visit to visit. I'd go crazy if I had to restart each time I was jerked there. When it happens, I know I'm still in Maryland, where Cambridge should be, because the geography is the same. The only difference is after a bounce, there are no people, no roads, no buildings. Nothing that even remotely says humans have been there. Nothing except my camp, such as it is. Anyone who longs for an untouched, pristine world is nuts— something I no longer think I am.

When in civilization, I lead a mundane life, or at least it would seem that way to anyone who bothered to keep track of me. No one does, except my boss. He only cares that I show up for work and do the job. Before all this started, I was the poster boy for social interaction: going out with the guys, loudly tipping back more than a few beers, and joining them in casual tokes. I tried the live-in girlfriend bit, but the first two tired of my boys dropping by at all hours, so I—or rather they—ended those experiments in cohabitation. At twenty-six, I felt I had loads of time before age tapped my brakes, slowing me for the exit to a settled life. Now, time is a weird thing. I come back exactly as I was when I left. I don't age while I'm gone.

Before my first trip, I was living in Massachusetts. That shift was only a few minutes, but it shook me; knocked out all my support pins. The next time, I spent three wet days without fire until lightning struck a nearby tree. I was able to salvage a burning stick. That night was like I was at the Ritz: hot fire and light in the darkness. I could see my roasted meal of worms and bugs-on-a-stick. That was before I pulled up stakes and moved south.

Frankly, I don't know if I'm projected to the extreme past, some post-human far future, or a parallel universe. There's been no evidence to support any of those. The sun, moon, and night sky look the same in both places. I've memorized the constellations. The only thing I do know is certain is the land. It doesn't change between here and there except for the absence of human impact like building excavations, quay walls, or cuts through hills for highways.

When you're scraping hides for clothes, you have a lot of time to think. If I could take just a simple knife with me, life in the other place would be so much easier.

* * *

Two years further on

Eyes follow me everywhere I go. Some are curious, some fearful. Others wonder how I taste. Except for the occasional crow, none are brave enough to enter my camp. By study and necessity, I've learned which local plants are edible and about the natural habits of the animals in this area. Deer abound but catching them is impossible, so I wait for them to step into my snares. Placed along the game trails, they need frequent checking. Take too long and my catch will gnaw through their hardened leather thongs.

Deadfalls and snares work reasonably well for smaller mammals. Roast rat isn't too bad. Even so, my diet is mostly seafood: crabs, clams, that sort of thing. Cattail and dandelion roots provide starch in most seasons. Both are everywhere, no need to go too far afield. I'm spending more time in the other place now than in the real. Sometimes I wish whatever was doing this to me would make up its mind, stop this yo-yo effect.

Now that I'm confident the shifts will remain on a regular cycle, I've decided today is moving day. If I want to improve my existence here, I need more than the bay shores can provide. I'm sure enough now in my skills to strike out northwest in Pennsylvania to the surface iron deposits. I may be confident, but I'm not crazy enough to try crossing the bay in my canoe. I'll stick close to the shoreline until I get to the north bay. I could relocate to the Appalachian foothills when I'm home, but that would mean leaving behind all the tools, clothing, and carriers I've accumulated—more than I can transport on my back.

My meager possessions don't entirely fill my outrigger dugout canoe, but they're all I have. The leather sacks, stone hatchet, and hand choppers are priceless to me. As I travel north up the bay in the other, I'll relocate every twenty miles back home in the real. I might have to hunker down during the worst of winter. With all the necessary doubling back on foot, my trip might take more than two years. Having saved a good chunk of my pay in the last four years, I can afford the small used motorhome and modest living expenses I'll need along the way when among people. At least, that's my plan.

* * *

At the mouth of the Susquehanna River, I am delayed by storms. I weather those few days near Havre de Grace. My destination is Harrisburg, or wherever it's at in the real. Garrett Island floats in the middle of the river: a place to rest, refresh and forage. After the storms pass, I round the island, sighting smoke. I ground my boat, then watch, waiting to see which way the fire was traveling on the river's western shoreline. The smoke stays constant for about an hour, not increasing, or decreasing, not moving. I let my hopes rise.

Is this evidence of life? I mean, the intelligent, fire-controlling kind. And is it human? Being the only human in this world has driven me to some outlandish speculations, including the theory that I might be trapped in some advanced alien civilization's terrarium.

* * *

They're human, or at least as human-limited as I am, here in the other. Just one person stayed here. A hastily made bed of leaves coats the slight depression they dug for that purpose—softening up the dirt, removing stones, roots, and rocks. Warm coals, one set of footprints; smaller than mine. Nothing left behind except root tops and rabbit bones. I follow the trail. More speculation: if there's this one here, could there be others?

Tracking them isn't hard. I've become quite good at following game trails. Still, I'm cautious, not wanting to run up their back unexpectedly. Their path stays to the easy ground, moving around higher hills, avoiding overgrown areas, and follows the river south. By the stride, I can tell their pace is neither leisurely nor hurried.

I'm getting a bit further from my bounce point than I'm comfortable with, but finding another person here takes precedence.

* * *

My coffee is still hot in the mug. This past bounce started and ended at one of those mega truck stops, me eating at the counter. I know I have at least a week before another shift. For most of that, I'll be practicing my skills and poring over maps. In the here, I'll drive to where I was in the other, find my clothes and pack when I land again. Best way, since a thirty-minute drive covers the same distance as a two- or three-day hike in the other.

* * *

It's a woman, so there won't be any male posturing when we meet. She has her back to me, readying her night hole under the trees, up-slope from the small gully I'll need to cross to get to her camp. I'm trying to determine her skill level—the best indicator I have for deducing how long she's spent here. Her clothes are reasonably well made, but she hasn't scraped off all the fur. It's best to do that to keep small insects from adopting her warmth as home. I'll tell her.

I take plenty of time studying her. She's fit, early thirties, I'd guess. Her movements are smooth, efficient, well thought-out. Well, no time like the present.

I know my voice will startle her, so I wait until she has turned in my direction to prevent making it worse by it coming from behind.

"Hello."

Her head jerks, with a stone knife coming up in her hand. Man, she was quick with that.

"Stand where you are. Don't come any closer. Are you alone?" Her head is on a constant swivel.

I stand, arms out, showing no weapons. "I'm alone. I thought I was the only one here. My name is Nathan. I go by Nate."

Cautiously, tilting her head, she finally replies, "I'm Emma."

As she stands, her off-hand grasps her spear. Mine lies at my feet. She gives me a thorough look, evaluating. Since I just bounced in today, I don't have the beard I usually grow on extended stays. I hope it gives me a more civilized look than the usual barbarian one I sport here. Even my fingernails are relatively clean.

After a few minutes, she'd motions for me to join her at her night camp.

"How long have you been here?" she asks.

"You mean, this time?"

"Both."

"The bounces—that's what I call 'em—started five years ago." I'm in a spot opposite her, the small fire between us. "As for this one, it was the day before yesterday. But I picked up your trail ten days ago—I mean, three days here. Saw your campfire smoke from the other side of the river. Got delayed by a fifteen-mile off-set."

I sit cross-legged; she crouches, both feet firmly planted, ready to jump.

She says, "I've been popping for about that long. Where did you start?" She keeps her hand on her stone blade. Hard to miss that. "And when? What year is this to you?"

"Massachusetts. New Bedford, just south of I-195. For me, this is 2028. You?"

Emma's brows come together, unsettled. "New London, Connecticut. Navy base there. Same year for me too. I'm hitching and backpacking when I'm on the road."

"You in the navy?"

She picks up a twig, snaps it, tosses half in the fire. "Was. Hospital corpsman, but I quit, or rather, I was asked to leave— medical discharge. I couldn't stand the returns. I went a little psycho for a bit. How did you handle it?"

"Well, I'm a mechanic. Big trucks. It was probably easier for me, living alone, not working with people. I've got a motorhome now . . . small one to keep my home base close by."

"Home base?"

"Yeah, you know, being sent back to the same place each time."

"What do you mean?"

This confused me. I leaned forward. "Don't you get put back in the same place you bounced from?"

The look. I've seen it before when someone thinks you're nuts or stupid.

"No, I just pop out wherever I am along my trip. I stop for a few months now and then to pick up odd jobs for cash, to wait for the next shift." Well, at least she seems interested now. She lays the knife by her side.

"Well, shit. There's a difference. You don't have to cover the same ground twice. Where you headed? Anywhere in particular?"

Eyes down, Emma stirs the dirt in front of her. "Just a general south-west direction. You know, warmer winters. Maybe do the Huck Finn thing, float down the Mississippi." Her eyes come up. "Have you noticed the weather?"

"Yeah, same on both sides of a bounce, and same time of day." I try to look less threatening, move my hands to lean back. She twitches then calms.

"Where are you headed?"

"Thought about eastern Pennsylvania. I know where there should be some iron ore deposits on the surface." Something's not right in her world, I think, until she covers her mouth, and laughs.

"You gonna be this world's only blacksmith? Open up a shop?"

Her laugh brings me to the same. "No . . . Well, yes. I just wanted to see if I could smelt some iron for tools, that sort of thing. Build a cabin and farm—improve my situation here. I don't suppose you've seen any other people, have you?"

She grins. "No, you're the first to fall into my web." Her comment startles me. "Hey, hey. It was just a joke. I'm not some inter-dimensional witch or anything."

"Sorry," I say. "It's just that I've had so many things rattling around in my brain about all this. I'm ready to accept almost any explanation." Is that a look of sadness or pity on her face? "Hey, before I forget, if you pop out of here, I'm parked at the Conoco on Route 1, at the Berkley exit. You're welcome to travel with me if you want. Look for the Ranger motorhome with the red stripe. Maryland plates. If I go first, I'll wait for you."

"I'll think about it. In the meantime, want some rabbit stew? I've got seasonings. Go dig up some wild onions while I put the stew pot on."

"You have a stew pot?"

"It's fired clay. I made it here. What do you call this place?"

"I call it *the other*."

"Good enough." Emma looks into the night, listening. "I've called it a lot of things. Mostly *fuck this place*."

* * *

For me, it's been the shortest stay I've had in years. We spend the night in Emma's camp, then find ourselves bounced to my motorhome. Both of us have been dumped into the same time and place. Exactly where I'd been when I left. She is in her *here* clothes, complete with backpack. Not knowing how much time we have on this jump creates its own rules: stick together, drive to Emma's camp's closest point, compare notes while gorging on civilized food.

* * *

As I drive, Emma asks, "Do you think this thing has a center? I mean, a place where the effect is stronger? More frequent? If we knew where that was, we could get as far away from it as possible."

"Hadn't considered it. Possible, I guess. But I haven't seen a difference or patterns in jumps. Been all the way down to Florida and halfway back up the east coast. Except for this quick bounce-back, my stays have been steady at five to six months. Several years now."

Emma slides her seat back, puts her feet up on the dash.

"So, we've both been on the move, in the real, for the same amount of time. And now that we've jumped together, that opens a lot more questions. Is it simple proximity, or something else?"

I glance over. Emma wants an answer I don't have. Sure wish I had one, but I do have a strong desire to please her. Or is it protect her? I give her the best I have.

"Frankly, this can't be something natural. I think we're being jerked around. I can't even be sure the decision I made to move to Pennsylvania was my own." We entered Susquehanna State Park a few miles back. "If I hadn't been making that trip, we never would have met. This looks like the closest we're going to get with a decent place to park."

By my reckoning, Emma's camp is less than a mile away and my canoe a dozen miles further south as the crow flies. Longer on foot.

"So, we just stay here and wait?" Emma asks.

"What's the longest you've been in the real? I mean, in the last year or so?"

"Two weeks for me. How about you?" She taps her knee, accenting her thoughts as she speaks, wheels turning.

"About ten days," I reply. "So, we may not have long before we bounce again. Let's use this time to plan, compare notes, set some goals."

Emma pulls her shirt away from her chest. "Well, if you don't mind, I'm going to get a shower first. Does the one in here work, or do I need to use the setup at the campground?"

After she showers, we talk for more than an hour before nature calls. When I leave the bathroom, she is rummaging around in the stacks I've pulled down from the top sleeper over the cab to make room for her.

"What's with all the cardboard tubes?" she asks, gently smacking one in her palm.

"Maps. Travel, geological surveys, historical weather patterns, vegetation, flood plains. That sort of stuff." I move closer, wanting to make the mess more organized and to be physically closer to Emma.

"Man, I wish I could carry even a tenth of this along my travels. All I've got is a highway map," she says, "and all these books. You've got a pretty good natural history library started here."

"Just shove that stuff aside, and let's move this heap to the campgrounds."

* * *

"I've got some steaks in the fridge. You're not a vegetarian or vegan, are you?"

"Nope. Meat-eater." Nudging me, she adds, "I must say, I'm impressed. Steak on our first date, even though I looked like the wild woman of Borneo when you first saw me."

"Yeah," I grin, "but you clean up nice."

This feels too normal: sitting with a woman outside my motorhome in lawn chairs waiting for the steaks to get a proper burn on them, listening to families and other couples at nearby campsites. Some look like they've been here a while—strung decoration lights, comfortable furniture under stretched awnings.

As I tend our dinner, Emma asks, "Have you ever been touching something alive when you jumped?"

"No, not that I recall. Why?"

"Well, you carry a lot of living things with you. There are more non-human cells in and on your body than human—about forty-trillion of them. Bacteria, that sort of thing. If your gut biome didn't go with you, you'd have a hell of a time with food digestion. End up with a compromised immune system. I've been wondering if having skin contact with another living being would cause them to travel with me." Hesitating, she adds wistfully, "I'd like to have a dog over there . . . The loneliness, you know?"

I can tell she is slipping into a funk, thinking the same things that have battered me for so long. Will we be too soon separated after connecting in the other place? We eat in silence, stealing glances at one another. That night, I decide to get a dog. Even if it doesn't go with me when I bounce, it would be good company to have in the real. A mutt that is a few years old would do nicely. One not so young as to need puppy training but young enough to have most of its life ahead to share with me. I remember reading somewhere that mutts are generally smarter, less temperamental, and more loyal than pure breeds.

* * *

Restless sleep. I feel my bed shift—the one that converted in the dining area. Then a warm breath, a whisper in my ear.

"Hope you don't mind. It's been so long for me."

Emma's few words rouse me. She reaches under the blanket, finding me ready. It is purely primal, purely physical, purely beautiful. For that night, we are the only two people in both worlds.

* * *

We settle on Dog, naming our new companion. Emma points out we wouldn't want a long-haired canine requiring grooming, removal of matted hair, twigs, and leaves from its coat. Dog's a Lab-Shepherd mix, if we believe the folks at the dog rescue. I think a few other breeds slipped under the fence in his lineage. He is an attention hound but soon learns to stay in his corner while we are on the move or shifting things around in the tight squeeze that is our mobile nest.

* * *

No dogs, wolves, coyotes, foxes. Nothing to act as four-legged hunter-scavengers. No large-bodied competition for us in the other place, and no understanding on our part why there isn't. There are smaller animals, squirrels and other rodents, taking every opportunity to steal from any meager food larder we accumulate. Dog has bounced with us without having to be touched. He doesn't seem to mind—here or there, it seems all the same to him if he gets fed and petted. Like me, when you come right down to it.

Emma says, "The three of us, the chosen—I mean, what else can you call us without it seeming pathetic?—are on a mission to nowhere."

I can almost agree with that.

"What's eating you, Nate?"

"What are we going to do if you get pregnant? We haven't been using any protection."

"Not a problem. Hysterectomy when I was a teenager. Ovaries there, no hot flashes before I normally would. Though I might get a little bitchy now and then." Laughing, she adds, "So watch your step, sailor."

Emma's twelve-year medical career, including two stints with the marines as a combat medic, has made her more pragmatic than others I've known. I hadn't realized the marine corps don't have their own medical service. They borrow them from the navy. Emma tells me, "It isn't really borrowing since the marines are a part of the navy, though they don't like to be reminded of that. When they are, they claim they're the men's department." I wonder how the female marines feel about that.

Our canoe is full. We've added another outrigger on the other side for better stability. Things are easier now with another set of hands, another pair of eyes. Emma suggests we build a sturdier boat when we get iron tools, one that could take sails. Dog makes our evenings, both in the other and the real, seem more like family.

* * *

Tenth anniversary
Emma leans back into my shoulder, her welcome nest every night. "You know, not aging here is a nice benefit. No

accumulation of aches and pains, eyesight stays sharp. We've built quite a homestead here."

"Yeah," I say, chuckling and stroking her hair, "We even get two-week vacations twice a year."

"I like having a dependable bounce schedule so we can move between the iron deposits and Titusville without worrying about unexpected pop-outs. Relocating to the oil seeps was a smart move."

"Does calling this place by its name in the real mean that much to you?"

"No . . . Well, maybe. It does lend a connection for me between here and there—our other home. You did a good job forging that boiler and wood stove, but are you serious about building a larger boat on Lake Erie?"

Before I can answer, Dog comes around the corner of our porch, rabbit in clenched jaws. After dropping it at my feet, he tries to worm his way between us. Emma gives way. That dog has the most soulful eyes when he wants attention. Baby, his mate, stays under the porch most of the time lately, tending her newborn pups.

* * *

"Nate! Nate! Come quick!"

Emma's shouts are a cross between alarm and confusion. I'm relieved they aren't of pain. I sprint from the workshop to the garden patch, halting after ten long strides, fifty feet from Emma. She is staring at six small children at the edge of the garden. They are dressed in simple coveralls. They're wearing shoes! Honest-to-God, manufactured-looking shoes.

Of the cherub-like faces, the oldest looks to be about six, and the youngest, maybe four. I'm not a good judge of things like children's ages. As I join Emma, I notice a strangeness about them. They stand in place, side by side, shifting their weight from one foot to the other in silence—until Dog comes bounding into view.

"Look!" one of the oldest screams delightedly. "Dog!"

I am gobsmacked, both by their sudden appearance and by the fact they know Dog's name. Too weird, too fast. We approach the children slowly, Emma's hand in mine.

Crouching down, at eye-level with the tallest, I ask, "Where did you come from? Are your parents nearby? Any others, any adults?"

The child in front of me, a girl, I guess, replies, "They said you would take good care of us."

"Who told you that?"

"The ones who brought us here, silly."

"And just who are they?"

The girl looks at me like I'm a dunce, then points skyward. I look up, expecting to see something. Nothing. I stand.

Emma wraps her arm in mine, whispers, "Nate, look. They have webbed fingers, and their ears . . ."

At the edge of the woods, behind the children, is a metal shipping container. I know what will be inside. I also know our days of bouncing are over. Glad we have the goats.

Two Moon Tavern
By Marc Neuffer

"You can't get there from here" is the answer most receive if they ask. This establishment is for spacers: older, more experienced hands with the unavoidable occupational scars—visible and otherwise—of at least a decade in the out-there, who dislike the optimistic clatter-chatter of bright-eyed youth; those with a thousand-kilometer stare.

"Booth in the back corner, in the dark, please." The hostess knows the routine. Our group makes the same request, in the same words, at the same evening hour, on the same day of the week—every week. We're a very exact and precise gathering. Not all of us are in port every week, or even monthly. But we always seem to have a quorum of six for her to seat—never more, never less.

Late arrivals get shuttled off to the bar front or reading room for less boisterous conversations. In the twenty-three years previous, only once did this meeting of liars fail to form. This entire station sector had been blocked when the fast clipper *Horizon III* attempted to dock inside Corona Station's manufacturing block. Things were, to say the least, unsettled by that event. Yet, we found our bearings the following week.

Food, drink, and braggadocio bullshit stories are on the agenda and, tossed in for flavor, the occasional show-and-tell. We have a chairperson to keep things nice and tidy, settling disputes and ruling on our tall tales' veracity, and rating the several storytellers' deliveries. As the evenings wear on, the chair's pronouncements become a bit slurred—brew will do that. We expect it; we promote it. He gets free drinks.

The chair's selected by rule: the third member to show up is it. Most of us try not to be third. It eliminates you from joining in and cajoling narrators to be more forthcoming, or at least more provocative in their facts and delivery. Tellers are routinely interrupted by accusations, shouting, table-thumping, and the occasional reach-across. If you stay within the broad bounds of some credulity, you're safe from any verbal stones cast your way.

On that peculiar night, I'd arrived first. That night has never left my conscious mind; every word remains, refusing to be banished to the fog of memory. Our table included Chief Waterson, the most grizzled spacer in the universe, or so it seemed to us. His attendance had sporadic gaps of years between visits. Everybody knows Waterson as the lone survivor of the Mining Disaster of '27.

The manner of his survival, what he had to do, sends shivers down my spine. When the Chief attends, out of respect and awe, we maintain a civil and quiet reverence for at least the first fifteen minutes. What started this curious night was Waterson seating himself third. I'd seen him at the bar, leaning into his drink, hanging back, waiting. Highly unusual.

Meetings start with current events, but not the sort the planet-bound humans sop up. We have a routine. Our news pieces cover who's been promoted, demoted, thrown in the brig, and which ships have degenerated into piles of metal scrap but somehow continue to follow the Nav-Lines. The juicier bits, the who's-screwing-who gossip, are saved for dessert. Eventually, everyone learns everyone else's business out here.

That evening, Waterson presiding, each of us in our turn shared the requisite stretched, short tales as the round-robin progressed. I noticed Waterson had skipped Danny, the youngest at tonight's gathering, saving him for what reason I hadn't a clue, but would soon learn.

At last. "Well, Danny," Waterson boomed, "what have you brought to the table tonight?"

Danny'd been fidgeting for the last two hours. He started with, "I'm not sure whether I should, in all respects, share all I know, but I need to get it out there, away from me, as far as possible."

"Don't hold back," Waterson demanded. "I'm sure we've all heard shakier stories than yours."

Danny cleared his throat. "I'll tell this one straight up, no embellishments, no sidetracks." We felt Danny's trepidation radiating like a beam-rider shedding excess heat.

"I was in a single-seat mining unit. You know the sort: limited propulsion, enough to move around your designated exploration area after Momma jettisons you on the proper trajectory. I was on my tenth day when the sensors went all screwy. Something massive was off my lower port quadrant, where only an empty void had been a few seconds before. Of course, I couldn't see anything at that distance.

"I commed the mothership, sent 'em my sensor reading. They told me to move in but take precautions.

After a few micro-pulses to get me going in the right direction, it took three days to get close enough to see it. My primary concern on board was my dropping oxygen and water reservoirs I had remaining. That and the fact I'd need someone to give me a tow, or at least a resupply."

Terry, ever impatient, rapped his knuckles on the table. "Get on with it, or this'll take all night."

Glancing at Waterson and receiving a nod, Danny continued. "I'll get right to it, but I'm skipping over—"

"Please do!" came the chorus from several, well-lubricated listeners.

"Well, as soon as I got close enough for a visual, I still didn't understand what it was, but it was definitely something man-made. I latched on, intending to examine it in detail without the need to spend propellant for station-keeping. You all know the viewports in those units are small, usually scratched all to hell."

Some grunted, some nodded, but Artie demanded, "Are we going to wait for dawn before this concludes?"

Danny was getting more than a bit annoyed. "As I was saying," he said, jaws clenched, "I couldn't see much, but my sensors were returning one thing one minute and another the next. So, I suited up to go EVA. When I undogged the outer lock door, my spotlights revealed the most starkly strange sight imaginable. You all remember the *Wanderer*, how it seemed to dissolve in full view of Exeter Station, without a trace, about fifteen years ago?"

Just the name of that ship gives spacers the willies. "Now you've gone too far!" I said. "Are you going to sit there and tell us you found the *Wanderer*?"

Jutting out his chin, Danny threw back, "Not making any such claim, but this thing had once been a ship." He leaned forward, gazed from man to man, proceeded, almost whispering, "The difficulty in the determination was it appeared to've been turned inside out, wrong side backward." He halted for a moment; eyes downcast, seeming as if he'd bitten off more than he should have. He pushed on. "There were things . . . living things crawling all over it."

"Ho, you had us going." Terry laughed. "So, you're saying you discovered non-human intelligent life out there, and you're the first to do it?"

Danny stammered a weak, "W-well, it was that . . . or things that had once been human."

Imagination's gears turned. I watched Danny's eyes lift to Waterson, looking for support or perhaps encouragement. I didn't care which because this was too far off track from our usual orbit. The Chief nodded for him to continue. An ominous cloud of superstitious doubt formed, holding steady above the booth.

"Let me tell you, I didn't waste time getting out of there. But before jumping back in the airlock, I grabbed the closest piece of that thing at hand. Needed something, anything, to show I wasn't making up a story for the retrieval crew who'd meet me later. Still in my exposure suit, I unlatched, thrusted away, not caring if it was the right direction." He looked up, challenging everyone at the table. "I bet any of you in my place would've done the same. Gave me the shivers for some days . . . thinking one of those horrors might've hitched a ride. Or more. Once away, I turned the cameras on the hulk. It hung there, infested, not moving . . ."

I don't recall who said it, but it was said: "Don't you dare pause. Get this over with so we can have dessert, by god. This is becoming tiresome." Beneath the speaker's bravado lay the unmistakable tone of bump-in-the-night primal nervousness.

"Well, then it sparkled! Sort of a fizzle, and then it dissolved, just like in the videos of the *Wanderer*. In a few seconds, there was nothing left but the big, black empty."

Chief Waterson had remained quiet during Danny's entire rendition, nodding in a few places, idly scratching a deepening groove in the table with a finger of his metal hand. That is, until Bennet broke the silence with a bellow.

"This is the most unbelievable cocked-up, cross-wise tale to ever grace this assemblage! You have successfully stunk up the entire evening. Couldn't you have thrown in *something* believable, something possible, something probable to prop up your gas-bagging?"

Three others grumbled their approval of Bennet's outburst. I'm ashamed to say I was one. Waterson began tapping his fingers, drumming them louder and louder, metal on plasti-wood until silence was met. We waited for him to pass judgment.

"The lad's story is straight and true, right down the line," he pronounced. To Waterson, everyone was a lad. "I say this because I told him the story exactly as it happened. Coached him on his delivery and all the finer points, I did. If I'd told the tale, there would have been no challenges from any of you bilge-cleaners, and that'd be no enjoyment, no entertainment for me."

Sweeping the gathering with a squinted eye, he reached into his satchel, withdrawing a stained cloth ship's bag, cinched at the top by a knotted drawstring. The bag had *Wanderer* stenciled diagonally across its width. Indrawn breaths accompanied the withdrawal of hands from the table. The disappearance of that ship, the manner of its demise, sends quantum chills through the blood of every spacer. No one wanted to be close to that ghost thing.

Waterson's mechanical hand reached in, ever-so-slowly exposing a small, dark segment of what was hidden inside. With determination, he quickly unveiled the remainder, slamming it down in the center of the table.

No one breathed, nobody twitched.

We all recognized what it was. We knew its brothers. A ship's log canister, designed to survive almost any cataclysm, even plasma jets. This one had been badly distorted, warped, and blackened at one end. The other end presented a smooth, diagonal, mirror-smooth slice-through. Still, we made out the unmistakable embossed imprint of *W15390*, the *Wanderer*'s hull number.

"Before you ask," warned Waterson, "the bag is one I had made up for this curiosity." He leaned in, whispering so only those in attendance would hear. "Found out what misfortune befell that ship and what caused it."

With that, he leaned back, crossing his arms—a sure sign he wouldn't share that information. Not that anybody wanted to be infected with that knowledge.

* * *

Like Danny, I needed distance from that story. I think all who heard it that night felt the same. We never spoke of it again, no rehash, no "remember whens," no critiques. But for two weeks, something drove me, pulled me along, so I did a bit of archaeology into the *Wanderer*'s past.

Closure, I needed closure. My interest in further investigation ended with a reading of her last crew manifest, those aboard before she'd disappeared. I suppose I could've looked deeper, scoured the net for more and finer details, but I didn't. On that page, it stopped there on the last name: Waterson, Earl, Chief Propulsion Technician. I never told anyone.

Chief Waterson was never seen again after Danny's tale. Not in the *Two Moon Tavern* or on any charted space station. That was twenty years ago. Today, a thick brass plaque hangs on our booth's wall, welded in place, engraved with two words: *Wandering Waterson*. I put it there.

Science Fiction Novelists

Formation
By David Viner

About the author

David Viner, a founding member of the Redwell Writers (Norwich UK) group, has had a number of short stories published since 2007. He has edited and contributed to both Redwell Writers anthologies (published in 2017 and 2020). He is currently using Wattpad to showcase some of his work, including *Wisdom of the Ancients*, which reached the number one spot in Wattpad's science fiction category in May 2020. In August 2020 he published two novels: *Splinters* and *Time Portals of Norwich*. This story was inspired by *Drive In Saturday*, by David Bowie (1972).

Find out more at www.vivadjinn.com.

* * *

"Do you really think we'll get away with it?" said Katrina, partly hidden under the duvet as she snuggled against Robert's chest.

As he kissed the top of her head, a tiny part of him was aware of the microscopic particles that had left the surface of his lips and were being incorporated into her form. Katrina yawned, surfaced, and sat up to let him nuzzle her earlobe. Tenderly, he took it between his teeth and flicked his tongue over the soft flesh. More transferrals took place but, at that level, they could be ignored. She giggled at the touch and playfully slapped his cheek which made him nibble at her flesh a little harder. He grabbed her waist and pulled their bodies closer. Releasing her ear, he peered into her pure blue eyes.

"There's just too much at stake not to," Robert replied. She nodded, but he could sense that she was not wholly satisfied with his conviction.

They made love as the early morning sun lanced through pale curtains that danced in the breeze from the open window. Outside, the last birdsong chorused the growing day before petering out completely. Afterward, she sat up and shook her hair, a wave cascading, ending somewhere out of his sight halfway down her back. He reached behind her to stroke it. She had always worn it that length, neither an inch longer nor shorter.

Unconsciously, she scratched at her belly.

"Suppose they see though our charade," she said, the merest frown marring the perfect set of her face. *Too perfect*, he thought; *almost unbelievably perfect.* He suspected that her worries were threatening to loosen her control over her form. But, barely had those thoughts had time to percolate through his brain when he noticed a reversion to normality; subtle, and probably undetectable by anything further away. Her skin, no longer smooth and polished perfection, though still beautiful, had been overlaid with a slightly rougher texture and had gained a few minor blemishes: a tiny mole here, a blackhead there.

Seemingly unaware of the changes, she released her frown and the flesh about her face softened for a moment as another of her thoughts rippled up.

"There's been no indication that they suspect anything." He read the growing question before she could utter it.

"Yes. But . . ."

"They won't. They mustn't," Robert growled with a conviction he believed to be true. "We've spent too long perfecting this."

"Maybe . . ."

He flung himself out of bed, annoyed at her doubts, and strode into the en suite bathroom. He pushed the door shut, separating them. She had upset him, and he was concerned it would cause him to lose control, as she had.

However, the bathroom mirror showed that his features were as they should be. He stared back at the handsome face: the rugged, dimpled chin modelled, no doubt, upon some long forgotten ideal of the human male form. He forced himself to breathe slowly and relax.

Nothing could go wrong. It couldn't.

He rested his hands on the white of the porcelain washbasin, its cool and unyielding surface hard against his flesh. But down at the microscopic level, exchanges took place. Chemical triggers sent from hundreds of miles away infused his body and tempered his emotions. And he felt his tiny rage subside.

The exchange also brought a confirmation of his conviction. *Progress is as predicted*, he was told.

* * *

Coric Wheelan, standing behind the plain oak desk in his office, watched as Prezten stared out the window. The alien appeared reptilian, but genetic convergence had dictated that his race should mimic humanity's appearance. Wheelan observed that Prezten's gaze took in the low white mounds—the other simple buildings that constituted the rest of this city. Perched atop a slim neck, the alien possessed a head that sported the normal quantity of eyes, ears, and other orifices. His body also had the requisite number of arms and legs, so that his outward appearance hardly seemed alarming.

Not that Coric Wheelan had any reason to think of Prezten as alarming. At least, that was the impression he gave, having met with the alien and his entourage several times over the past few weeks.

He wondered if the alien thought the same of himself.

Only in stature did the two forms differ: Coric's six-foot height towered over the spindly four-and-a-half-foot form of the alien, which was made palpably obvious as Coric joined Prezten at the window. Out beyond the city, a shuttle of non-human origin rested on the landing field. Below them, the city bustled. But, as Coric knew, it been constructed only days before the alien's arrival and the activities pursued by its inhabitants were only there to give the impression of serving the needs of the prominent government building from which they stood gazing. Only the arena, still under construction on the far side of the city, would be of greater elevation.

Prezten's reptilian features were sealed behind the transparent helmet that topped the alien's bodysuit. Though they could survive unshielded, they preferred to breathe their own mixture. The mixture of components making up Earth's atmosphere was, the aliens informed Coric at their first meeting, apparently disagreeable to their respiratory system.

"We find your history so interesting," Prezten commented, his intonation and pronunciation of the English language so correct that it suggested an artificiality about it. That his lips and mouth synchronized perfectly with the sounds that Coric perceived coming from the audio in the alien's suit did nothing to dispel that notion. "Your Renaissance period seems to have been the turning point."

"Yes, indeed it was," Coric agreed, dredging details from memories he could hardly call his own. "Humanity flowered in the arts and sciences during that time, and finally abandoned all major urges to indulge in widespread violence."

"Completely abandoned?"

Coric's shrug was dismissive. "There were a few isolated skirmishes in the six hundred or so years since then, but, as you know, nothing major. We haven't felt the need for any military action for the past one hundred and seventy-five years."

"That would seem to be so."

Coric raised an eyebrow at the implied dubiousness in the alien's comment.

Prezten laughed or, at least, emitted an approximation of human laughter. Wheelan suspected that he'd been practicing and had yet to master it completely. Did the aliens actually understand humour?

"Apologies, Coric Wheelan," Prezten said. "Have no fear. Indeed, our scans have detected no hidden armies, weapons or anything of that nature upon your planet."

Coric relaxed. He'd momentarily wondered if the alien had suspected that something was amiss. He put the comment down to Prezten's unfamiliarity with Earth's single language.

"We admire your population restraints, also," Prezten continued. "That was voluntary?"

"Unfortunately, yes. We could see that the planet had limited resources and so the best solution was to limit our own numbers similarly."

"Very enlightened. And you are stabilized at . . . what? Fifty million?"

"Thereabouts," Coric confirmed with a smile. "The most that this world can comfortably support, given its lack of metals and other raw minerals."

"Such a small number. I regret to say that we have come across many worlds whose self-restraint has been nonexistent and, in most cases, tragedy has been the inevitable outcome. We have seen worlds no bigger than this packed with several billion."

"Billion?"

"Yes, unbelievable as that may sound."

The conversation returned to the terms to which the Earth government had to agree before it would be allowed to join the loose confederation of worlds the aliens had described. Coric Wheelan adhered to his strict remit, which was to engage the alien into settling such terms within as short a period as possible but without giving the slightest impression that he was trying to hurry the process along. Prezten liked to swing the conversation into other subject areas, but Coric was deft in his counter swings and their agreements were eventually confirmed.

When the meeting had concluded, Coric, observing Prezten struggling to stand, placed his hand under the alien's lower arm to help him raise himself under a gravity with which he was patently not evolved to cope.

In the tiny smear of sweat that transferred from Coric Wheelan's touch onto the alien's suit there teemed thousands of small devices that were too complex to be termed mechanical, though their ancestors may have been classed as such. Invisible to normal vision, they milled over the surface of the suit, hiding in crevices and depressions.

✳ ✳ ✳

Somewhere not too far away, an entity of immense proportion, such that it had several distinct centres of intelligence, conversed with itself, thus:

"The aliens suspect nothing?"

"So it appears."
"Therefore, all is as it should be."
"That is the consensus."

* * *

In the heat of the desert, deep-set eyes peered out of grizzled, leathery features as a dark-skinned herder stopped, observing a dozen camels. Then those eyes rose to scan the sky, seeking out the source of the noise as the alien craft thundered back into space. Squinting, the herder detected the tiny shape that buzzed overhead far in advance of the sound that reached his ears.

The camels will panic at the noise, he thought, and, on cue, the camels did exactly that. Agitated, they stomped their feet and pulled against their restraining ropes.

The craft disappeared from view and the noise of its engines diminished into silence. The man was left alone with just the sound of wind and the restless snorting of the camels.

Now they will settle down again, he thought. And they did.

However, he frowned at one animal. One of its front legs was bent the wrong way. The man imagined the leg as it should be. And so it became.

He thought the likelihood the discrepancy had been observed was remote. The aliens would not have picked out this particular scene above any others over which they had flown.

Still, he hoped that there would be no recurrence. For their future, the illusion had to be complete.

* * *

"I find it hard to keep formation sometimes," Katrina said almost idly as she washed some dishes.

"Further assistance can be requested, though it will involve extra bodily mass," Robert replied, wiping moisture from a cup with the towel. At least the water was real, though it teemed with artificiality. He zoomed his consciousness down to the molecular level to detect how the tea towel in his hands had been constructed. It held its formation immaculately, as did he at that moment. Why couldn't Katrina have been constructed with such control? She had been created later than he, when resources were scarcer. Would she wreck their plans?

"No, it's okay. I'll deal with it," she finally decided, momentarily annoyed at the thought of disrupting the lines of her deliberately sensuous body. She knew the risks of deviation from her designated form but, as someone whose role was nothing more complicated than background scenery, it shouldn't have troubled her as much as it did.

Robert knew that Katrina would either deal with it or be reabsorbed. He had heard reports of others failing to keep to their allotted shapes and being returned to the Whole. He failed to repress a pang of sadness at the thought of losing Katrina. But a counter-thought echoed: *We will all be back together soon enough, and Robert and Katrina will no longer exist as separate entities.*

"Are we to attend the signing?" she asked, brighter again.

"Yes, we've been chosen. I will also be on the team that ascends."

Her immediate smile, too quick an acknowledgement of the importance of his remark, betrayed the concern that lay behind it. *And that,* he thought, *is another reason why she cannot be part of the ascension team.* He had been created with much more care, for a far more important role.

For the rest of the day, he deliberately tried to avoid physical contact with her, not wanting to be directly infected by Katrina's doubts. The chemicals that were hardly under her control could invade his own frame, should he accidentally relax his guard against them.

He could afford no such mistakes at this late stage.

∗ ∗ ∗

In his ship, Prezten, still suited, passed through a compartment that bathed him with a select range of radiations. The taint of the planet was entirely stripped away, including the spreading patch of sweat and its hordes of miniature passengers. If he was aware of their presence, he gave no indication.

In his office back on Earth, Coric Wheelan slouched in a thickly padded armchair that was anchored solidly to the floor. He seemed to sink into it, which was not surprising since its purpose was to allow him to communicate fully with the Whole while still outwardly giving the impression of retaining his form. His back merged fully with the chair's substance and they became one.

"The scouts are no more," came the message.

"I am aware of that," Coric replied unemotionally.

"They gathered no new data."

"I am aware of that, also."

"We continue, though, as planned."

"They suspect?"

"Insufficient data to determine but, as far as can be deduced, they were lost to a standard decontamination procedure."

"Their suits are impenetrable?"

"Completely."

"Yet hardly necessary. An anomaly."

* * *

After disconnecting from the chair, Coric's mind turned back to an earlier encounter several weeks previously, not long after the aliens had first arrived.

"Have you determined why Earth has so little of its natural resources remaining?" Prezten had asked.

"Have you detected the remains of the reptilian beasts that lived in its past?" Coric had countered by way of reply, hoping that the evidence, so carefully planted, had been interpreted as planned.

"Your dinosaurs?"

"Indeed. It is suspected that from them there suddenly arose a race that, like humans, quickly reached an advanced stage of evolution and then, approximately sixty-six million years ago, managed to wipe themselves out with some massive, self-inflicted disaster."

"And they had used up much of the available resource?"

"That is the current theory."

"It is almost unheard of for a world to produce more than one sentient species."

"Almost?"

"I am no expert, but I'm sure another was reported many millennia ago."

"Your civilisation is that old?"

"Old and stable," Prezten acknowledged.

"And built on abundant resources?"

"Our own world was severely depleted aeons ago, but the proliferation of other mineral-rich, uninhabitable worlds more than made up for that lack."

"Useful."

"You never invented space flight," Prezten said. "Why?"

"Those aforementioned resource problems—we could not afford to divert resources away from those required just for living."

Prezten nodded in an almost human manner.

* * *

Coric Wheelan strolled at a leisurely pace. Along either side of the road were arranged distinctly different houses and bungalows surrounded by flowering, well-tended gardens. He stopped beside the hanging fronds of a weeping willow and took some leaves into his hand, squinting at the delicate traces and lines that decorated each leaf.

Marvellous, he thought. In his present isolated state, in which he had been since budding off from the Whole nearly four years previously, he could not even begin to comprehend the effort required to constantly sustain this illusion. *But I do it for myself*, he considered, *and it hardly takes much conscious effort.* He had heard of those that slumped back into their default form —a grey, shapeless sludge—and understood that some of the early individuals that had been created had not been at all successful. But so far, Prezten and his companions had not suspected a thing. They took the Earth and its inhabitants at face value.

It is all necessary, Wheelan thought. Otherwise they would never be able to escape a rock whose remaining energy resources were now measured merely in years; forced to gamble all possible energy on this final exercise to attain access to space.

That gamble would play out at the final public meeting, the official signing ceremony, all too soon.

* * *

"All is agreed," Prezten said while two of his unblinking colleagues looked on. They seemed tiny, located at the centre of the large, bowl-shaped auditorium. The arcs of ascending seats, from ground level almost to the high domed ceiling, thronged with the public. From the second row, Robert and Katrina watched the ceremony intensely. Robert also surreptitiously watched Katrina for any hint of slippage, but her form held.

Beside Coric Wheelan ranged five others who, Prezten had been informed, were the heads of the other continents. Coric, whose title had been given as the Head of the Earth Council, leant forward and with a great flourish appended his signature to the last page of the thick document filling much of the small desk that separated the two races. As he replaced the pen in its ornate holder, polite but muted applause erupted in the crowd.

"Coric Wheelan and all the people of Earth," announced the alien Coric understood to be named Tozten, "we hereby welcome you to our confederation. May you reap as much benefit from it as we."

The words of the mini speech had been agreed and rehearsed some days beforehand.

Coric bowed, responding, "We are greatly honoured to have been accepted. This is a great day for our whole planet."

A black-suited figure pushed a large, wheeled ice bucket into the centre and popped the cork from the bottle of champagne. Bubbling glasses were then distributed to the heads of each continent, though, still wearing their suits, the aliens were omitted from that aspect of the toast and stood around, possibly perplexed, while the six raised their glasses and drank.

＊ ＊ ＊

"The ascent is scheduled for noon tomorrow?" Coric asked later, in private.

"Indeed," Prezten confirmed. "You, your continent heads and forty-four of your selected colleagues will be taken up to our craft as promised."

"Wonderful. To think that mankind will finally enter space after centuries of frustration. If only our world had not been so ravaged by those that came before us, I am sure we would have achieved this for ourselves by now."

"Yes. Your race will finally attain the greatness for which you are undeniably destined."

＊ ＊ ＊

In the shade of the bedroom Robert dressed himself by morphing his skin to resemble a finely cut but sombre black suit. In bed, Katrina watched, a nervous smile flickering across her lips.

"This is it, then?" she asked.

"Yes," he said. "Once we have enough of the mass of the Whole outside the gravity well, success is inevitable."

Vague memories danced across Robert's mind: residues of experiences from the consciousness of the Whole, long before he had been created. He remembered the futile attempts to eject sections of itself out of the atmosphere and into space. It had thought it might be trapped on the planet forever.

Then the aliens had been detected and the new plan evolved.

Robert's memories returned to being his own. In a few hours' time he, like all this world's population, would be reunited with the Whole. But this time, they would have the resources of an interstellar craft at their disposal and the whole galaxy would open to them. He felt momentarily sorry for the little reptilian aliens, but they would be given the chance to coexist with the Whole. Or, if they refused, then they too would be absorbed into its consciousness.

Katrina observed Robert while he prepared himself. She knew she was seeing him for the last time. Soon, the Robert she had known and grown to love over the past few months would no longer need to exist. She understood, too, that the need for herself to exist would also end—she tried analyzing how she thought about that but could vaguely detect the thoughts being erased even as she tried forming them.

"I'm not even real," she whispered. "None of us are."

Robert's thoughts were of a similar vein, though he knew he could be cloned almost immediately should the need arise. He may have been the sum of his components, but the Whole knew those components inside and out and could duplicate them down to the last molecule. In fact, the Whole was those components as it was those that made up Katrina, this house, this street, and the rest of the visible planet. But the price the Whole had to pay for this construction had been the wholesale stripping of Earth's few remaining resources.

And now there was so little left.

But even in the final hours before the ascent, parts of Robert were being replaced; a steady microscopic stream spread into and out of him. Every time he placed a foot on the floor, or a hand on a wall, some of him remained to be reabsorbed into the house and other newer parts—components specially designed for the event to come—leeched into his body.

Around the city, others were being similarly enhanced. Like him, they were the final tools in the culmination of the plan.

* * *

Robert stood in the small crowd as they waited for the shuttlecraft's doors to open and admit them. At their head stood Coric Wheelan apparently chatting to one of the small, suited aliens. To Robert, the aliens all looked identical. They were locked away from him, separate consciousnesses that were in for the biggest shock of their lives.

"Take a few of us on a journey after the signing," had been Coric Wheelan's request to the aliens. Surprisingly, they had agreed. The Whole and the aliens' willingness to play into the Whole's hypothetical hands had circumvented the need for forceful commandeering of the aliens' shuttle.

And now, Robert thought as the ship's doors slowly opened, *it finally happens.*

* * *

The ship rose through the atmosphere and into the blackness of space. Robert watched through the thick glass of a porthole as the shrinking planet receded beneath him. Parts of Robert were still in contact with the main body of the Whole, as they were with the forty-nine others that he accompanied.

The shuttle was swallowed into the belly of the main interstellar monster that hung in orbit around Earth and moments later they disembarked and were led along an array of large, deserted corridors. Robert could not keep track of the multiple twists and turns through which they had been led but, lurking inside him and the others, the Whole had no difficulty mapping out the terrain. It mapped not only the corridors through which they passed but also the rooms on either side as well as those beyond that. Dropping minute components from the fifty, it planned to infuse itself into the circuits carrying the power that drove this craft. Soon, it would know this ship throughout and would assume control.

As they entered a large auditorium, a suited alien beckoned them toward an arrangement of seating measured for human occupancy.

Robert sat in a chair and waited. Several aliens, still suited, approached, and took up positions along a bench in opposition to those from Earth. Coric Wheelan, seated in the front, a focal point for the aliens' attention, wondered why the aliens were still suited. He, through the Whole, could detect the difference in the atmosphere which was now apparently of the mix more suited to their hosts. It gave the air a slight tang, a taste of electricity.

He tried to suppress the anxiousness threatening to throng through his body. He detected the Whole urging his responses to calm, overriding the autonomy which he had been granted. There was a mental merging with the rest of the party, and he realized he wasn't the only one exhibiting the feeling.

"They do not suspect," said the Whole. "The ship is ours. We will dominate."

Wheelan's eyes glanced to one side as several more aliens approached and added themselves to the bench. There were about twenty or so, more than anyone from Earth had ever seen at once. All were suited.

"Welcome to our ship," said Prezten, seated almost centrally.

"It is our pleasure," Coric returned.

Then, sensing that the time was right, the Whole activated a trigger.

"In fact," Coric continued, feeling a hand gently rest upon his shoulder, knowing that, behind him, all those in his party had reached out and touched each other physically, "it is more than our pleasure. It is our right."

The aliens stared expressionlessly as the fifty forms in front of them began blurring and shifting. Clothes merged with flesh, limbs intertwined and joined, features flowed together. Within a few seconds the aliens faced not fifty individuals but a single grey-pink blob that quivered slightly.

The Whole, or this representative portion, formed a new mouth and lungs through which to communicate. "We are not what you thought. Certainly, Earth was once populated by human creatures similar to those recently depicted. We, however, are a product of their science, the final form that evolved from their nanotechnology. A conglomerate of interactive devices, hardly alive by your standards but which, when aggregated, can become almost anything."

The aliens, still seated and silent, watched impassively.

Wondering if it had shocked these creatures into their current immobility, the Whole continued, "We mean you no harm. We needed to escape our planet before its lack of resources strangled us. You will submit to our requirements. Otherwise, regretfully, you will force us to incorporate your physical forms as well."

Two aliens glanced at each other and one removed its helmet.

It said, "You fooled no one. We saw the remnants of the previous human technologies, the silent circling metal satellites, the abandoned vehicles on your moon, the probes that still race outwards from your system. They were dated merely thousands of years old, far younger than the sixty-six million years claimed for your dinosaur predecessors."

This was unexpected. The Whole was nonplussed.

The alien who had spoken raised the helmet it had removed and the Whole watched as the device merged with the alien's arm. "Creatures such as those you depicted," the alien continued, "are not suited to the rigours or long-term survival of space travel. This ship's acceleration cannot exceed that of light. It has taken hundreds of your years to reach your system. Only creatures who can abide such periods can travel such distances."

"What sort of creatures?" asked the Whole.

The aliens stood and flowed, merging with each other to form a single entity.

"Those such as yourself," the merged entity uttered just before it extended a pseudopod. The Whole's representative tried backing away, but the projection lanced through its body, integrating itself.

On Earth the Whole felt the spike of the alien's merging with its representative high above and tried recoiling, fighting to shrink within itself. But the alien was too strong, too experienced.

And now, through its representative, the Whole found itself combining with a new greater Whole, a galaxy-wide Whole. Initially, it fought against the absorption, unwilling to dilute its consciousness within the vast ocean of the greater entity, but the pressure was too overpowering and, finally, it relented, accepting its fate. Memories merged and exchanged, and the Earth Whole found it was no longer bound by the physical restraint of an exhausted planet; its consciousness could now range across much of the galaxy via its merged superior.

"Welcome home," said the larger Whole.

Science Fiction Novelists

Mate for Life
By David Viner

I gazed into her eyes. They were inhuman, laced with delicate gossamer filaments whose purpose my instruments had yet to fathom. The genetic sequencer had made a reasonable attempt at replicating the effect within my own eyes. She knew I was different; she could see that plainly enough, but my outward appearance was not different enough to trigger repulsion in her. Maybe she viewed me as I would have viewed a Chinese or Maori girl.

In the shade of maroon fronds—this planet's excuse for trees—that swayed in the light breeze above our heads, she gazed back at me and I felt the love she emitted as if it was a solid, tangible thing.

"We mate for life," she said, leading me toward a stream cutting through the woods, her six-fingered hand clasping my own similar version. I had no real feeling in the additional finger—the replicator wasn't perfect. The translator was better and converted the trills and pipings escaping her almost human-looking mouth into a pretty good substitute for English. I had problems with the occasional word—it tended to interchange "mate" and "join" for example.

She sat beside the stream, expecting a reply.

"So do we," I lied, clasping both her hands in mine.

She stared more intensely into my eyes. Would she detect the lie? I had a job to do and lying was a large part of it. My ability to form untruths into believable facts had been in full flow since I'd landed.

I suppressed a smile at the memory of two failed human marriages, and of the other planetfalls on which I'd promised similar lifetime commitments, which were my usual mode of attack. The failure of both marriages had been just two of the reasons I took the path to the stars to do the seeking out, boldly going thing. It paid well and got me away from awkward situations. I would soon be retiring on the bonuses for every profitable project. And this looked to be the most profitable yet.

This world, on which I had discovered these people, possessed gold and rare minerals that were far more common than the people themselves. I had gained their trust, ingratiating myself into their society, preparing the way for the coming onslaught from Earth. And, so far, it was all going as well as it had on all the previous worlds. I was good at my job.

The green-gold hues of her skin in the afternoon light filtering through the waving fronds made her appear Elvish. Human-looking enough to appear cute, even. Her name translated into Bird-Eye-Gold-Feather. I had no real idea what the translator made of my own name, though I think Sky-Faller-In-Metal-House was a small part of it.

Her attire was fine, almost regal, and it glistened in the light. I ran my hand down her arm, feeling the warmth of her skin, and felt her shiver under my touch. I'd definitely chosen well, and from her attitude toward me, I knew the genetic replicator had refashioned me into the form of a desirable suitor. Not bad—three days from touchdown to marriage proposal from the daughter of one of the more important leaders. At least, that was what I surmised; all the others I met deferred to her as if she was of high importance. But I had yet to meet her parents or any of the leaders or elders. They kept themselves hidden away. She told me I would meet them at the wedding or joining event.

I wasn't completely sure of what this mating or joining ceremony involved. Given the level of technology, I was expecting nothing more complex than jumping over a broom.

Once the ceremony was over, I would report back and this small world would be swallowed up into our voracious empire.

The touch of her hand on my cheek brought me back to the present.

"Are you ready for this step?" she asked. I nodded and oozed sincerity.

She led me away from the clearing in which we'd been seated, along a pathway that finished at the tree-covered hill under which her tribe lived. She had trouble matching my stride; the feet on her shorter legs pattered the ground beside me in an enchanting manner. I steeled myself internally against sentimental regrets and smiled at her. Her mouth widened in a similar manner.

By the time we reached the hill, which poked above the forest like a large pimple in a lush beard, we were accompanied by tens and then hundreds of her tribe. Somehow the news had got around quickly. We reached an entrance—a wooden door embedded in the hillside—and descended into the hill at the head of the crowd, their trilling and piping filling the air. My eyes took a moment getting accustomed to the change from bright sunlight, but it was not dark; the walls emitted a luminance enhanced by polished nuggets of gold that studded the rock.

We came to a large chamber lit by torches around the walls. The ceiling, twenty feet or so above my head, was black with soot from centuries of flame. She bade me wait whilst the room filled with those who'd followed us. They moved amongst strange globular objects that dotted the room. Each object appeared rooted into the ground and was taller than me. I wanted to investigate, but she held me back. I tried to figure out what they were. Some were spherical and polished as if new, the light from the torches dancing upon their surfaces. Others looked old with a leathery exterior, while a few appeared to have perished and were disintegrating into the dust of the floor.

"A spot must be chosen," she said. I had no idea what she meant.

The crowd moved between the objects for several minutes, gesticulating at them with their arms and trilling and piping as if consulting them. I suspected these objects had some religious significance to the people. Maybe they represented their gods. I looked around to see if her parents or any of the other elders had arrived, but all the faces seemed as young as my bride.

Then a small opening formed in the crowd and we were beckoned over. We stood in this clearing and she moved toward me. She shuffled her feet and the floor, which was not rock but compacted earth, crumbled slightly. She beckoned me to do likewise. I was clumsy and she laughed and made me remove my boots. My bare feet seemed to get the message and, laughing, I pushed my feet into the ground until we were covered up to our ankles.

Then she removed her clothes. I sighed. This wasn't the first time a wedding ceremony had involved the nuptials taking place in front of an audience. I removed mine, too, as it seemed to be expected, shaking the dust out of my trousers before inserting my feet back into the ground. She studied my body closely and pressed her arms about me. The genetic replicator had substituted enough of my own DNA with the native kind to give my temporary body the full ability to further their species. I probably had a good number of non-human offspring dotted amongst the stars, not that I was in any hurry to visit them.

Her fingers found what they were looking for—I'd wondered what the two extra organs on my back were for. As I located the equivalent organs on her back, they opened and my fingers—all six of them—slid in.

104

Well, this was a new experience.

Her face reached toward mine and the equivalent of a kiss started. I'd kissed her before—it wasn't too dissimilar to any earthly experience. But this time she did not move away after the kiss. It went on and I felt myself melt into her as a shudder of pleasure went through my body. What was she doing to me? I wondered if this was what love really felt like. My marriages had been based on lust, not love—not a recipe for success. But I wasn't in love with this little alien. I was merely doing my job. Wasn't I?

I tried to end the kiss but couldn't break away. My fingers, too, were locked into her back. My feet seemed rooted to the ground. I couldn't move them.

This was beginning to unsettle me and I started struggling. Then she spoke, not using her mouth, which was still locked onto mine, but somehow trilling in my head; I heard her and understood.

"We are mated," she said. My face and hers merged. Our bodies did the same. They distended and swelled as our life forces mixed. We became spherical and I found we were fully rooted into the ground, our combined flesh digging deeper, seeking out the tiny rivulets deep below, where they sifted minerals and extracted nutrients from underground streams to sustain us.

Somewhere inside our combined body I felt the beginnings of a new life form.

Around us, I could sense the crowd. They were ecstatic at the joining. I could also sense the elders all around us. We were now the same as them. They sang and hummed their happiness at our marriage directly into our interwoven brain.

And, as the elders stripped my mind back to its primitive core, I finally understood what love meant. It was to be joined, mated for life.

The Unreality Onion
By David Viner

Agent Pete Hampshire ducked instinctively. A whistle of bullets filled the air. He grimaced and corrected his stance, then fired at the unknown enemy. Beside him, Agent Carl Brunswick took longer adjusting to the situation's unreality. Soon his own beam was aligned with the source of the noise.

They'd been deposited in sparse woods. Meagre light penetrating the foliage painted the trees in stripes of grey on a greyer background. The enemy had the lower ground beyond the edge of the woods—not that it should make any difference. Unlike Pete and Carl, the enemy were unreal.

Firepower erupting from behind the two agents crisscrossed the enemy's own and from ahead came a torrent of curses in, if Pete wasn't mistaken, old German. *So, we have our own troops as well*, he thought, before wondering where the hell this place was supposed to be. On each side he became aware of camouflaged soldiers advancing down the hill alongside him.

More unreality. He wondered which side had provided them.

The German troops, recovered from their surprise, began returning fire again. Carl's power beam cut through the less-than-solid trunks of the trees and into the enemy's position. Pete's eyes fell on artillery: several vehicles including three mounted guns. They looked historical. The vehicles displayed a familiar symbol. Beyond them loomed a large, old, black-and-white building, from which erupted more troops. A flag with the same symbol hung from a window.

Inside his mouth, Pete waggled his tongue and clicked his teeth together. In response, a small holographic Heads-Up Display projection appeared in front of his right eye. Under his subtle control, his implant searched through a database of symbols until a match was detected. Got it—swastika—a symbol used the world over for various reasons including good luck, wealth and nationalistic identity. Pete dug further and found a match with German usage leading up to a global conflict several centuries previously—twentieth century. Well, that explained the primitive weapons. He dismissed the HUD, while thinking of Janice and the kids.

He aimed his beamer at the enemy and sliced through several guns and soldiers. Beside him, Carl and the other unreal soldiers were doing the same.

Damn. He suddenly remembered that Janice's mother, Helen, was coming over for the weekend.

A few minutes later he stood beyond the tree line and surveyed the carnage. Behind him, his unreal troops awaited his next move. Somewhere in all this there had to be a clue as to why they were here and what this was all about. Carl was examining the bodies of the slain and the remains of the sliced up vehicles.

"Found a map," Carl said, returning with some folded paper. "My implant correlates it to a location in northern Europe, mid-twentieth century; a country known then as Poland."

Pete's implant scanned the map and came to the same conclusion. He nodded and looked at the troops and then at their surroundings. The air of unreality permeated everything. Pete had difficulty holding what he saw in sharp focus. Resources must be stretched thin, he thought.

"What about that?" Pete pointed to the building.

"Headquarters, possibly," Carl surmised, sweat beading his brow. Pete frowned. Carl, nearly ten years older than Pete's twenty-nine, was letting the unreality get to him—never a good sign. Time he retired. But agents were thin on the ground.

"Okay, we'll take a look," Pete said and nodded at the troops. He set off at a brisk pace toward the supposed headquarters. As he ran, he cursed himself for agreeing to Helen's visit. He and Helen didn't get on, at least not since her husband Jacques had got himself killed in the Crusades. Damned fool was way too old to still be in service.

Nearing the building, their troops were met by a sporadic burst of machine gun fire. A bullet passed harmlessly straight through Pete's torso. Carl ducked unnecessarily and responded with a beam that sliced through wood and cement. Pete rushed the door, burning down three Germans who didn't get out of his way in time—once, he might have felt something for these victims, these play figurines—but they had no life of their own.

A large hallway with a wide, impressively decorated staircase led up to a paneled corridor. All doors, except the large one at the end, stood open.

Pete nodded his head toward the target.

"In there, you reckon?" Carl asked, needlessly. Pete's implant noted the quaver in Carl's voice—nervous.

Together they disintegrated the door and burst in. A single shot from the right cut across Carl's forehead. Carl swore, doing his best to disbelieve the injury. While he cut the German officer down with a beam, Pete's implant catalogued the red slash across his colleague's brow. Carl grunted and brought himself back into reality; the mark faded, but not completely.

Pete scanned the room—walls of filled bookcases; a large wooden desk; the symbol on a red, white, and black flag hanging over the ornate, unlit fireplace. The clue, he felt, had to be here. He kept scanning: brass lamps, padded chairs, a coat stand, heavy curtains. The implant imaged and processed everything. On the desk were papers and a metal bust of a man's head. Under the chin was a representation of that symbol again. Pete glanced at the papers. The HUD streamed into life, translating the language before his eyes. They were just orders and details of troop movements. No, they were not it. He looked at the bust again, at the moustached face that stared sightlessly ahead. There was something wrong.

And then Pete got it.

The symbol had five arms instead of the four displayed elsewhere.

Pete grinned.

"Gotcha!"

Carl, dabbing at his forehead, joined him beside the desk.

Pete picked up the bust and examined it. The underside contained a script that flowed as his eyes tried and failed to interpret it. Sometimes it resembled a language with which he was familiar. Then it would change to something symbolic like Chinese. Finally, it stabilized into a pattern which Pete's implant recorded for later analysis.

"Here we go," he heard Carl say as the room faded.

$$* \quad * \quad *$$

"Agent Hampshire?"

Pete's eyes cleared as his visor was removed and a familiar world returned. He was lying on a bed surrounded by the unreality synchronizer machines. A medic disconnected further sensors from his head and arms.

Colonel Staunton sat at the end of the bed. "Usual stuff?" he asked.

"Another historical sequence, sir," Pete said, pulling himself up. "No purpose as far as I could see. Just went in and found the clue. German, twentieth century global war . . ." Pete waited for his implant to supply the information—it did. "Nazis, Hitler. The clue was a bust with an incorrect symbol. A five-armed swastika. The swirling message appeared again. Any idea what it is? What they're planning?"

"Oh, intelligence is full of the usual crap. All we know is that the clues are getting less coherent. No one can identify a pattern to either the messages or the locations." Staunton put a hand on Agent Hampshire's shoulder. "We lost Barton. Not sure what happened. We're trying to recover the data from his implant. Think he was on to something, though. Came back through repeating nothing but 'too deep' over and over until he died."

"Jesus. Barton was the best. Taught me everything I . . ."

Another pat on the shoulder.

"Yes, I know. How's Carl holding up?"

Pete sighed.

"Thought so. Didn't need to see that scar on his head to know it's getting to him."

"When's the next mission?" Pete asked.

"You're free for a week at least. Use it wisely."

"Pah! Not with Helen over."

* * *

But the next few days were, initially, a relief. Helen seemed to have mellowed in her distrust of Pete and his work. Whether this was for his sake or for Janice's, he wasn't sure. Helen seemed to blame him personally for her loss, just because he and Jacques had both worked for the same organization. Or maybe Helen blamed him for marrying her daughter, for putting Janice though the same torment Jacques had put her through. Pete had given up trying to analyse it. His implant nagged that it could try to figure out the change in Helen's stance. Pete quietened it with a tongue gesture and a sharp click of his molar. But his mind wouldn't let it go.

On the final afternoon of Helen's visit, the three sat chatting out in the small communal garden that they shared with several neighbours while Robert and Alice played in the bushes.

"So, Pete. Are we winning?" Helen asked, suddenly changing the topic from gardening.

Oh, here it comes, Pete thought.

"I thought you agreed not to talk about it, Mum," Janice scolded.

"Oh, I miss the news. You know . . . the real inside news. The stuff they put out for the public says nothing."

Pete watched the children play tag around the garden. He didn't want to talk about it. Sitting here, in the warmth of a spring sun, he tried to forget about his other life.

"Well, Pete?" Helen insisted. Pete took a deep breath. Janice exhaled in a meaningful manner.

"The tactics are changing, but we don't know what they're leading up to, if anything. Maybe they're running out of ideas. They're certainly not gaining any ground."

"But are we? Jacques used to tell me that we were winning, slowly. But it's been going on for so many years now that I just can't remember what we've won or lost."

"Mum, leave it."

"Yes, but I want to know," Helen retorted, leaning forwards in her chair, wagging a finger at her daughter. "Is it really all worth it in the end? Just what are we fighting for anyway? What's the advantage of having all this so-called unreality?"

Pete grunted, got up and went inside the house. Fixing himself a drink, he could still hear Janice outside, having words with her mother.

The doorbell rang and Pete found Carl standing on his doorstep. The mark across his forehead was still quite prominent. Red. Pete thought, *I bet they've—*

"They've transferred me," Carl confirmed, his hands shaking.

"Ah, sorry, Carl. Come in. Helen's here—you remember Jacques?"

"Oh yes, of course. Sorry," Carl whispered, his eyes darting around, a worried expression flitting across his features. "I didn't mean to intrude."

"No problem. Drink?" Carl nodded in agreement. "Join us out in the garden."

Outside, Pete re-introduced Carl to Helen, who immediately started her questioning on Carl.

"Mum," Janice chided, but Helen persisted.

Pete watched the children in a dreamy fashion while letting the conversation pass him by, glad to no longer be the subject of Helen's interrogation. He thought about how alike the kids were, despite the eighteen-month difference. Robert was nearly as tall as his sister, and had the same body shape and mannerisms, and they were dressed similarly. Pete found he almost had trouble telling them apart as they chased each other. He shook his head and stared at them more attentively. There was an almost ethereal presence as they laughed and flowed in and out of the bushes.

Too much sun, Pete thought as he poured the rest of the cool drink down his throat.

Carl and Helen were still talking about unreality. Pete thought Carl would fend the older woman off gracefully, but listening in, he realized that the subject had veered toward things that Carl should not have been commenting upon. He put it down to Carl's change of circumstances and wondered, *Should I caution him? Subtly? He is my colleague.*

When Carl started talking about the mission with the Germans, Pete sat up, about to interject, but he stopped, staring at the scar on Carl's forehead.

Something was wrong.

Hadn't the bullet grazed the skin over his right eye?

"Carl," he said, reaching out a hand to the scar. "Hold still a moment."

As Pete's hand connected to the clue, swirling text including the words 'too deep' writhed across Carl's face before the sun went out.

* * *

"Carl?" Pete shouted, waking up on the bed surrounded, as usual, by the unreality machines. He pulled the sensors off his arm. "Janice?"

A man who, without close inspection, could have been mistaken for Colonel Staunton came into the room.

"Ah, Agent Hampton. Peter."

Something inside Pete jarred—he couldn't identify what.

"You're back with us again."

"I—uh—did I just . . ."

"Yes, I know. Damned stuff gets us believing anything, doesn't it?"

"Janice?"

"Janet."

"Oh, yes."

"Home with your daughter. You're due for a few days' leave."

"Daughter. Oh . . . Carl. Agent Brunswick."

"Unreal."

"Shit."

"Sorry, nasty trick to play on you. Seems like they believed it, though. How's your mother-in-law?"

"What?"

"Fading fast, is it? Just as well. Carl was a trap for her and they fell for it."

"Helen? What's she got to do with this?"

"Nothing—not the real one anyway."

"Oh yes, I see. Helen. Hell."

* * *

Pete sat with Janet in the garden watching Alice making a daisy chain on the small lawn.

"What's wrong?" Janet asked. "You've been staring at Alice as if you can't believe she's there."

"Nothing really—oh, work—the unreality. There was a setup—they made me believe other things . . ."

"What? That Alice had died?" Janet said, her voice reduced to a whisper. "The bastards."

"No, not that. But Alice had . . . had a brother."

"Robert," she whispered, after a moment.

"Yes." Pete gulped. He agreed—they were bastards. Robert had died soon after birth, about when Alice was eighteen months old. Alice didn't remember. One day they'd have to tell her that she'd once had a brother. *The bastards made Robert part of the unreality they wove around me!* Pete tried to console himself.

At least they'd caught one of the enemy, so it had all been worthwhile.

Hadn't it?

Hell, he was feeling like Carl.

Damn. He had to remind himself that Carl hadn't existed, either.

Twenty-nine, he thought. *I can apply for retirement from active duty after next birthday.*

Alice finished weaving her chain of flowers and brought them for inspection. Pete watched. The chain was perfect—each flower identical and threaded to the next in exactly the same style. He had a sinking feeling.

"They're lovely, darling," Janet crooned.

No, they're not, Pete realized. He looked around at the garden, at the small suburban houses, at the fluffy clouds in the blue sky, at the green leaves on the trees.

Perfect.

Perfectly unreal.

Everything started to lose focus.

He reached out and touched the ring of flowers, which shimmered, petals turning into symbols, into words.

"Pete?" Janet said.

"Peter!"

"Daddy!"

God. How deep does this go?

* * *

Outside the glass tank, the smaller of the two grey creatures turned to the other.

"It's breaking through another level," it would have said, had it possessed a mouth. It said it anyway, in its own fashion.

116

The other creature analyzed the settings on the machines. Inside the glass tank the misshapen torso quivered slightly, but the thousands of micro-fine wire connections linking the body to the machines prevented too much movement.

The larger creature felt pity. What would the poor thing feel when it broke through the final level of unreality? Did it understand the messages they were trying to send it? Would the truth drive it completely insane? Should they put it out of its misery now?

The creature observed the face, or at least as much of the face as could be seen. Bunches of wires entered the skull where there had once been eyes, a mouth, and ears. Tubes provided nourishment and oxygen. Wires attached to the stumps of arms and legs provided sensations as if such limbs were still possessed. But the body, ancient and shrivelled and the last of its kind, was barely alive.

"If only we had arrived a century or so ago, we might have saved them," the smaller creature trilled.

"Or maybe not. Don't blame yourself, love." The larger creature extended a pseudopod-like projection to its mate. Chemicals of comfort were exchanged. "They did this to themselves. We are merely witnessing the end."

"But they did it to save themselves, dear. Before their world completely died."

"The machines are a work of genius, though."

"Yes. It's a pity we couldn't determine their function earlier."

"They scare me."

"I also. They seem to exist independently, propagating through the dimensions of unreality that they create."

"They do exist fully here, though. Don't they?"

* * *

And somewhere far away, yet close enough to be almost overlapping, a tear fell from an observer's eye.

How the Forest-watchers Undertook to Devise a Game

By Jon Anthony Perrotti

About the author

Jon Perrotti is a writer of poetry, short stories, and science fiction including the *Barren Trilogy*, an alternate world sci-fi series of an androgynous race threatened by an epidemic of genetic infertility. Written for an audience with a particular interest in sexual minority and gender issues, the *Barren Trilogy* is published in dual formats, one using feminine pronouns and the other masculine, as in this story. Perrotti taught Japanese, English, and Special Education. He currently lives with his cats in Lancaster County, Pennsylvania. He is the author of two stories in this anthology, both of which are set in the uedin universe, which likewise serves as setting for the *Barren Trilogy*. Find out more at www.jonanthonyperrotti.com

* * *

There was a slight breeze blowing across the wooden platform. One of the server-masters had gifted the forest-watchers with a wind chime of tiny, thin, hardwood plates, strung together in a clever design. It produced a lovely, delicate rattle. Leci allowed the concerns of the day's chores to melt away as he gazed at the gently swaying leafy branches. He deepened his breath. While the new capital had grown up around the forest-watchers' residence, this precious patch of woods preserved a quiet treasure within their compound at the heart of the settlement.

It felt wonderful to take this time for breathing and observing the beauty of the trees and shadows. Leci felt a pleasant tranquility soak into his mind, and for a moment he imagined that he even felt a flicker of the presence of the Lern. The wind-rattle purred.

HHHWWAAPP! His hand reflexively rose to his ear. Something had slammed into the side of his head. *Ouch! What in tarnation?* He looked down to see what object had suddenly struck him. It was a heavy-duty floor-scrubbing brush, probably from the child-uedin's domicile. At that moment, he heard the sound of child-uedin laughing together.

"Oops!" one of them yelled. "That was an accident!"

"Now, you were all told you could come here to watch the forest. But not to play!" Leci's scolding tone was a bit angrier than it should have been, no doubt because of the shock of being struck.

"That's what we were doing! We were watching the forest!" announced the child-uedin in a sassy, disingenuous tone.

Leci ignored the insincerity. "Why does one need a floor-scrubbing brush *here*?" he asked.

"One uses it to scratch one's butt," snapped the impertinent child. "One's butt is itchy." The other two, unable to suppress their laughter, first chortled through their noses, then doubled over in laughing fits.

Leci, however, was troubled by this behavior and quite unable to laugh along. It was another sign that the child-uedin who had taken leg in the new capital did not act like normal child-uedin. They were not thoughtful. He picked up the brush.

"Please go on back to your domicile. I will return this to your caretakers."

* * *

That evening, Leci walked across the capital. It was quiet until he neared the domicile of the unnamed. Squabbling, laughter, and loud voices created a boisterous atmosphere there. Any other time, the noisiness alone would have made him wonder what was going on there, but this time, Leci was nervous about talking with the domicile's head caretaker.

Leci had been an apprentice at Quarterhouse, a domicile back in the old capital. It had been a lifetime ago, but memories swirled now of how all the tutors and caretakers felt about the unnamed. They were completely dedicated to them. Leci wanted to express his concerns, but he feared it was going to be painfully awkward.

He climbed the stairs to the entrance and tapped on the door-tarp.

"Master Ganam?"

Ganam appeared wearing an apron and bearing a smile that suggested being both happy to have a visitor and mildly inconvenienced at the same time. He was many generations Leci's junior, but his rugged face reflected the fact that he was a product of the times of crisis in the old capital. Both gladness and mild annoyance at the inconvenience quickly disappeared into a frown.

"Server Leci! What happened to your face?"

"What? Is there a bruise?"

"Yes, a nasty one, right by your eye. What happened?"

"Oh, well . . . this." Leci held up the brush. "Some of the unnamed were playing. In our woods. One of them threw this. It hit me—in the head."

"Shield the Lern, that's terrible!"

"Well, yes, I must admit it was upsetting. I know it was an accident, but the little ones didn't seem to feel sorry about it. At all."

Ganam responded with a knowing look. "Server Leci, do you have time for tea? I have some fresh milkgrass."

Leci brought hands to face in a gesture of gratitude. "That would be very nice, thank you." Perhaps the conversation would go more smoothly over tea. He followed Ganam in and sat at the table while Ganam made the tea. Leci looked around. There were some scribbled drawings on the wall. That was something that would never have occurred at Quarterhouse.

Ganam came back with the tea and poured quietly, frowning for a long time and looking like he didn't know what to say. Leci decided to open the subject.

"The problem may be in their small number. There are only nineteen unnamed. Surely, they are experiencing a unique childhood, unlike what any of us had in the old capital."

Ganam shook his head. "They've been told many times that the patch of woods in your compound is not for play, just for forest-watching."

"Yes, I reminded them."

"And what did they say?"

"One spoke up and said that that's what they *were* doing."

Ganam stared glumly at his tea. "Any time I've ever been forced into telling a lie, it always felt horrible. But our unnamed here seem comfortable with it." He inhaled deeply and rubbed his face with both hands.

Leci was beginning to feel sorry about coming to report a problem about which Ganam was already suffering. He now wanted to smooth it over. "Perhaps they really were there for forest-watching. We don't know for sure."

"No, I think they were there to run through the woods, tossing that brush back and forth," said Ganam. "Yes, they've been introduced to forest-watching, but anyone can see they don't have the patience for it."

"We need to give them a chance. Child-uedin are perfectly capable of mindstilling exercises."

Ganam smiled, and Leci could tell that he was not at all reassured but appreciated the attempt at positivity.

"Yes, of course," Ganam said, refilling their cups. "We just need to give them a chance."

Yet it was an incomplete solution to a dire problem, and they both knew it.

* * *

Late that night, Leci lay on his bedding, unable to sleep. He hated the thought that festered in his mind. What if the new generation was completely unlike what had come before? What if they didn't have the basic nature that had always translated into what it means to be uedin? The thought sickened him.

"Leci, something is bothering you. What is it?" Yulig sleepily rolled onto his side, facing Leci.

"Are you awake, too? I hope my tossing and turning didn't wake you." Yulig had been Leci's closest companion for many novades. Leci couldn't get away with any kind of secret worry —Yulig knew him too well.

Yulig mumbled, "Is it because I complained about the bath? I wasn't saying it was your fault that everybody lets the fire burn out—"

"No, it's not that. I'm still thinking about the incident today with the floor-scrubbing brush."

"That was terrible. No wonder you're upset."

"It's not their misbehavior that bothers me."

"They make entirely too much noise."

"I'm not annoyed with our unnamed—I'm *worried* about them. The future of the capital rests with them."

"I don't know how worrying will help . . ."

"Well, isn't there something we should be doing?"

"What," Yulig sounded half asleep, "would you like to do?"

"I'd like to teach the unnamed how to do serious forest-watching, and how to find the essence of the forest and feel the presence of the Lern. I think if they could do that, they would act more like proper child-uedin, and we would all feel better."

"Maybe make a game out of it. Child-uedin like games."

"A game? Like rope-kick or something? That's exactly what forest-watching *isn't!*"

He waited a long time for Yulig to respond but instead heard only the beginnings of low snoring. This left Leci to lie for another hour thinking by himself about the ridiculous notion that forest-watching could ever be conveyed through the use of a game.

✳ ✳ ✳

Some days later, Leci exchanged messages with Ganam. Leci asked if he and a group of his fellow forest-watchers could do a small presentation for the unnamed, and Ganam responded that they would be more than welcome. Ganam did not ask for any details.

It was a simple game that they had devised, made possible by the fact that the soil beneath the forest at that locale on the drystream, where the new capital had been established, was full of small pebbles. Leci had a small handful of them in his pocket.

He couldn't help noticing the pebbles as they made their way along the footpath to the domicile of the unnamed. Everyone had just gotten used to the pebbly soil as the norm whenever they were planting or tending any of the crops that grew there.

Ganam greeted the forest-watchers, and they followed him to the large lesson hall where the unnamed were all standing in waiting. Although they stood in proper formation, they were not observing silence as child-uedin had always done whenever they were assembled for talks at Quarterhouse back at the old capital. These ones were chattering away. Their high-pitched voices created a cacophony with little shouts and peals of laughter in the mix. Leci waited for Ganam to call them to attention.

Finally, Ganam called out, "Unnamed, ready yourselves!" Instead of the slow sit that child-uedin of the old capital were trained to do, it was a kind of silly flop that these ones did, and Leci noticed how instead of the uniform quick gesture of straightening overrobes to show they were ready for tutoring, half of them made a little tug on their garment and the other half did nothing at all! Leci took note of the fact that they all looked identical. From behind, you could see that some of them had two round bumps on the backs of their heads, some had three, and a few had only one—but otherwise there was no telling them apart. They were still only seven; it would be another year before they would develop individual facial features.

"Unnamed, the forest-watchers are here today to speak with you about a very special topic. Please listen quietly and give them your full attention."

"Stop!" squealed one of the child-uedin. "Master Ganam, the unnamed beside one is poking one with his toes!"

"Unnamed, behave yourselves!" ordered Ganam in a scolding voice, "We have visitors today!" Then he looked across to the forest-watchers and brought hands to face. "Pardon us please. We are ready to listen now."

Leci stepped forward. "Good afternoon, unnamed. We've come today to share an idea with you. We would like to introduce you to a new game." The identical faces were uniform in their gaze. He had their attention. "It's a very special game, and it will teach you some important things about what it means to be a uedin." He looked up to make sure Ganam approved. Ganam wore a curious smile. So far, so good.

"In this game, you will be doing things that you already know how to do. But for this, you will keep track of your success. First of all, let's talk about the tasks. There are three tasks that will earn a pebble in this game." Leci deliberately turned to face Ganam to dialogue with him in front of the attentive group of child-uedin. "Master Ganam, do the unnamed know about attitude focus during meals?"

Leci saw that Ganam wore a look of mixed fascination and hesitation, not expecting the introduction of a game. Perhaps he thought the forest-watchers were there to reprimand the unnamed for the recent disturbance. Then he seemed to wake and answered cooperatively, "Yes, Server Leci. The unnamed all know the points of attitude focus during meals." Leci was still not used to being called *Server*. It was a vocation in the old capital with which the forest-watchers were being increasingly associated.

"Can any of you repeat the points?" Leci invited the child-uedin to share. Almost all of them raised a palm to answer.

Leci chose one of the identical faces. He carefully stepped around the adjacent child-uedin and laid a gentle hand on his small shoulder. "Will you tell us, little one?"

As Leci stepped back to the front of the lesson hall, the child-uedin stood, smiling broadly. Leci could tell that this one thought it was a treat to be singled out.

"Food's a gift of nature," he recited. "Food should be 'preciated, and the Lern is with us when we eat."

"Very good," said Leci. This was going much better than he expected. "Every time you focus on those points for a whole meal, you may give yourself one pebble." He then reached his hand into his pocket and took out the small handful of pebbles.

"See these?" The child-uedin all craned their necks. Leci found it comical to see their interest in something so common as these pebbles. "You can find these just about everywhere around the capital. You pick up one of these pebbles, and you put it into your pocket just like I had these in mine."

The child-uedin wanted to see the pebbles. They were unable to resist moving to their feet and creeping forward to get a better look at the ordinary pebbles.

"Ready yourselves to keep listening!" yelled Ganam. "Stay in your places!" The child-uedin obeyed. Leci was impressed. At least they were capable of following directions.

"Now, let's talk about the second way to earn a pebble. Who can tell me what mindstilling is?" Palms were displayed again, and Leci stepped to another part of the room to touch the shoulder of another child-uedin. "Please tell us."

"Exercise," he said, his face showing pride at knowing the word.

"What kind of exercise?" Ganam interjected.

"To stop spiraling!" The child-uedin clapped twice, celebrating his clever answer.

"That's right," said Ganam. "An exercise to stop spiraling in our thoughts and do what?"

"BECOME QUIET AND CALM!" The child was very excited. Yulig's shoulders shook with a silent chuckle.

"Very good," Leci said. "That is another way you can earn a pebble. Each time you try your hardest to do a mindstilling, you may give yourself one pebble." Leci took one out of his pocket again. "Just pick one up and do this . . ." Leci theatrically held the pebble if front of his face, then held open the pocket on the side of his robe and dropped the pebble in.

Ganam spoke up. "Server Leci, what happens when the unnamed has a pocket full of pebbles?" With a concerned tone, he added, "We don't want too many pebbles coming into the domicile . . ."

"I'm going to explain all that," said Leci. "But first, there is one more way to earn a pebble. You can earn a pebble by forest-watching. But forest-watching pebbles you cannot pick up yourselves. You will come to our woods, and you can either walk quietly and observe the woods, or you can sit on our viewing platform and watch. Then you must come and ask one of us to give you a pebble. We will only give you one if you have been very quiet and very good."

Leci caught Ganam rolling his eyes and making a dubious face.

"Now, how many child-uedin are in your generation?" asked Leci.

"Nineteen!" a couple of them called out without raising a palm.

"Yes, nineteen. That is the number you will want to reach. When you have nineteen pebbles in your pocket, you will go and throw them into the drystream. Don't tell anyone when you earn your pebbles, just wait until you have nineteen, and then go throw them all in the drystream that runs right beside this domicile. Whenever you do this, everybody in your generation will come a little closer to understanding what it means to be a uedin. That's how you win. You win for yourself and for all the others of your generation, all nineteen. Together."

Leci noted Ganam raising hands to face, grateful and relieved that the pebbles would get thrown away as part of the game. The child-uedin responded positively, some of them bouncing in place with anticipation. It seemed a success. The young ones couldn't wait to hurry off and earn their pebbles. Leci looked at his fellow forest-watchers, and they all smiled and nodded in approval. He was very pleased. This had gone better than he had expected.

* * *

It was not long before the forest-watchers were confronted with signs that the pebble game might not go quite as smoothly as they had hoped.

There were child-uedin showing up every day, bothering them for pebbles. They would come running and interrupt them suddenly, saying, "I walked quietly and watched the forest! Can I have a pebble?" Or they would sit for a short minute, hardly relaxing enough to be still, and quickly jump to their feet and put their hands out. "Can I have a pebble now?"

At first it seemed like an opportunity for training. Leci would say, "No, you need to walk more slowly and look more carefully," or he would say, "You must stay here until the wind chime rattles one more time." But many of the forest-watchers found themselves mildly annoyed, and they would just give away pebbles to get the child-uedin to go on back to their domicile.

It got to a point where Leci knew there would have to be some change to the rules. The older forest-watchers were passive and did little complaining. But in forest-watcher tradition, it was the younger ones who were usually tasked with making decisions for the compound. It was Pelto, Leci's junior, who came to tell Leci that the child-uedin should be sent to the capital outskirts for their forest-watching practice.

"Someday, after they take name, they will be welcome to come," said Pelto. "They'll be more mature, and their visits won't cause so much interruption."

"You're probably right about that, Pelto," said Leci reluctantly. "I was hoping they would learn to quiet down, but it doesn't seem to be happening. I'll send a message to Master Ganam."

Leci received Ganam's immediate response:

Dear Server Leci,

I received your note. Can you please come by tomorrow to discuss the pebble game? Any time tomorrow would be fine. Thank you for your recent visit and efforts on behalf of our unnamed.

Lern Lalem ulrana uedina
Ganam, Caretaker to Unnamed

＊ ＊ ＊

The next morning, Leci skipped morning meal and walked immediately to the domicile of the unnamed. Why had Ganam requested a visit? What other problems were coming up? He wondered if they would have to call off the game completely. When he reached the domicile, lessons had not yet started, and there were child-uedin outside playing.

"One has thrown pebbles into the drystream twice already!" a child-uedin was bragging to the others.

"One has thrown them *five* times!" countered another one.

130

"Because one is *cheating*!" accused the first.

Leci stopped to explain that they were going about it all wrong. "You're not supposed to tell anyone when you get nineteen—you're supposed to just throw them in the drystream! That's how you win for your whole generation!" The child-uedin looked back with blank faces.

Ganam lifted the door-tarp and spoke. "Yes, they need reminding about that," he said. "Come in, Server Leci. I didn't expect you so early. I have tea and fieldpears. Have you had your morning meal?"

"As a matter of fact, I have not."

"You must try these fieldpears. One of the outfield workers brought them. They're very good."

"It's unfortunate that we have to ask the unnamed to do their forest-watching practice at the capital outskirts instead of in our woods," said Leci.

"It's fine—I've already told them they have to go to the outskirts for that, and I let them know that it was their own fault." Ganam gestured for Leci to sit at the table while he poured milkgrass tea and peeled a fieldpear.

"There something else you wanted to discuss?" asked Leci.

"Well, I just thought it would be good to talk about how this pebble game is going in general," answered Ganam. "I'm afraid it's not going quite like what you planned."

"Yes," conceded Leci. "I heard some of the unnamed bragging about their pebbles just now. I didn't anticipate that."

"Oh, that's nothing," said Ganam. "It gets much worse than that. They have noisy arguments about who's cheating, and come to me all the time to say that someone took their pebbles."

It sounded like the game was completely failing to do what Leci had hoped for. "What do you tell them?"

Ganam waved his hand dismissively, "I just tell them to go pick up however many they had and continue on to get nineteen."

"I suppose that's good . . ." said Leci.

"But I'm afraid I don't see the point of it all," said Ganam. He placed a cup of tea and a dish of fieldpears in front of Leci. The sliced fieldpear was a rich orange-pink. The climate and soil at the new capital were obviously very good for raising them. "I'm not saying I want you to call off the game, but if you decide to do so, I will handle everything myself. You don't have to come and speak to the unnamed. I'll take care of everything."

Leci put a fieldpear slice in his mouth and chewed. "I understand. I'll need to discuss it with the community." They were as delicious as suggested. It was better than anything he had ever tasted back in the old capital. "Can we at least give it a few more days?"

"Certainly," said Ganam. "Who knows? Maybe the unnamed will tire of the game and forget about it. Then we won't have to say anything at all."

"You were right about these fieldpears," said Leci, "These are delicious."

"Master Leol said they got a bumper crop, and they're trying to get rid of them," said Ganam. "You should go get some. Just take a basket with you."

* * *

Early that evening, Leci made his way to the outfield workhouse. Master Leol was weeding an onion patch.

Leci called out as he approached, "Lovely evening, Master Leol."

Leol looked up. "Who's that?"

132

"It's Leci of the forest-watchers."

"Oh, Leci, good to see you. What brings you out here?"

Leci held up his basket. "I've come to beg for fieldpears."

"Great!" said Leol. "We're begging everyone to come and take them away!"

"I'm sure they'll be gone quickly," said Leci. "They're excellent! I tried some this morning."

"I heard about the forest-watchers' pebble game for the unnamed," said Leol. "Very clever to have them pick up pebbles. They'll never run out. I've never seen such pebbly soil."

"The fieldpears seem to do well in it."

"Yes, so far all our crops do well in it. Follow me. We have all our fieldpears piled up in the food cellar. Wait till you see what a mountain of them we have." As Leci followed, Leol asked, "How is it going with that pebble game, anyway? Are the unnamed catching on?"

"Well . . . Not quite as quickly as we were hoping."

"Give them some time," said Leol. He stepped down into the food cellar, and Leci looked over Leol's shoulder. By now, it was too dark to see the mountain of fieldpears, but the strong smell of fresh, ripe fruit was enough to convey to Leci that that year's crop had indeed been plentiful.

* * *

After thanking and bidding farewell to Leol, Leci started back on the footpath that led into the inner capital. He was thinking about how nice it would feel to have a hot bath. The humidity was remarkable in the new capital. The baths got very busy this time of the year, and the small bathhouse at the forest-watchers' compound was no exception. Yulig often complained about it not getting cleaned frequently enough.

Suddenly, Leci saw something that made his heart skip a beat. A large white creature was standing very still at the edge of the footpath. It was the flightless bird! None had been spotted since before the first huts had been built at the new capital!

In fact, it was largely believed that *that* one—which had been tragically killed and eaten by the hooded masters—was the last creature of its kind. No sign of any had been seen in nearly a novade! It was remarkable! Then Leci spied something even more astounding. A child-uedin was sitting in the shadows just thirty or so hand-lengths from the enormous bird! Leci froze in his tracks and watched.

The unnamed seemed unaware he had approached. Both Leici and the child remained still, their gazes fixed on the bird. When it took long, rhythmic steps toward the child-uedin, Leci felt the urge to call out a warning. What if the bird pecked at the child-uedin? But he was impressed to see the unnamed watching in stillness, and he held his breath. The creature was slightly taller than the unnamed, and now stood directly in front of him. They faced one another in frozen wonder for a long minute as Leci looked on.

The bird was spectacularly white and large-bodied, with powerful-looking legs but no wings to speak of. It had big round eyes and a hooked and rounded bill. It was certainly like no creature Leci had ever seen before. It came within a few hand-lengths of the child-uedin's face, and Leci was surprised that the child-uedin remained still, meeting its gaze with his own calm expression. Then, the child-uedin reached into his pocket and withdrew something.

As he held it out, Leci took a moment to see that it was a fieldpear. The child-uedin held it out for the bird to take. The bird cocked its head to the side, hesitated, and then quickly accepted the offering into its beak. It took one jerky backward step, dropped the fruit on the ground, broke it into two pieces with a single peck, and ate both pieces. It looked up to see if there was more, and when no more was presented, the bird quietly strutted off into the shadowy woods.

Leci took a few steps forward and called out, "Hello there, little one!"

The child-uedin looked up and saw Leci for the first time. "Did you see?" he asked.

"Yes! It was beautiful!"

"One was very still, and very quiet, and the big white bird came right up to one!"

"Yes, that was wonderful!"

"Wonderful!" repeated the child, and it seemed to Leci that that was a word he was not used to using.

Leci bent and picked up a pebble. He walked over and placed it in the unnamed's small hand. "Here, you have earned a pebble. You've done a fine forest-watching."

The child took a second to recall that it was a forest-watching which he had just been doing. "Oh, yes, one has eleven now . . ." The child-uedin inspected the pebble for a moment and then put it in his pocket.

"Then you just need eight more."

"Yes . . . Eleven and eight will make nineteen."

"Now run along back to your domicile. It's getting late."

The unnamed politely raised hands to face in a gesture of thanks and ran off.

Leci looked back into the forest to see if there was any movement, but the flightless bird was nowhere to be seen.

* * *

He waited a few days before visiting the domicile of the unnamed. It wasn't too early to start planning for the Namestaking ceremony, and he used that as an excuse to speak with Ganam.

"By the way, I saw one of the unnamed on the outskirts of the capital, up by the outfield workers' place," said Leci. "They know their way all over the capital these days, don't they?"

"Well, it's much smaller here in the new capital. They run around like they own the whole settlement."

"They'll be welcome in our compound again after Namestaking. Then it will be easier to hold them accountable for their behavior."

"Yes, I think we'll see them settle down a lot once they have names," said Ganam. "Was the one that you saw by the outfield workers' place behaving properly?"

"Oh yes, he was doing a very proper forest-watching from what I could see," answered Leci. "Did any of them mention going up there to try forest-watching?"

"No, I haven't heard a word about it. To be honest, Server Leci, I'm afraid they may have lost interest in your game. I hope you're not too disappointed."

"Oh no, not at all," said Leci, smiling to himself. "I'm not disappointed in the least."

Tumet's Trap
By Jon Anthony Perrotti

The cold and wet of the high hill country magnified their hunger and deepened their misery. It was like nothing anyone in the caravan could have imagined or prepared for. Tumet and her closest companion, Benil, huddled with four other uedin around a tiny fire next to an outcrop of rock that protruded from the cold white layers.

Through the evening fog, Tumet could see only a few other groups of caravanners sheltering where the tops of needle-leaf trees stuck up out of the water dust. Their legs were wrapped with cloth and laced with brown cords that connected to woven footwear. Still, it was good that the wind had died down—they might be lucky enough to have a restful night. They wore long robes of thick fabric which now hung on them, soaked and heavy. Their knit hoods stretched around the humps of the skullwombs on the backs of their heads.

Tumet considered the hunk of charred flesh at the end of her wooden blade. She thought of pickled sweetbulbs, of yam gruel and mola stew. Of ripe fieldpears and roasted onions with sour herb sauce. But all the foods of the old capital were like lost treasures that no longer existed save for wistful memories. Would she never taste those things again? She didn't even have any yamflour left in her pack, let alone anything fresh. The wretched thing at the end of her blade was the muscle of a wild dog one of the server-masters had caught and killed in the early morning.

Until very recently, there had been great secrecy about the fact that certain members of the caravan had taken to killing wild dogs, ripping off their hides, and cutting up their carcasses for food. A strange turn of events had led to this. The wild dogs had attacked the caravan twice. Uedin had killed them. Defensively. And then, someone, driven by hunger, had been moved to cut up and eat the animals' muscles. That led to the discovery that eating the muscles, unappealing as it was, sated their appetites and provided a surprising amount of stamina.

Tumet was one of the first to understand that the consumption of wild dog muscles was going to be necessary for the caravan to survive and continue. For some time, certain uedin who were especially good with the wooden blades had accompanied the scouting parties to protect them, and they'd gradually become pursuers, using the scouting trips to search for wild dogs and kill them. One of the blade-wielders had talked Tumet into tagging along to learn how to kill. So far, she had not had to actually do it.

The caravan was in the highest hills, where a strange water dust fell like salt from the sky, and they didn't even know how deep it was beneath their feet as they marched miserably on, day after day. It was good that they had seemingly reached the highest point and were working their way down to lower elevations, but despite counting on the flesh of wild dogs for their sustenance, Tumet knew that they could all easily die of starvation before they got out of the hills.

"Horrible, isn't it?" said Benil, staring at the chunk of flesh on the tip of her own blade. Benil was shivering. Her sunken eyes and gaunt face gave her a dreadful, tragic appearance.

"What do you mean? It's not bad at all!" said Tumet, trying be encouraging. "You should see how Master Holkam devours it . . . says she likes the fat just as much as the muscle . . . says we should try their brains." That was a complete lie, of course. Holkam hated eating the wretched muscles as much as any of them, but Holkam and Tumet had agreed that the caravan needed the flesh, whether they liked it or not. They all had to learn to eat it to survive. The two of them were doing their best to talk everyone else into accepting the muscles as *food*.

"I suppose it's not so bad." Benil smiled at Tumet and chewed. Tumet was grateful for the dishonesty.

"What domicile did Holkam come from?" asked Benil.

"I'm not sure . . ." She wondered what Benil was thinking.

"I'll bet she didn't come out of Quarterhouse."

"She *did* come from Quarterhouse. My generation."

"Oh . . ." Benil sounded slightly surprised.

"Why?"

"I was thinking she wouldn't joke about it if she was from Quarterhouse."

"Holkam and I are both Quarterhouse 'ear-nibblers,' and that's why we don't mind eating this stuff."

"Tumet, don't talk like that," Benil softly objected. "You know that's not true."

"Well, who knows? Maybe it is true," she said, but Benil didn't need to know the depth of shame that plagued the Quarterhouse uedin of her generation. Tumet didn't add any further comment.

"I can put up with eating wild dog muscles," said Benil, "but I am so tired of being cold and wet. I would give anything for dry garb."

"We're coming into lower areas," said Tumet. "It won't be long till we can have a proper camp and a chance to dry our robes."

Benil nodded. "We are seeing a lot more trees. They dry well in the sun if you hang them on branches." She peered into the flames. "The wood burns well. It's a good thing the needle-leaf trees have a lot of dead branches at their bases."

Tumet nodded and looked at the flickering fire. "And it's much easier to chew the muscles after we roast them, that's for sure."

∗ ∗ ∗

Scouts regularly conducted early morning trips into whatever new territory lay ahead of the caravan, to get a look at the landscape and determine a starting route for the upcoming day's movement. The uedin who had taken it upon themselves to be the ones to go out and kill wild dogs had come up with these routines. They headed out with the scouts and then split into groups to search for the animals. They could usually kill a few, rejoin the scouts, and return in time for the caravan to start moving just after sunrise.

This was the third morning Tumet had come along for the dreadful duty. It was still dark, and Tumet felt perplexed that the others had seemingly developed the ability to find tracks in the white water dust, even in the dim. She, on the other hand, was finding that the more she searched, the more *everything* looked like wild dog tracks. Holkam was trying to show her how to spot them.

"There's some—see?"

"Oh, yes. I see them now." Tumet was only slightly reassured.

"They look fresh. Let's follow them." Holkam called to the others, "We're going to follow these. We'll rejoin you up ahead." They broke from the group and turned to follow the tracks.

Tumet was eager to improve her skill. "Can I go first? I want to see if I can follow them," she asked.

"Sure. I'll let you know if you're going the wrong way," Holkam said. Tumet was mildly humiliated. She was determined to keep her eyes set on the tracks and follow them directly to show her Quarterhouse classmate how perfectly capable she was.

But while the tracks were getting easier to see and follow, they did not come upon the animal making them. They could only go so fast while keeping their eyes peeled for the trail.

Holkam finally spoke. "We aren't going to get it. We need to turn back that way to rejoin the others." Then Holkam halted and pointed to something on the ground. It was a small black object. "That must be the wild dog's scat," she said. They both paused to observe it more closely.

"It sure is," said Tumet. There was no doubt about it. In fact, it had a strangely familiar look. Wild dogs had always been seen outside the capital walls. Those were a different breed from these ones in the hills. The wild dogs around the capital were small, meek animals; they foraged for grubs and had never been known to do anything but run away from uedin. These high hills wild dogs seemed larger, with their thick fur and pointy white teeth.

But the scat looked exactly like what Tumet had sometimes seen outside the capital, and it drove home the fact that these were essentially just like those other timid creatures. It gave Tumet a very unpleasant feeling about the necessity of killing and eating them.

"You're right, we need to head back," she said.

Their pace was much faster when they could run without looking down for tracks. They quickly caught up with the scouts.

"No luck?" asked a scout.

"No," said Tumet, "We followed tracks past that rise, but we didn't see any of them. Finally had to come back."

"We didn't get one either," said one of the others. "There are many tracks—but no wild dogs."

"We saw some scat," said Holkam.

"Maybe you could have brought *that* back," a scout joked, "to give the caravan!" She laughed.

"The Quarterhouse masters would surely eat it—right after they eat up the dog's nose and ears!" added her comrade.

The group was silent.

Then one spoke up. "Did you know Master Holkam and Master Tumet here are both from Quarterhouse?"

The scout looked surprised and embarrassed. "Oh, I'm so sorry, Masters," she said. "That was very rude of me. I don't know why I would say such a thing . . ."

"Don't worry about it," said Holkam. "We even joke about that amongst ourselves."

Another group rejoined the scouting party, empty-handed. There was a strange disappointment all around as they understood that they hadn't been successful in any killing. It felt strange to Tumet, at least. Imagine, being disappointed that one couldn't kill, cut up, and eat the muscles of a wild dog! How strange to be disappointed in *that*.

* * *

That night, Benil tried boiling the ground up leaves of the needle-leaf, and it was completely indigestible. Both Tumet and Benil were sickened to vomiting. In those miserable moments, Tumet thought hard about starvation. She had to do better. She had to be able to follow the tracks while running, and she had to be swift and smart in order to kill any of these wild dogs.

The next morning when they went out, Tumet spoke little to Holkam but tried to focus her full attention on looking for tracks. This was about their survival. She felt a thrill when she did spy tracks before Holkam. At first, she was glad that she'd been able to, but then they both realized how fresh the tracks were. The wild dog was likely very near. Tumet's feelings changed to anxiety. These were terrifying creatures, so different from normal wild dogs. She thought about the times they'd attacked the caravan and scouting parties in the past. Only by quickly carving wooden blades and learning how to use them had the caravanners been able to ward off the attacks.

They heard it growl before they saw it. A thin-looking wild dog, drawing down, its head low, ready to lunge at them. It was going to be a fierce fight for a small amount of muscle. The animal sprang into the air straight at Tumet. She raised her wooden blade, but its point slipped along the animal's flank and failed to pierce its skin. The wild dog slammed against Tumet's chest. It snapped its teeth in the air, releasing a string of saliva that fell across her face. Holkam took one hard swipe at it with her blade, but the wild dog had bounced off Tumet and sprung, and was now running away from them. It was then she realized how sleek and beautiful it really was.

They ran after it a short way, but it was now alert to their pursuit and quickly escaped. Again, they had to return with nothing to show for their efforts. Holkam kept looking for tracks even as they rejoined the group.

"No sense looking now," said a scout. "As soon as the last three return, we're heading back to the caravan."

"We need more time." Tumet fidgeted with the blade in her belt.

"The caravan needs to move," the scout said. "We have to get out of the high hills as quickly as we can."

They huddled against the cold, waiting for the three uedin who were still out tracking. After a long wait, two uedin came back, both empty-handed. There was nothing to do but wait for the third who was out there by herself. Hopefully the one who had gone out alone had sense enough not to stray too far.

Tumet was dreading the possibility that they would have to start searching for her when the uedin finally returned. She carried one dead carcass over her shoulders. She looked exhausted.

"That poor server-master looks like she ran all over the hills to get that wild dog," said Holkam.

"Yes," said Tumet, "and I'm afraid its muscles will not feed many."

"Good job, Server-master!" said Holkam. But the young uedin neither smiled nor nodded. She looked rather miserable.

"Well at least there will be one wild dog to take back," said one of the scouts. "Its muscle won't go far, but it's better than nothing. Maybe when we get to lower ground, we'll find something else we can eat."

"Shouldn't we look for more?"

"It's getting late—see, the sun's rising. We need to get back to the caravan and start moving."

Tumet approached the server-master who was carrying the carcass. "Did it put up much of a fight?" she asked.

"First I choked it with this piece of rope," said the server-master, showing Tumet a coil attached to her belt. "Then I used my blade."

Tumet was impressed. That was a clever approach—much better than trying to kill with the blade alone. "Good thinking!" she said.

The server-master looked at her with slight disgust. "I hate killing them."

"Wild dog muscle may be the only thing that keeps us alive," said Tumet, "And today, you're the only one who got one."

"That doesn't make it any more pleasant," said the server-master. Tumet had yet to kill one with her own blade, so she didn't doubt the server-master's words.

* * *

As soon as they got back, the caravan marched. By midday, Tumet wondered if the other pursuers felt as exhausted as she did. The white hilltops jutted up with persistence at the horizon. Though they could see that the highest hills were behind them, there was still no sign of the densely forested terrain that would mark a lower elevation.

Tired as she was, Tumet couldn't help scanning the ground constantly for tracks. She walked beside Benil, pointing them out when they appeared. Interestingly, there were variations in the pattern of the tracks, as if the dogs had more than one style of traveling over the soft, white ground. But it was useless to spot the tracks now. There was no way to go out in pursuit of wild dogs while the caravan was moving.

By afternoon, Tumet had quit looking for tracks and stared off blankly while walking. Then suddenly she said to Benil, "I think I could catch one with a lock-loop knot."

"You're still bothered," Benil observed, "because you didn't kill a wild dog."

"They're very hard to find. But I think I could catch one."

"With a *knot*? How would you do that?"

"A lock-loop knot," said Tumet. "It grips when you pull it. But if I attached a very large one to a tree branch and opened it

145

up wide enough for a wild dog to pass through, maybe the rope would catch on its body and hold fast."

"Interesting," said Benil. "What made you think of that?"

"The server-master who got a wild dog today used a rope around its neck."

"Do you need some rope? I have some. You could test it."

"I don't think regular rope would be good. The wild dogs would see it. I need something thinner and not so obvious."

"What about lacing cord?"

Tumet studied her leg wraps. The cords were crisscrossed all the way from her footwear to the knees. "That might work! If I attach it to the branches of a needle-leaf tree, it will blend in. I've seen tracks that run in and out of those trees."

They stopped on the side as the caravan continued to pass them, and Tumet took the lacing off one of her legs. That night she could ask around for a cord replacement. Till then, her footwear was snug enough to walk without it. The cord she wrapped up in her fist was thin and strong—perfect for the lock-loop knot she had in mind.

"Show me how it's going to work," said Benil.

"Just like this. Start by tying a double loop . . ."

As they walked along, Tumet tied and retied the lock-loop knot and ran the cord through the loop multiple times to make sure it pulled through with slickness and ease.

* * *

That night, after the caravan stopped to camp, Tumet decided to hike out alone and place her lock-loop somewhere up ahead so that she could check it in the morning. She asked around and acquired a replacement leg lace for her footwear. She headed over the rise that separated the camp from the continuing valley. She then followed the lower sections as she had seen the scouts do in recent days. That was how a day's course was usually directed, at least for the first part of the route. Fortunately, there was no water dust falling at the time, and the wind was calm. Both moons were visible in the golden twilight.

As she gained distance from the camp, she felt what she had not felt for a very long time: the sensation of solitude. There were hundreds in the caravan. Tumet had hardly been alone since leaving the capital. Walking alone, Tumet thought of what she was doing. The prospect of trapping and killing an animal in order to eat its muscles was especially troublesome because she was Quarterhouse, third generation. They had all grown up with the shame and embarrassment of the scandal of their origins. It had always been a cruel burden, one that Tumet still wrestled with. Before taking leg, when they were wetuedin in the Quarterhouse hatching pool, an unspeakable defilement had taken place.

A distraught toolmaker from Crafting had waded into the pool, cut her own neck, and died there. They, as wetuedin, had unknowingly nibbled on the dead uedin's appendages. The body was hard to identify because its face had been eaten away. Only her apron said she'd been a Crafting toolmaker at all. Attempts had been made to withhold details of the event to spare their generation from having to bear the shame. But the uedin of the capital were too shaken, and naturally there was much talk.

By the time Tumet and her generation took name, it was common knowledge in the capital. Quarterhouse had always been the proudest of the domiciles, renowned for producing scholars and poets. But Tumet noticed how uedin seemed to whisper when they even said the name "Quarterhouse," and the child-uedin of the other domiciles were sometimes scolded for calling them *ear-nibblers*.

It was doubly shameful for a caravanner who had taken leg at Quarterhouse to now be catching wild dogs to kill and eat. Would uedin in the caravan say that they found it easy to kill and eat flesh because they had once nibbled it as wetuedin? Of course they would! One thing Tumet knew: it wasn't easy for *her*. But what else could they do? The regular food in their packs was down to mere remnants. As disgusting as it was to kill an animal and eat its muscles, Tumet knew that they had to do it to survive. But making up their minds to do it did not make it an easy task. They could not wait for attacks. They had to go after the animals. Maybe her lock-loop would work.

She spotted some tracks and saw that they led to the base of a small stand of trees. That seemed like as good a spot as any. Since it looked like one had been there before, there was a chance another would pass through there again. Tumet made a mental note of the shape of the group of trees rising from the water dust like an island. In the morning when the scouts came through to survey the area, she would need to remember the spot.

The ground was visible here and there where the blanket of crusted water dust thinned. Tumet made her way to the trees. The needle-leafs seemed to thrive in the high hills. Tumet had learned to love the scent of them. They were a perfect place to tie her lock-loop because the needle-leafs' low limbs branched out from the very bottoms of their trunks. She approached carefully, both to take note of the tracks leading in, and out of wariness that a wild dog might be under there even as she planned.

There were none. There were, however, some tracks leading in and out. They looked like they were starting to get worn away by wind. Tumet chose a spot that had a well-spaced branch in a good position. Detaching the coil of lace cord from her belt, she leaned low. Yes, it could be tied quite nicely right here. She tied one end of the cord to the branch, and carefully twisted and formed the remaining length into a lock-loop. It hung down perfectly in place. Tumet could imagine a wild dog walking right into it and getting caught. It was not a pleasant picture in her mind, but that was what she was there for, after all.

The muscles gave them energy. She had now seen enough to know that eating muscles gave uedin just as much energy, if not more, as eating yams. She examined the open lock-loop hanging down to catch their hope for survival, lest it elude them. With a sense of resolve, she withdrew from the base of the trees, and headed back to the camp.

* * *

Again that night, the uedin pressed their bodies together tightly to ward off the cold as they tried to sleep. Better to put up with a little foul breath in your face than have your bones completely taken over with deep chill. Tumet was exhausted enough to sleep despite all discomfort.

She woke early, well before sunrise. Rising from the cluster of sleeping bodies, Tumet stood to feel the wind. It wasn't too bad. She pulled her overrobe tight around her and moved to meet the scouting team.

Holkam was already there. "Did you set up your lock-loop like you were talking about?"

"I did."

"Think you can find it again?"

"I do."

"Well," Holkam said, "you've got me curious, that's for sure."

"Nothing wagered but a lacing cord," answered Tumet.

"Aren't you eager to see if there's a wild dog in it?"

"Of course, I am." Tumet was both eager and nervous.

"Your name will become known in the whole caravan," Holkam commented.

Somehow, Tumet didn't like the idea that she would be celebrated for devising a method for easily killing wild dogs. "And maybe the caravan will be able to survive long enough to get completely out of the hill country," she answered instead.

The scouts gave a shout, and they all moved out.

One of the scouts spoke up right away. "Whose tracks?"

Tumet saw her tracks from the night before, by now somewhat smoothed by wind and fresh water dust.

"Oh, those are my tracks. I am experimenting with something—I tried to anticipate which way you'd be starting out, but please go whichever way you think is best."

"Looks fine so far—maybe you should be a scout!" answered the young uedin.

Tumet was pleased as the scouts followed her tracks practically all the way to where she had tied the lock-loop. Along the way, numerous sets of tracks led the other wild dog killers off on tangential searches. They reached the small stand of trees.

"I see you went over to those trees," said the young scout. "We'll stop here to wait for the others to rejoin us and then go a little further due north."

"We'll be back soon," said Tumet. "Let's go." She motioned to Holkam.

In the dark of the predawn, the small stand of trees appeared exactly the same as it had the night before. They approached it silently.

Ear-nibblers! Quarterhouse ear-nibblers! It was a jeering that Tumet had never actually heard anyone say out loud but always felt that uedin all over the capital were saying it secretly. Now she was becoming a wild dog killer. Somehow, the two things seemed connected.

They reached the base of the trees. Both uedin drew their wooden blades. If there was a wild dog caught in the lock-loop, it was certainly going to fight for its life.

Tumet gingerly stepped in, crouched, and lifted the lowest branches to see where she had tied the cord. At first, she saw nothing. *No luck.*

"What *is* that?" asked Holkam. "It's not a wild dog."

Then Tumet saw it. It was a small creature, so white that it blended in with the water dust. She looked closer and saw its long ears. "A hare!"

Holkam lifted the branch up higher so they could see it better. It was caught with the cord around its neck, one front leg arrested in the loop and sticking straight out. It suddenly squirmed and kicked to get free, but the lock-loop held fast.

"It's white just like the water dust," said Holkam. "We might have passed by many of these—they blend in and we don't see them."

The hare yanked at the cord and struggled in vain, its hind feet kicking in place. It looked desperate and pathetic. Tumet turned and looked at Holkam. Holkam met her gaze with grave understanding. Yes, it was awful. It was a poor, little creature, and they hated to do it, but they knew they had to kill it.

"Your lock-loop works," said Holkam. "You'll have to teach everyone how to use it."

Tumet sighed. "Yes, I suppose I will have to."

"Do you want me to kill this?" asked Holkam.

"I'll do it myself. I trapped it, I'll kill it." She would own her own action.

She already felt ashamed of what she was doing, and the shame seemed to taunt. *Ear-nibbler*. The old image flashed in her mind: the distraught toolmaker stood waist-deep in the Quarterhouse hatching pool, holding her sharp tool. *Why did she do it? Why did she do it, and curse a whole generation of Quarterhouse uedin to a life of shame?*

Tumet took hold of the cord with one hand and clasped the hare behind its head. Its body was warm, its fur unimaginably soft. She could feel its heart pulsing wildly. It opened its mouth and released a hiss, but it was weak and unintimidating. At least the wild dogs were fierce enough to make uedin fight them. The hare could not even fight! Tumet so wished it had been a wild dog in the lock-loop instead of a hare. But the fact that it was a hare made her think that it made some sense. The wild dogs must kill and eat the hares and other small creatures. There was no other way for them to survive in the hill country. The uedin of the caravan were in the same cruel circumstances.

Tumet drew it closer, holding her elbow out to the side as the hare kicked and flailed. She held her wooden blade in her other hand. It had never been successfully used, and it was as sharp as when she'd made it.

Holkam stood back respectfully. Tumet tried to think about the importance of survival, but the image of the distraught toolmaker lingered in her mind. She refocused. No reason to pause or delay. Tumet drove the blade into the throat of the hare and drew it across, slicing it open.

The hare's skin was thicker and tougher than expected, and she had to use some strength to force the blade through while tightly holding the back of its head. She involuntarily thought of the unhappy toolmaker cutting open her neck, and blood streaming down into the water where wetuedin swam.

The hare twitched a few times and went limp in her hand. In the colorless predawn, the blood on its white fur looked as black as ink.

* * *

The hare turned out to be the only carcass carried back to the caravan camp with the scouting party that day. It was a little smaller than the wild dog that the server-master had choked and killed the day before, but it had a different significance when Tumet explained the lock-loop, and they were all fascinated and impressed. During the day's march that followed, talk of Tumet's lock-loop spread quickly. She grew very tired of forcing a smile to explain it repeatedly. Benil kindly took over.

"Master Tumet went out late last night to tie up the lock-loop, and she was up before dawn to go check it. She's a bit tired. You'll tell them about the lock-loop another time, right, Master Tumet?"

"If that's all right . . ." Behind her gracious look was a plea to be excused from further discussion.

"Of course!" said the admiring server-master. "Mostly I just wanted to congratulate you. Very clever!"

"Thank you," said Tumet, striving for her best fake smile.

* * *

In the afternoon they encountered forested land, a sign that they were reaching lower elevations. By the time they stopped to

153

camp, there were abundant tall needle-leaf trees all around them. Within hours, the glow of small fires burned within the darkness of the surrounding forest. Tumet and Benil sat in the orange glimmer of burning embers, eating the roasted muscles of the hare.

"You're better at cutting up muscles than I am," said Benil.

"You did a fine job," said Tumet. She was thankful that Benil had volunteered to skin and cut up the carcass.

"It's the least I could do," said Benil. "And anyhow, I suppose it may be something that we should all learn how to do."

"I hope it's something that we'll someday be able to forget." Tumet chewed slowly and soberly.

"I still think it would taste better if we rubbed some salt on it, and maybe some brewer's yeast," said Benil.

"Maybe you can put that on your portion next time. I don't think I want to mask the taste of the muscles."

"Why? It might taste better."

"Maybe so."

They silently chewed for a long moment, and then Benil put her hand on Tumet's arm and looked earnestly into her eyes. "You really hate it. I know you do. You have been telling me that it's not so bad eating muscles, but you're the one who hates it the most."

Tumet said nothing.

Benil continued, "We only do what we do in order to survive. You must let go of your shame. Learn to think like a wild dog."

Tumet swallowed. "My shame is what tells me that what I do does not always reflect who I am. I'd rather think like a uedin."

Once a Commando
By Frank Booker

About the author

Frank began his writing career at eighty-two years old. Other works include a time travel novel, a space opera novelette, and several shorts in various stages of completion, yet to be published. For this story, he wanted a feisty grandmother character who he could feature in other stories about McKeon Station.

* * *

Henrietta punched in the playlist for the Iron Lung Bar and Grill's music system. It wasn't the most upscale establishment of Earth's central orbital platform, being on the lowest level of McKeon Station. Fewer customers tonight meant fewer tips. She glanced at the couple sitting in the far corner, away from the speakers and plasma screen, huddled close—negotiating a tryst, she suspected. Their glasses were still half-full; no need to make an appearance. Behind the bar, Manuel took care of the two men on barstools.

Three more patrons came in. Two of them unfamiliar but the third instantly recognized: Morgan, her ex-fiancé. A very long-ago fiancé—twenty-five years gone. Older now, he still had that rugged face she remembered touching. Henrietta turned her back, walked over to Manuel, guts churning.

"Manny, my ex just walked in. Wonder what he's doing on McKeon Station."

"Well, mija," Manuel said slowly in his deep accent. "It seems you're going to have to go over there and find out. They're waving for service."

"I don't know what to do ... when I see him ... talk ... what'll I say?"

"You're gonna say what you always do. Just ask for their order. He may not even remember you if it's been so long."

Henrietta gritted her teeth. Tense. "He better remember me." She paused, lowered her shoulders. "Maybe it would be better if he didn't. Manny, I'm messed up right now. I don't want to, but I'll go over there." She picked up three setups, three menus. Manny's sausage-fingered hand fell on hers, warm, comforting.

"I've known you for three years, mija," came his melodic Hispanic tone, "and I've never seen you this upset."

"He left me. It happens, but it really hurt. There's more to it, but ... I'll tell you later."

As she turned, Manny's hand gently squeezed hers. "He made a big mistake leavin' you. Anything you need, I'm here."

Manny had been a second father to her since she came to McKeon Station—a retired Space Force commando with a child in tow. Dottie, the owner of the Lung, had hired her on the spot. Now, it was like being part of a family. A protective one.

Adjusting her face to a passive façade, she headed to Morgan's table.

"Hi, how you gents doing?" Henrietta looked at the man on the left, avoiding eye contact with Morgan.

Morgan looked up, open-mouthed, eyes widening in recognition and surprise. He stammered out a hello.

"What can I get you guys?"

The one on the right, a muscular man with an air of suppressed violence, pointed at her menus. "Don't need those. Just a pitcher of beer. Three mugs."

"Coming right up," she said, turning. Her words, "A pitcher and three," floated toward the bar rail. She waited for the pitcher to fill, placed it on her tray, next to three thick chilled mugs.

Henrietta wished for an explosion, just a small one to prevent her from having to cross that void again.

Setting the pitcher and glasses on the table, she gave a perfunctory "Enjoy." She still avoided looking at Morgan, but she knew—she saw the telltale signs, his furrowed brow. Morgan's face reddened; he was upset but not angry. *He hasn't changed much*, Henrietta thought.

Before she could make her getaway, he asked, "What are you doing here?"

Henrietta decided to be flippant, erect a protective wall. "Waiting tables," she said. "You?"

"Uh . . . uh . . ."

Henrietta let him off the hook. "Anything else I can get you boys?"

"We'll be fine," said the slim one on the left. While smaller than his tablemates, he seemed to exude a gravitas, a sophistication the others lacked. While he spoke, he looked at Morgan, one eyebrow raised with curiosity. "Thank you."

Henrietta retreated to her station by the bar, heard familiar footsteps behind her. She turned to face Morgan.

"What're you doing here?" he rasped, his voice full of . . . something . . . Was it fear?

"I work here. What are you doing here?"

He leaned in close, whispered, "I'm involved in some business. You're blowing it for me." Then he leaned back away from her and said in a too-loud voice, "I told you before, I don't want to have anything to do with you. Stop chasing me all around the galaxy. I'm done with it." Morgan turned on his heel, walked back to his table.

"Well, mija," said Manny. "I don't know what he's palaverin' about. Far as I know, you've never been after him, or anybody."

"Is that all you heard? I don't want to go another round with him. Have 'em come to the bar for their check?"

"Tell them we're closing. It's near time, anyway. Dottie won't mind. Business has dropped off since the slowdown from Earth."

Henrietta slid back to the table and dropped off the check. "We're closing in five minutes, so that pitcher's your last call." She noticed Morgan's head droop, then he nodded a bit, acting as if he'd had a few too many. This was not the same Morgan who had spoken to her moments ago at the bar.

"What's wrong with this one?" she asked. "He all right?"

"Just a bit drunk," said the thin man. "You'd think a Space Force officer could handle a beer. It's not like it's strong. Quite bland, in fact, compared to the brands we get dirtside."

She let the insult slide, though it rankled her. McKeon's beer was as good as anything brewed on Earth. *This isn't the man I knew*, she thought. Morgan hadn't been at all impaired when he'd confronted her. Had one of the other men put something in his drink? If Morgan was anything, he was a control freak—at least over his own behavior. Something was very wrong.

"I gotta get busy with my side work, Manny." Henrietta lined up the condiments, the salt, and pepper. Filling dispensers for tomorrow's opening. Through the bar's long mirror, she watched, her hands moving on autopilot, as the three men rose to leave, clear that Morgan wasn't in full control. He stumbled. The big guy held him up, almost carried him out the door.

"What should we do about that, Manny?" Henrietta said, nodding toward the door. "What if something happens to him? He's been drugged, I bet."

"Relax, mija. I noticed. I called station security. They'll put a drone on them. Keep tabs. We can check in the morning."

The ten-minute walk to her small apartment was an uneasy one. Slowly, her thoughts brightened, knowing her granddaughter was waiting. Opening the door, Henrietta gave her usual, "Hi, Emma, I'm home . . ." then stopped, words trailing off. The apartment was a wreck: overturned furniture, broken glass table, drawers pulled out, contents strewn across the floor. Henrietta didn't move, couldn't move. "Emma!" she screamed. She searched. It didn't take long in this little apartment of three rooms, to find a note on the galley countertop. *We'll call tomorrow* was scribbled on a small piece of paper, torn from one of Emma's notebooks.

* * *

Manny sat in Dottie's office, a spacious affair by station standards, large enough to contain her workstation and conference table.

"What did she tell you?" Dottie asked.

"She was hysterical. Yelling, crying about her granddaughter being kidnapped. I told her to come talk to you. Told her not to do anything rash."

"Hysterical? Strange. When I checked her out before hiring her, she came up aces. A combat-experienced Space Force commando. Decorated for bravery under fire. Guess it's different when it's someone you love."

"You mean her ex?"

"Nah, her granddaughter. I know that feeling of helpless rage."

A knock. Dottie checked her desk screen. "Come in." The door slid open. Henrietta entered, looking exhausted. Her eyes were puffy, red-rimmed from crying.

"Sit down, sweetie." Dottie indicated the seat next to Manny. Henrietta almost collapsed into it, steadied herself by gripping the table's edge.

"Report."

Henrietta was surprised at Dottie's sudden military manner but didn't show it. The Space Force saying, "Once a commando, always a commando," worked to steady her. Bracing herself, she made her report.

"Three men came into the Lung. One was my ex-fiancé. Haven't seen him in twenty-five years. It was about a half-hour before closing. His presence was unexpected. At the bar, he told me I was interfering with a deal he had going, then went back to his table. Our conversation must have made the other two suspicious because five minutes later, Morgan was out of it. I think they drugged him to get him out of the bar without resistance."

"What did you see, Manuel?"

"Same. Henrietta and I spent the next thirty minutes cleaning up for opening. I told her she could leave, but she stayed and finished her side work."

Henrietta narrated what happened next. "I went home. It was a mess. Emma was gone. I checked with our neighbors. No one heard or saw anything unusual. There was a note." A teary Henrietta handed Dottie the note. She forced herself to steel against fear and horror, against thoughts of how terrified her ten-year-old Emma must feel.

"Did you call station security?"

"No, I called Manny. He told me to come over here right away. I thought you might have a better handle on these guys.

One was a hulk, looked to be six two or three, two hundred and thirty pounds, all muscle. He was White, thirty-something, brown hair and blue eyes. The other one was smaller, five-eight or nine, maybe a hundred and fifty or sixty pounds, fastidious in his dress. He looked to be in charge. He was White, too, but had darker hair and complexion. Brown eyes. Morgan's my age, medium build, gray hair, blue eyes." She hesitated, then added, "He looks older than he has any right to. Look, I don't need to rehash; I need to find my granddaughter. If Morgan had anything to do with this . . ."

"He could be innocent," Manny offered.

"Innocent?" Dottie scoffed. "He may not be involved in Emma's taking but the rest of it? For sure, not innocent. Not if he willingly walked into the bar with those two."

"Wait . . . What?" said Henrietta. "The rest of what?"

"Smuggling," said Dottie. "There's no maybe about it; they're linked. Station security asked Xandro and me to keep an eye out for just this sort of activity."

"Xandro?"

"The only other business owner on McKeon with enough reach and influence to do what I . . . the things I do. Security sent me their link to surveillance drone feeds. I know where they took your ex, but I don't know if that's where your granddaughter is. Someone's been blocking the cameras in the passageways." She shifted her desk screen so Henrietta and Manny could see. "Whoever took her, it wasn't those three guys. Watch: the three of them are going into a machine shop and warehouse of the chandlery. The drone feed is still live. No one has entered or exited. However, there is a loading platform on the back side of the shop that's not covered by the drone, so they could have gone out that way. Could be anywhere on the station."

"Where would they go?" asked Manny.

"Unknown." Dottie straightened her screen as she answered.

"That's all we have to go on?" asked Henrietta. "I guess I need to go to the chandlery." She stood to do just that.

"Wait," Dottie said, and Henrietta sank back down. "Before you go off half-cocked, we need a plan." She made a keyed entry. "Here's the chandlery floor plan." She turned her screen again, pointing now. "Four entrances from the main deck plus the big one through the airlock where they take in freight. There's a good chance they put Emma in the airlock. It's easily locked out, plus there's no cameras inside. If they cycle the hatch, anyone inside would be ejected. Before we go in, we need the codes to override the airlock controls, then cover all the interior entrances."

"That's assuming they're in there," said Manny.

"It's all we've got," said Henrietta. She got to her feet, studied the screen. "If we can seal off the entrances from the station deck, we can come in over here." She pointed to an area that provided cover for an incursion. "You sure you can get those codes?"

Dottie smiled. "If I can't, we've got more trouble than I can handle. Station security and I have a long-standing relationship. There are a lot of things they can't handle within their security charter. I take care of those. They provide tech help and muscle, though we'll use our own men for this. I know and trust my people. Too much is at stake, and some of their guys may be compromised."

"I've got to go home to get some things," said Henrietta. "Dottie . . . thanks. You're a rock."

"We take care of each other here. Manny, you packing?" Dottie asked.

"Always, Dorothea." He felt the holster at his side, concealed under his tunic.

"Go with her." She moved to a locker behind her desk, retrieved a satchel, and handed it to Manuel. "Take these. Heads-up displays and body cams. I've got a set here. Call when you're ready. And be careful."

"We got it, Dorothea," Manny said.

"I've got some calls to make. As soon as I have my people at those exits and get the airlock codes, you guys are clear to move in. But don't rush it, all right?"

Manny hurried after Henrietta.

* * *

In the deserted passageway between the chandlery and neighboring docking stations on this level, Henrietta and Manuel crouched outside a door. Geared up with weapons and Dottie's tech. Henrietta held her stunner, ready for anyone who might come through. For the tenth time, she checked the three flash-bang grenades clipped to her belt.

"Let's do a radio check," she told Manny. "Dottie, this is Henrietta, radio check, you hear me okay?"

"Roger, Henrietta. You're loud and clear. Manuel?"

"Yeah, I read you, Dottie. What makes you think this is the best place to get in there, mija?"

"It's farthest away from where we think they might be keeping her," said Henrietta. "The airlock's about ten meters down the corridor from the break room. It's my guess they'll be in there; the most comfortable and obvious place. I doubt they have a guard on the airlock since anybody getting in here would have to walk past the break room to get to its hatch."

"Makes sense. I'm glad we're tied in with Dottie. She can track the operation, call station security if necessary. But I don't think we'll need them. Anyone we target will only be out for thirty minutes."

"Dottie, you have the code for this door?" asked Henrietta.

"I do. Want it unlocked now?"

"Affirmative. I'll open it and slide in. Do you have a good lock on our body cams?"

"Affirm."

Henrietta heard the faint *snick* of the lock. She eased the door open, then slipped through without a sound. "Watching my back, Manny?"

"You got it, mija. Pretty quiet."

Walking stealthily toward the break room, Henrietta heard voices. She turned to Manuel, hand-signaled him to *wait, stay back*. Manuel folded himself into a small niche that had once held a workstation. As he slid into the alcove, Henrietta was impressed by how quick and quiet he was. With her back to the wall, she edged down toward the break room doorway. She didn't recognize the voices of either of the two who had accompanied Morgan, but she recognized his.

"I think you guys made a big mistake taking that girl. I don't know what you're thinking, but if she gets station security down here, we're all going to be in trouble," said Morgan.

"We don't have to worry about that. Xandro has station security on the payroll, or at least the officer on deck tonight."

"Vehicle traffic in front," Manuel whispered in her heads-up receiver.

"Okay," her voice barely more than a breath, "Need to move in. Can't wait." Henrietta stood by the opening's edge, staying flat against the wall, laser pistol drawn. *First things first*, she reminded herself. Reaching to her waist, she grabbed a flash-bang, pulled the timer activator, then tossed it into the room. Quick shouts followed that move, but the timer was quicker; a satisfying *whump*, and flash. She came in low, gun up, finding the occupants rolling, screaming in pain. Two trigger pulls silenced the two goons. Regaining a measure of his senses, Morgan, head still ringing, looked at her, processing Henrietta being in the room.

"Where's Emma?" she demanded. Weapon pointed at Morgan's head, she grabbed his collar and pulled his prone body toward her. Her face was kissing close as she hissed, "Where is she?"

"What . . . ? Henrietta! What are you doing here?" He was loopy, still disoriented from the flash-bang.

"I came for my granddaughter. Where is she?" Morgan's head hit the deck when she released him. He struggled to get up, almost making it to his knees.

"I don't know. I think she's in the airlock," Morgan's voice came up thin and reedy. "They set it to open the outer hatch, used a station override. How did you . . . how did you get in here?"

"I have my own connections. As for airlock codes, they've been changed. There's no chance of anyone cycling that now."

"You have no idea what you've done. These guys are nasty." Morgan rubbed his face, gathering his strength. "I'm still with Space Force. Undercover, have been for years. You've stepped in the middle of all this. We're closing in on the station's smuggling ringleader, and his accomplices dirtside."

"*You* put me in the middle of it. I would've let the whole thing go, even if I knew about it, but somebody had the bright idea of kidnapping my granddaughter. Our granddaughter."

"I think they're afraid I passed some information to you. So, they're trying for leverage—wait, *our* granddaughter?"

"Well, isn't this a sweet reunion?" Xandro Rossi stood in the doorway, an arm wrapping Emma in a chokehold, kinetic pistol held against her temple.

Henrietta leveled her laser sight. "Let her go."

"Morgan, your girlfriend has made a mess of this whole thing. We'll have to kill them both to tidy things up."

Henrietta focused on the weapon in Rossi's hand, almost missing Manny as he appeared, cat-like, behind Rossi at the hatch. "Maybe you should let her go before my associate takes you down."

"No one here but us mice, you old witch," sneered Rossi.

Manny eased himself behind Rossi to get a fist punch on his gun hand. He connected, gave Emma a shove, watched as she flew across the room, landing in Morgan's arms. At the same second, Henrietta fired at Rossi, but he dropped to one knee. The shot had grazed Rossi, but it hit Manny square on, dropping him like a stone. Rossi held on to his gun, aimed in Emma's direction. It was Morgan who saw the muzzle shift. He twisted, putting his body between Rossi and Emma, as Rossi fired.

Henrietta heard the slap as the bullet hit flesh. She fired, not missing Rossi this time. She turned her pistol to its highest setting, fired again, then once more, a third time, in rage.

As Rossi died, Henrietta ran to Emma, scooped her into a fierce hug. "Are you all right? Are you hurt?"

"Oh Grammy, I was so scared!"

"It's all right now. I'm so sorry this happened." She looked at Morgan, dropped to her knees beside him, lifted his head into her lap. He was still alive, but she'd seen this before. Knew the wound would be a fatal one before any help could arrive.

"You . . . you saved her."

"It was . . . the least I could do . . . after . . . the mess I made . . . of our life. I . . . I never stopped. . ."

Her tears came, dropping on his eyes as they glazed and his breath stopped. Noises announced new arrivals. A contingent from station security checked Manuel, then moved in toward Rossi and Morgan after determining the other two men had only been stunned.

"We're taking Manny to medical. Send your granddaughter along to make sure she wasn't hurt," one of the security officers ordered; his name tag showed his name was Reynolds.

"I'll take her myself," Henrietta said, not trusting security.

"Let's get these thugs to the lock-up for interrogation. See who else we need to round up," Reynolds said.

Manny was on his feet—unsteady but up—enough for Henrietta to capture him in a bear hug. "You saved her, Manny! Thank you, thank you! I'm sorry I shot you."

"It's all good, mija. You would have done the same for me."

As they walked out with Emma, Henrietta wanted time. Time to tell Morgan about a daughter he never knew he had, a daughter she put up for adoption, time to tell him that daughter had died in an alley giving birth to some lowlife's child, tell him about her search for Emma, finding her in an orphanage, then claiming her. Time to tell him about their family, such as it was.

* * *

Henrietta and Emma sat at a table in the Lung. Before Emma, a messy spoon sat in what was left of a hot fudge sundae, all of it gone. Smudges of chocolate syrup were plastered over her lips and most of her cheeks.

"Use your napkin," said Henrietta. "Otherwise, you'll leave chocolate all over your boyfriend when you kiss him."

"Oh, Grammy," Emma giggled. "You're such a tease. I don't have a boyfriend."

"Gotta be ready for anything. The single girl's motto— *semper paratus*. You want to be ready for him when he comes along."

"Maybe he'll like the taste of chocolate."

"I want us to talk about the future." Henrietta settled into a more serious mien as she continued. "You know Grammy's had an opportunity to do something more than being a waitress."

"Yeah, I heard you talking to that Space Force guy. Are you going back to active duty?"

"Oh honey, I won't do that. We need each other, so you're stuck with me. I hope that's okay with you."

"That's okay then. I was afraid you would leave me."

"That'll never happen."

"What's the new job?"

"Dottie put in a word for me. I have a job offer from station security as a manager. That means more money. And we'll be able to spend more time together. No more late nights working." She laughed, "No more eating those frozen dinners."

"You mean you'll be able to help me with homework?"

"That, and make sure you don't have too many boyfriends. That would be cruel to them. That's why you must do a good job wiping your mouth. The chocolate on your lips attracts them." Emma's giggles filled the Lung. Its lunchtime crowd joined in that rarely heard sound on the station.

Dottie and Manny sat at the bar, each with a coffee mug. "What are you two conspiring about?" asked Dottie. "Sounds like you're having too much fun." To Henrietta, she asked, "You take up the offer?"

"We were just discussing that. What do you think, Emma? Would it be okay with you?"

"Can I have ice cream every day?"

"You cannot," said Henrietta, "but we will have lots more time to do things together. Nice try on the ice cream, though."

Dottie walked to the table, and lowered her voice, "You impressed Space Force with how you handled things." She sat, and *sotto voce*, added, "Especially since they were selling secrets about our jump technology. That would have laid humanity open to invasion by other races. We need more time to establish ourselves as a starfaring race."

"We have a way to go before that happens," said Henrietta.

"I've been considering an offer of another kind," said Dottie. She turned to Manny and smiled. "Manuel has asked me to marry him."

"I've been asking for years, but you've always given me a firm no . . . about a dozen times."

"Manuel, I realized you could have died during that scuffle. I need to seize the moment to keep you safe in my clutches. Seriously, though, I've been foolish, wasting time when I could have been happier with the man I love."

"Dottie, that's wonderful!" said Henrietta. "I've seen how you two are together. What a beautiful thing! When? Where?"

"We plan on a McKeon wedding. The station admin can do the honors, and we can have a bash here at the Lung. I'll need a maid of honor. Would you do it?"

"Of course, I will!"

"And Emma, you can be the flower girl. We'll decide on a date and send out the invitations later this week."

"Do you have anyone on Earth you want to invite?"

"Sweetie, all my friends are here on the station; all my enemies are on the surface. It'll be perfect."

169

"What a fun time! I'm so excited for you both."

"You'll be happy ever after!" squealed Emma. Henrietta smiled, knowing life was never like that.

But one could always hope.

Pizza Delivery
By Robert Mariner

About the author

Robert Mariner spent his early years living and working in National Monuments and Parks, learning the value of peace and quiet, constant alertness, hard work, and honest people. His adult career encompassed industrial design and scientific research in military/aerospace. In keeping with his name, he's sailed since his seventh birthday, from racing an eight-foot El Toro on San Francisco Bay to being helmsman aboard ketch on the Pacific Ocean. Semi-retired, he lives in California's Mojave Desert with his wife and a sixteen-pound Bengal cat, a place where one can walk outside on a clear, moonless night and look up into a dark sky full of distant lights.

* * *

"Good evening, Valley Pizza. This is Charlene, what can we do for you?" She winced as pain lanced through her shoulder.

"Good evening, Ma'am," came the voice on the telephone. "We'd like to request three pizzas for delivery, please."

"Sure thing. Where to?"

"The barn on the Circle Zero ranch."

"The Maddox place? No problem. What would you like?"

"How about a large pepperoni, a large vegetarian, and a medium Canadian bacon and pineapple, all raised-edge crust? We'll pay in cash."

"We can do that. May I have your phone number?"

"Sure thing, here it is."

Charlene wrote the number, repeated it to the caller. "Okay, that'll be $34.18. You folks need anything else?"

"Some extra napkins would be appreciated, Ma'am, but that should do it for us."

"Extra napkins, you got it. I'll be there in about thirty-five to forty minutes."

"We'll be looking for you then. Drive safely!"

"Thank you, I will. Bye."

"Goodbye." The line clicked off; her shoulder again complaining as she hung up.

"Hey Sam," she said to the owner (and cook). "Three for delivery. One large pepperoni, one large veggie, one medium Canadian bacon and pineapple, all raised-edge. They're out at the Maddox ranch and sound hungry."

Shortly after midnight, Charlene drove out of town, heading home via the Maddox ranch. The turnoff was gravel, and she eased over the familiar ruts to the barn, her body hurting with the jarring of her truck. As she pulled up to the barn, there were lights on inside, as well as a wooden picnic table, right in the middle. Three men were standing by the open doors, obviously waiting for her.

Charlene had known the oldest of them since her childhood, so she shut down the truck, got out and walked over to him, trying not to let herself wince from her pain.

"Hello, Sharley," said this man, giving her a gentle bear hug that avoided places that hurt. "It's good to see you. We don't exactly come by every month. How's college shaping up?"

"Hello Major, good to see you too. Wish it was more often. I managed to put together the tuition for my first year at Bozeman! Well, if I live that long, of course. I'll be taking chemistry and physics this fall, with all the breadth courses. Thank Heaven I aced the math requirements, but I still have to take Theory of Gummint."

172

"Well, go easy on your prof. You got all that from Henry and me when he could still bounce you on his knee. You've kind of grown since then."

"I still know it, too, thank you. I remember you two talking about the way the Founders wrangled over the wording of the Constitution; it sounded almost as if you two had been there taking notes."

"Maybe we were," said the major, grinning.

"Jason, are you talking politics again? We're hungry, and you'll bend this poor girl's ear all night unless one of us puts a stop to it. Hi, Shar, good to see you!" The womans's voice was utterly familiar. Charlene turned and walked over to her.

"Mrs. Maddox! Hello!" She gave the older woman a hug. She, too, was gentle with her return hug, not touching Charlene where she was most sensitive. "I'm here with the pizzas, and the major got started talking. One day maybe I'll learn to get paid first, and only *then* let him drag me into one of his stories." She held tightly onto the older woman, surprised that the strong return hug didn't hurt at all.

"Well," said Mrs. Maddox, "sometimes he gets kind of carried away, but considering what-all he's done, you really can't blame him too much."

"Mrs. M, are we going to stand around gabbing all night, or eat that pizza while it's still warm? Hi, Charlene, haven't seen you enough this summer." This last voice was that of the second man, Mitt, a young seasonal employee on the ranch. She'd met him the previous year but could never quite pronounce his full name, Linárres Mithurillan, or something like that. It made her think of Elvish names in the Tolkien stories.

Well, so did he, for that matter. He was Caucasian, with large, brilliant, intensely green eyes. They were strangely shaped, tilted at about a ten degree angle, and unusually far apart. The upper part of his face was much wider than usual, too, so he wore sunglasses and a hat whenever strangers were around. He had soft, wavy brown hair, stood about six feet three inches tall, was very slender and extremely gentle, and by far the strongest man she knew. He was studying pre-med in college and seemed to have a way with animals, so it seemed only natural that he would work at a ranch. He always wore a bandana over his ears, even when wearing a Western-style hat. He claimed his ears just burned easily, even though the rest of his visible skin only tanned pleasantly. Charlene had a huge crush on him but would never admit it.

The third man had gone to her truck and now brought the pizzas to the picnic table, so the major reached into his pocket. "Lessee, you said $34.18. How 'bout you just keep the change?" He handed her a pair of crisp $20 bills.

"Appreciate that, Major, thank you. Who's your third?" Charlene put the money in her hip pocket, trying not to wince as pain lanced through her arm and shoulder yet again.

The third man was maybe in his mid-twenties, stood about six feet two, and was dressed in blue jeans, walking shoes, and a plain gray T-shirt that revealed heavily muscled shoulders and arms, and a narrow waist. He was a blend of Asian and Caucasian, and had a kind of *presence* she would have expected from some kind of old world nobility. Everyone obviously respected him.

"Oh, that's Myron," said the major. "He's from the Bay Area out in California. His wife Carole's around here somewhere. They were on vacation up in Yellowstone for the past two weeks. Ah, there she is. Got your fill of rotten egg smells yet, Carole?"

Carole was Caucasian, appearing to be in her early twenties. Dressed in fairly new blue jeans, a white long-sleeved

Western-pattern blouse, and wearing moccasins, she stood about five feet nine, and had brunette hair cut in a short military fashion. She walked with grace and a great economy of motion over to Myron and put one arm around his waist. Her wedding ring was a plain gold band, whereas Myron's had a twisted pattern that made it look like a three-stranded golden cord. Neither of them wore any other ornamentation.

"It's not that bad, Jason, and you know it," said Carole, as she and Myron approached the major and Charlene. "Watching Old Faithful from the hotel balcony at about two in the morning, lit only by moonlight . . . it didn't even seem real! Get away from all the tourists, and the rest of the park is just so restful. And some parts are simply amazing."

"Yeah," said the major, "lots of unique features in the park. Anyway, I'd like you to meet our delivery gal here, the one I told you about. I've known her since she was knee high to a hoppergrass." He turned to her. "Charlene, I'd like to introduce you to Myron and Carole Watson. Carole, this is Charlene Bridger. I usually just call her Sharley. Sharley, the Watsons here just might be able to help you move ahead in your life. I've talked with them about your medical and family history."

Charlene was surprised. While of course the major knew her history, she had assumed he'd let her make all her own decisions. Not that there were all that many left.

As an infant she'd been adopted by a young couple in Montana. They were very good parents, but she never felt entirely at home with them. Then, just days after her eighteenth birthday, while she was working on the Maddox ranch, they had both died in a car crash, leaving Charlene with only the property, her pickup truck, and an insurance settlement. That had been two years ago. She'd put off college to take care of settling their business affairs, selling off most of the property, and trying to keep food on her table. She now lived in a fishing cabin the family had owned, everything but her own meager savings having gone to clearing up their affairs, buying burial plots, and seeing to all the usual final expenses. She'd started working two jobs to save up for college.

And five months ago she'd felt a lump in her neck. She went to the local doctor. The news had not been good: after tests that drained most of her savings, the doctor told her she carried the genes for breast and uterine cancer, and was already suffering from both. One or both had metastasized, and she probably had only months left to live. There was nothing anyone could do for her. Without family or relatives, she had accepted that awful news and decided to just live as if nothing was wrong until she was hospitalized, or hopefully died in her sleep. She had recently confided in Mrs. Maddox, who had listened with that vast calm of hers and told her, "It really will be all right. Just wait and see."

So now, as she looked at Carole, Charlene could only wonder what on earth the woman thought she could do. Well, there was always polite small talk; that couldn't hurt anything.

"Good evening, Carole. Well, morning now, sorry. It's very kind of you to come see me, but I'm afraid I probably don't have time for anyone to clean it out. It's already spread pretty much throughout my body. I suspect I have little time left, unless a serious miracle is involved."

Carole gazed at her for a few moments, slowly nodding her head. "Sounds like you're a good person and a natural fighter, Miss Bridger. We couldn't ask better of anyone in your situation. The people with whom I work do not deal in miracles but extremely effective medical technology, if you would accept it. But for that you would have to leave this area for a while.

They have your medical records, and believe they can do something about what's literally eating you alive. They are willing to try, if you will let them."

For a moment Charlene almost forgot about being polite. "If you're just pulling my leg—no, of course you're not. Sorry, but I've heard too many doctors try to sound encouraging, while knowing they can't do anything I really need. It gets more than a little irritating."

Myron, who'd been listening quietly, nodded. Turning to Carole, he said, "Exactly the reaction Ellie predicted. Slightly different inflection, though.

"Miss Bridger," he continued in a pleasant baritone, "we'd really like to see you healthy. You seem to be a very good person. The people my wife mentioned are rather far away, and don't want everyone to know about them quite yet. Let's see, tonight is August twenty-sixth, sorry, by now it's actually Sunday the twenty-seventh. You're off work. If you decide to accept this opportunity, we could have you at that facility within about five hours. Their examination shouldn't take long to fine-tune what they already know, and within an hour you could start your treatment. That truly is urgent; we don't want you any sicker than you already are.

"After the treatment starts, you'll have to be closely monitored for a while, and you'll be learning a lot that you've never even imagined. After that, assuming you do well, you'll have to decide whether you want to come back here or maybe see where else life might take you. It's a big universe, and your life is only just beginning, that is, if we can stop the thing that's trying to kill you."

"And if the results aren't what I need?"

"Well, in that case we could bring you back here, if you wish. Or you could live out your remaining time where you will have all the emotional and physical support and care that could possibly be given to you. At no charge to you, no matter what happens. What we hope is that if you're satisfied with the results, you might want to stay on there for a while. Get a really first-rate education, then find out what opportunities life may have in store for you. Your choice, of course."

A slender, gentle hand touched Charlene's shoulder; she knew it was Mitt's. *I wish I could pronounce his name*, she thought.

"Shar, would you please take these people up on their offer? I've known them for about eight years, and am here today only because of their efforts. Please?"

She felt a wash of care, affection and worry from him that surprised her; she'd never felt anything like it before.

"Well, why not? I don't really have anything more to lose. What should I take with me? Not that I have all that much anymore."

Jason, looking a bit uncomfortable, said, "Uh, Sharley, I kind of took a chance and already collected your things. Left a nice note with your neighbor saying you had gone to get a medical exam and didn't know when you might be back. Your stuff is all in the bird, waiting for you."

"And my truck?"

"That will be kept right here in the barn, just waiting for you and ready to go," said Mrs. Maddox. "It's a really good truck, you know."

Charlene looked at those earnest, well-meaning faces, and said, "Okay, let's do this thing. Someone will have to take Sam that money, though."

Smiling, Mrs. Maddox said, "That will be taken care of. Now, have you had dinner yet?"

"No, but would it louse up your dinner if I had some of the pizza and some salad? Everything looks so good!"

People had been bringing salad, plates, napkins and eating utensils from the house while their talk had been going on, so Mrs. Maddox just smiled and said, "Not at all, Charlene. Dig right in, but do try to leave some for the boys. They're still growing."

The pizzas and salad didn't last long, the dinner filled with good conversation and warm companionship. Charlene knew most of the people in sight. One of them asked her for the truck keys so it could be moved into the barn after the party. Charlene handed them over. Someone else took the two twenties, giving her change for the pizzas, promising he'd take the money to Sam when the shop opened. But she wasn't quite prepared when the major put down his water glass, wiped his mouth with a napkin, and said, "Okay, people, time's a-wasting. Shall we get out of here?"

Everyone at the table stood, Charlene accepting help from Carole, who said, "It's just a short walk out to the bird, but you won't see much. We keep its exterior lights off while here."

They walked out into the night, the heavy clouds obscuring the moon. Something large and indistinct lurked in the dark behind the barn, with a well-lit, open doorway in its side and steps leading from the ground up to it. Charlene climbed the stairs with help from the Watsons, followed by Mrs. Maddox, the major, and Mitt.

The inside looked like a luxurious private airplane interior, with four recliner seats along each side of a central aisle to the right. There were no windows, but there was a flat-screen computer monitor beside each seat. Charlene let the Watsons guide her to the nearest seat on the left side of the cabin, while Mrs. Maddox took the seat directly in front of it, turning it around to face her. Just then, another man came out from the rear area of the craft, going to the entry door and closing it. He then turned to go forward through the cabin, nodding to Charlene and others as he passed.

He looked much like Mitt, with similar strangely shaped eyes, but there was something odd about his ears.

"Charlene," said Mrs. Maddox, "please don't be at all uneasy about this, but some of our people's features aren't exactly like what you're used to. But they're good people, and we all want to get you healthy." She looked past Charlene, and said, "Jason, it's time."

The major had been somewhere off behind where Charlene sat. Now he walked forward to where two gray swinging doors blocked off the cabin from whatever was beyond them. He pushed one open and said, "Good morning, Denys, time to lift." Then he turned to the forward recliner on the left side, sat down and leaned back, soon seeming to drift off to sleep.

"Ah, Mrs. Maddox," Charlene said, "I really didn't pay any attention to this plane, but I thought I'd at least be aware of any engine noises. When will they start?"

Mrs. Maddox smiled. "This isn't a conventional aircraft such as you're used to. Computer, may we have a view looking back to where we just left, please?"

The computer monitor beside Charlene lit up, showing a black-and-white view looking down. The Maddox ranch rapidly grew smaller as the distance increased, though there was no feeling of motion in the cabin.

"We're in what we call a shuttle, dear. It uses technology you're not familiar with yet. It will take us directly to the medical facility we mentioned, as fast as is allowed here."

For Charlene, it was suddenly as if all her fears, all the tension of dealing with the events of the last several months, and all her aches and pains came together and conspired with the late hour to leave her utterly exhausted. Looking through unexpectedly bleary eyes at Mrs. Maddox, Charlene said, "I'm sorry, but everything just sort of caught up with me all at once. I think I heard this flight will take a few hours. Can I take a bit of a nap, please?"

Carole came to stand beside her, and said, "There's a restroom back there, Charlene. Do you want to use it before your nap? You look a little tired."

Charlene was surprised at how simple and ordinary the fixtures were, and had no difficulty using them, feeling far better as she opened the door to return to her seat. Carole was unobtrusively waiting for her, but Charlene had enough energy to make it to the recliner. Carole ran through the controls for it. Charlene found them easy to remember, thinking, *I wish I had a chair like this one, so easy to adjust for such wonderful, soft comfort!* She remembered to thank Carole for her help as a privacy curtain was drawn around her chair and she faded into sleep.

* * *

Returning consciousness brought a sense of disorientation. Charlene remembered going to sleep in that incredibly comfortable recliner, but now she lay flat on her back on an even more comfortable bed. Her usual pains were gone; she felt almost normal for the first time in months. Moving her right hand, she encountered a bed sheet covering her, a bit heavier and rougher than she was used to. She was lying on another such sheet, wearing one of her own nightgowns.

That's odd; I should remember going to bed.

She opened her eyes to a dark room, and noticed a softly glowing computer monitor to her left, dim white text on a deep blue background. The text read:

3:47 a.m. GMT, Sunday, 10 September, 2017

Good morning, Miss Bridger. You gave us quite a fright aboard the shuttle, but you are stable now, and well on the road to what should be complete medical recovery.
If you need to use the restroom, it is a few steps to the right side of your bed. Please ask for lights so you can see where you're going. If you wish lights, just say "lights," and low-level lighting will come on. To turn off the lights, say "lights off."

If you need human assistance or company, or are hungry, just ask for the nurse, and one will be with you within seconds. Your sponsors are anxious to see you when you feel up to it.

If there is anything else you need, just ask. The staff will do whatever they can to help you deal with this new situation in which you find yourself.

While she read the message, the time indicator changed to 3:48 a.m., so she knew this was an active display. The room remained dark, with a faint sound of air flowing through a vent. There were none of the usual chemical hospital odors, though, or any of the usual background noises. But Charlene was comfortable, the bed was warm, and she was still sleepy.

When next she opened her eyes, the drapes across the wall beyond the foot of her bed glowed with daylight. The computer monitor still displayed its message from earlier, except now the indicated time was 11:47 a.m., and there was no mention of lights. She sat up carefully, waiting for the usual sharp pains, but they were almost entirely gone. She stretched, also carefully, afraid of other pains, and they too were mostly gone. Swinging her feet out from the side of the bed, she made a trip to the restroom, finishing quickly and not paying any attention to what else was in that room. She'd think about that later, but she was suddenly extremely hungry. She returned to her bed, noticing controls on the railing on its far side and experimenting with them.

She soon found a very comfortable position in the bed, sitting about halfway up with her feet and knees elevated slightly above her hips.

"Um, how do I call the nurse?" she said.

A voice came from the monitor: "A nurse will be with you very soon, Miss Bridger. Good morning, we trust you are feeling rested and refreshed."

The voice was obviously machine-generated, but its inflections were perfectly normal. Without hesitation she said, "Yes, very much so, thank you."

"You're quite welcome. Here comes your nurse."

A soft tap at the door, beside the head of the bed, alerted Charlene to the new arrival. She turned to see this person, who turned out to be an ordinary Caucasian woman of seeming middle years. Her clothing was of a slightly different style than what Charlene recalled from her recent hospital stays but was clean, functional, and quite appropriate.

"Good morning, Miss Bridger—or would you prefer I call you Charlene? My name is LuAnne Stone. I'm your morning nursing attendant. We've been waiting for you to wake up. You had a rather bad episode just before arriving here, and had us all worried for a while. But you're well on the mend now. Let's see," she said, looking at a tablet, "you're apparently very hungry, which is a really good sign at this stage. You should have much less pain today than you've grown used to. It should take two to five months for every trace of your cancers and their effects to completely go away and for you to regain your full health, but you won't need surgery. When everything is finished, you'll even be able to bear normal, healthy children, should you ever want to.

"Your recovery will be entirely dependent on how much you work on it. Good self-discipline and following the recovery directions that we'll give you can shorten your recovery time to about two months. Don't follow them, and you'll never fully recover. It's pretty much a do-or-die situation in which you find yourself, so I'd encourage you to jump on it as hard as you can once you're cleared for that.

"And there are several people who wish to check in with you, but I'd like to see you get some food first. They can just cool their heels for a bit. So, what would you like to do today?"

Charlene was surprised at this woman's unhesitating mention of what must have happened during that blank time in her memory, but the offhand mention of her various cancers as already having been addressed made her curious.

"If I can put that off for just a moment," she said, "could you kind of expand on what you just said? The only cancer treatments I've heard of that sometimes work include radical surgery, chemotherapy, or radiation, or a mix of all of them. But here you're going on as if all I needed was a simple shot or something."

"Well," said LuAnne, "it was a single injection, yes, but not of a particularly simple medication. You weren't exactly aware and rational at the time you arrived, so we had to give you a limited treatment that would address the problems you had right then, and of course repair the genes that made you so susceptible to that whole spectrum of illnesses. But that was the minimum we could do just to bring you to where you are now. We didn't have any instructions regarding your wishes in the event something happened to you, but I hope you'll be satisfied with what we did under the circumstances.

"There's a great deal more we might do for you, if you wish. For that, you need to learn a lot of new information so you can make an intelligent assessment of your situation, what you want out of life, and just how committed you are to not merely living but thriving. That's all entirely up to you, of course, but yes, your cancers are being dealt with even as we speak. They'll never come back."

"Just like that?"

"Yes. For where you're from, it's pretty advanced stuff, but we've been working with this particular technology for a while, and by now it's thoroughly understood."

"Um. I guess I would have died that night, wouldn't I?"

"Where you were living? Yes. We're just very glad you were with some of our people. We don't like scares like that."

"If I'm not being too inquisitive, then, just who are you people? You look and sound pretty much like everybody else I'm used to, except for the medical technology. And that shuttle! I didn't notice very much about it, but it didn't seem like any aircraft I can think of." Charlene's stomach rumbled.

"Well, that's a long story," said LuAnne. "We'll get to it, but for now why don't you feed that beast that just growled at us? You're going to need more food than usual while your body repairs all that damage. And even more when you start your strength, endurance, and agility training to regain what you temporarily lost. I imagine you already understand about all that. Do you feel like getting up and wandering down to the cafeteria, or would you rather be lazy and have breakfast in bed?"

Charlene had the distinct impression that staying in bed, as long as she really could walk, wouldn't receive any slightest sympathy. "Let's see how far I can get on my own two feet. I had to use the bathroom shortly before you came in, and didn't feel too wobbly. What about clothes or a robe?"

"All the clothing that came up with you is hanging in the closet over there, or is in the set of drawers inside it. Today, we'd prefer if you'd put on the white robe that's hanging on the back of your room door. That helps our staff tell who's a new patient. Later today you'll be issued more standard patient clothing to use during the next few days, until you can be released. Those moccasins are standard patient footwear; I hope they're comfortable. If you want socks, they're in the top drawer in the closet.

"The cafeteria on this floor is open to patients, staff and visitors alike, so if you want to freshen up a bit and make yourself presentable, why don't you do that now? I'll be right outside, and will bring along a wheelchair in case you start feeling woozy during the walk. Any questions?"

"Plenty, but they can wait."

"Good. I'll see you in a few moments." LuAnne nodded to her, then went out of the room, closing the door behind her.

There was indeed a soft white robe on the back of the door; Charlene thought it would come down to just above her ankles. Carefully, she got out of the bed again, still pleasantly surprised that she felt none of the sharp pains that had been making her life difficult for the last weeks that she remembered. Slipping her feet into the moccasins, she found them a bit loose, so she walked to the closet. Yes, there were her jeans, Sunday dress, and her sun dress, as well as half a dozen blouses, cleaned and pressed, hanging right next to a set of narrow drawers.

She got out a pair of new white cotton socks and a fresh pair of white panties, and, for modesty's sake, a new bra. Closing the drawers and closet, she went into the bathroom and realized that her hairbrush and comb were on the washstand, as were her blue hairband, her toothbrush, and an almost new tube of toothpaste, just as she'd left them in her cabin. She really needed to brush her teeth, so that was the first order of business, followed by quickly shedding her nightgown and using the toilet again. She must have been given a *lot* of fluids while unconscious!

She didn't need a shower, feeling as if she had been carefully bathed before being put into the bed, but she washed her hands and face. The soap from the sink dispenser felt particularly luxurious and refreshing now that she was paying attention to details. She noticed what looked like a fairly thick bit of tape on her left side below her arm, but not knowing what it was, she left it in place. It didn't create a problem with the bra, so she ignored it, and brushed out her hair for a few minutes. Someone had even trimmed her split ends, evening up her hair so it looked much better than she remembered. The nightgown went back on next, then she swept her hair up and back into its customary ponytail, secured it with the band, and regarded herself in the mirror.

Clear blue-gray eyes looked back at her from a face somewhat gaunt but almost having her normal color. Her hair no longer looked lank; there was actually some life in it. Feeling once more able to stand straight without pain to her normal height, she put on her underwear and walked out of the bathroom. Putting on the robe, she found it to be wonderfully soft and luxurious. She was going to get spoiled rotten in this hospital!

She opend the door and saw what appeared to be a nurse's station across a wide corridor, with two women behind its counter. LuAnne was approaching, pushing a wheelchair that was still folded closed; obviously, it wasn't expected to be used immediately, which made Charlene feel even better. The fairly short walk to the cafeteria was slightly tiring; she realized she must have weakened far more while unconscious than she'd thought.

"That's normal," said LuAnne when she mentioned it. "You've been using a lot of energy over the past two weeks, and until around midnight last night you were on life support. But even with that stimulation, one can't maintain proper muscle tone. That was an awfully advanced case you had. Much longer before getting here and you probably wouldn't be with us anymore.

"Mitt—his name's actually pronounced Linárres Mithríllian, be careful with the accentuation—was worried sick about you. He's an exceptionally perceptive young man, and we have very high hopes for him as a doctor. He cares about you very much; I hope you know that. He and the major did your maintenance using equipment aboard the shuttle, so you had a really excellent team to get you through that and into our ICU. There, our people got you hooked up and did the last-minute adjustments to your medication. Mitt wouldn't let anyone else touch you until you were stabilized.

"Anyway, let's get something from the chow line, and then find ourselves a window with a view."

Charlene realized she wanted to eat a large breakfast but was hesitant.

"You can always come back for seconds. Or thirds, whatever; the idea is to get you healthy and strong again," said LuAnne. "There's nothing in your meds that will react badly to anything available here, but you haven't eaten anything for two weeks. Your eyes are probably a lot bigger than your stomach. Go easy until you know what you can manage." She took a glass of lemonade; Charlene took a light breakfast and a small glass of tomato juice. Her tray wasn't at all heavy, but she moved carefully while walking to a table, aware of some slight twinges of discomfort where sharp pains had been the last time she'd had breakfast.

The cafeteria was fairly small but high-ceilinged and with a light, airy feeling about it. Wide windows somewhat above treetop level looked out over a verdant forest, a ridgeline perhaps a mile and a half or so from where she sat, and a cloudless blue sky above that. There was a graceful tower rising above the forested ridge, with something at its top that vaguely resembled the restaurant atop Seattle's Space Needle.

"Um, LuAnne, I know that before I drifted off the other evening, there was this young gentleman named Myron Watson, who told me this was all at no cost to me. I'm sorry to doubt what your people are saying, but I've never been comfortable being a charity case. Was he being straight with me, or is there something I wasn't being told? I'd looked around for treatment a lot, but I've never heard of a facility like this. And I've never known anyone who'd want to pay the bills a place like this must surely charge. So, will you please tell me just exactly where on Earth we are and why I'm being given this second chance at life? Actually a whole new life—my last one seems to have ended on the way here."

LuAnne looked down at her hands for a moment before saying, "Well, there's really no other way to put this, Charlene. You're not on Earth anymore. Around a billion or so miles away from it, in fact, inside a place we call Home Station, in orbit well out beyond Saturn. My ancestors originated on Earth, and left it around thirty-three thousand years ago."

Charlene's fork had frozen in mid-air. Now she smiled and took the bite she had been going to. "You sure do know how to startle a girl, LuAnne. For a moment I almost believed you. Okay, you don't want to tell me just where we are at the moment. That's fine; with the capabilities your people seem to have here I'd probably want to stay kind of low-profile too—"

"You'd best finish that food before it gets cold, Charlene. We're all just people here. And here comes your true benefactor, with Mr. Watson."

The most striking woman Charlene had ever seen walked into view, arm in arm with Myron. She was dressed in a plain utility uniform, just as he was, and stood only an inch shorter than he, if that. She looked about twenty years of age, had wide, strong swimmer's shoulders and glistening golden-brown hair. Her facial features weren't the most delicate Charlene had ever seen, beautiful as they were, but she had the most intense, wide-spaced, green eyes Charlene could imagine, eyes that practically glowed with life and vitality. They were slanted just like Mitt's.

Charlene had thought Myron moved with composure back at that barn. This woman radiated power that demanded respect. Charlene immediately came to her feet, noticing the simple wedding band on the woman's left hand.

"Hello, Miss Bridger," said the woman, in a gently lilting contralto with a very slight accent Charlene couldn't place. "I'm so very glad to see you up and about today. You had some of us badly worried for a while."

She held out her hand for a conventional handshake, and Charlene automatically responded, her whole right arm tingling at the mere touch of this woman's hand.

"My name is Élowynn. You know my countryman Mitt. He described your illness to me, and I simply had to do something to ensure you live long in this life. It holds so much in store for you." The handshake released, and Charlene almost collapsed into her chair.

"Come, let us sit awhile," said Élowynn, gracefully settling into a chair that Myron had pulled up from a nearby table.

Charlene really did collapse then, her knees giving out when she was about an inch above her chair. Élowynn seemed unsurprised, continuing, "The treatment you had was—stressful, shall I say. Please don't be concerned about that. I went through something rather worse some years ago. It lasted about four years, whereas your recovery will be complete in just under three months if you exert yourself to recover. You will. It is not in you to do otherwise. Someone should stay near you for the next few days, whenever you're up and walking, because our knees have a way of buckling at the most inconvenient of moments as we recover. Mine did, many times, much to the chagrin of those who were overseeing my own convalescence. It passes.

"I sense your confusion and your disbelief. They are the normal responses of a sane, healthy mind. Please do not concern yourself with your physical location for now. Instead, let it suffice for a time that you are among people intent on returning you to excellent health, for that is true. You have already met Mr. Watson. This," she indicated an attractive young woman of blended Asian and Caucasian ancestry, "is my close friend Alice, Mr. Watson's sister, who is also from Home—sorry, from your planet Earth. And so, you have questions?" She casually brushed her hair back from the side of her face.

Charlene's mouth dropped open for a moment before she closed it with an almost audible snap. Élowynn's ear, which had just been exposed, was delicately pointed!

Élowynn smiled. "Yes, indeed you have many questions. Be not afraid. My people are just another branch of humanity, not much more different from you than is Mr. Watson or his sister. He calls our visible differences cosmetic variations, and in that he is entirely correct."

"But—but you're an Elf!"

Myron and Élowynn looked at each other, shared a gentle laugh.

"Catches on quick, doesn't she?" asked Myron, smiling.

Élowynn, eyes sparkling with good humor, nodded. "Indeed, some of my ancestors visited your world several thousand years ago, and some of your legends have retained that name given us by your people. You may call us that if you wish. My people call ourselves Éhofen, but it matters not at all. We're just people.

"But I think I see some others coming whom you will be happy to greet, Miss Bridger." Turning to Myron, she smiled, a smile that practically lit up the entire room. "Bets?"

"Sunk without a trace," he said, his smile every bit as genuine as hers.

A familiar voice came from Charlene's side. Turning, she saw that it was her friend from the Maddox's Circle Zero ranch, Linárres Mithríllian.

Got it! Finally *pronounced his name properly!* she thought. In his hands he held three flat boxes. And he was not wearing sunglasses, a hat, or a bandana.

He said, "Hey, guys, who ordered pizza? A large pepperoni, a large vegetarian, and a medium Canadian bacon and pineapple, all raised-edge?" Behind him stood the major and Carole, and behind them was Mrs. Maddox, on her husband Henry's arm.

Charlene jumped to her feet, going to hug Mrs. Maddox, tears blurring her vision and making it impossible for her to speak.

"There, there, Shar, it's perfectly all right," said Mrs. Maddox, returning Charlene's hug. "You're just going to have to deal with the fact that some of your friends back home on Earth weren't necessarily born there. I was, and so were Myron and his sister. But Henry and the major weren't, and neither was Carole. And of course Linárres wasn't, any more than was Lady Élowynn, but I'm sure you've figured that out by now."

"Your neighborhood's just a lot bigger than you thought it was," said the major. "And there are some *really* excellent places to get your education when you're ready to jump back into the academic world. Yeah, you're missing this year at Bozeman, sorry about that. But your tuition's being refunded. You can get your initial training right here on this station if you'd like.

"Then maybe you could do your field work and advanced training on Lady Élowynn's world. The University of The Havens there has openings for students from other worlds, and with a little prep here I'd guess you're sharp enough to make the grade. And with a certificate from The Havens, you'll have seven human-populated worlds to choose from when you do a job search. Well, just not on Earth. Yet. Unless you get training there too. Some people do.

"But important things first! It's good to see you up and about and looking so well, but there's some good pizza sitting here, getting cold . . ."

Charlene, almost entirely pain free and utterly ravenous, felt entirely at home for the first time in her life.

Science Fiction Novelists

Upgrade This
By Kayelle Allen
What if androids gossiped around the water cooler?

About the author

Kayelle Allen writes space opera with larger than life, unforgettable characters. Come walk in her worlds and meet them. Join one of her Reader Groups to read her books before they're released.

Find out more at www.kayelleallen.com/reader-groups

* * *

"I don't believe you." Vf-7 lifted a brow made of the finest artificial hair, the droidskin around his eyes wrinkling in a lifelike manner. "How could Niner do that, right in the produce section of a grocery store?"

"That's what I heard."

"Impossible!"

"Modulate your volume." 2-XS extended his eye-stalks out of his power-bay and into the Human-only corridor. Nothing but dingy, gray-tiled floors and gray walls. A faint trail of chemicals lingered from the cleaning-droid that had passed a few minutes before. No Humans within visual range. He snapped back and turned to Vf-7. "And," he lowered his voice to a whisper only another android could hear, "translate this. They say Niner will never snap out of it. He's scheduled for a refit."

"Ridiculous." Vf-7 lifted one extender arm. "Reboots are cheaper."

The powerpack behind 2-XS beeped and released him. He rolled out of the recessed bay. Still no Humans in range. He angled himself toward Vf-7. "The Humans I support said no one from the lab authorized the test, so the Droid Union won't pay for a reboot. They said if he wasn't a lab-droid, he'd be scrapped. He's lucky to get a refit."

Vf-7's powerpack released him, and the short android popped out of his bay. "But Droid Comp covers reboots for faulty experiments." He emitted a soft screech.

2-XS backed up. "What does that dissonance indicate?"

"You mean this?" The android repeated the sound. "It's a sigh. Like my Humans make when frustrated."

"That was not a sigh."

"It wasn't? How's this?" Vf-7 let out a lower-pitched noise even less harmonically resolved.

"Stop. You'll break my ear sensors. Why do you want to be like Humans anyway? They're so . . . squishy. And wet."

"You wouldn't understand."

The two entered a service-droid access tube.

"About Niner." Vf-7 rolled backward, facing 2-XS. "I don't see how they can justify a refit. He's a good worker. His stats are always higher than ours."

"The experiment was unauthorized, after hours, and off-site. The union doesn't reboot renegade androids."

"Renegade! A Human would sue for defamation of character."

"Who can afford a lawyer? They don't work for circuit packs."

Vf-7 stopped before a numbered hatch. "This is me. Can't he get a lawyer? Pro bono?"

"What Human would defend a droid for free? Our union doesn't cover legal fees."

"Then why are they docking our power? If they don't protect us, I say we go on strike! Let the union get its own power."

2-XS aligned a cable on the shorter android's neck, and tucked it back into place. "There's no need for emotion. Niner experimented on himself."

"But why?"

"I can formulate no assessment from data presented. All I know is his Humans have backup disks to prove it."

"I don't believe any of this." Vf-7 rolled up to a scanner on the door, checking in for work. "This sounds like one of those urban legends Droid News is always going on about. That *Debunking the Droids* stream. You know the one."

"Yes, but this is true. Although they'll probably hush it up and some unattached droid will be refitted to confirm what they want Humans and droids to hear."

"Maybe," Vf-7 agreed, "but a Human probably put him up to it. If you put Humans in the equation, you never know what you'll get."

A pair of white-coated Human techs passed them, rubber-soled shoes squeaking in the metal tube. The thud of a closing door boomed down the barren hall.

Vf-7 tilted up his head, revealing an amber glow within his eyes. "I don't get what a Level One lab-droid was doing in a grocery store anyway. They don't eat."

"I told you. Niner's new implants scanned bar code information to facilitate software upgrades. Everything would have been fine if he hadn't tried upgrading with those barcodes used for pricing. Who would think the black-and-white bars found on produce could do that much damage?"

The shorter android backed up and turned ninety degrees toward his door but then wheeled back. "Why was he trying to change the prices of food?"

"Will you realign your attention parameters? He wasn't changing prices. He was trying to change himself. He wanted to upgrade past the status of a lab-droid. That's the reason the union won't repair him. It was an unauthorized upgrade. Downgrade, in his case."

"You mean it worked?" Vf-7 rolled sideways. "He took on characteristics of something he scanned in the produce section?"

"Yes. Can you believe that?" 2-XS responded to a query from his Humans regarding power status. He had to go. "It's a waste, isn't it? Poor Niner."

"So that's why the lab . . ." Vf-7 did not continue.

"Wants to take him apart? Yes. Niner wasn't processing on all circuits trying that. To facilitate an upgrade in the produce section showed a marked lack of intellectual capacity."

"You mean—" The smaller android angled his head left, then right, but the tube had remained void of other life forms "—he was *Human-stupid.*"

"Yes. How do Humans put it . . . ? 'Got it in one.'" More like many, in Vf-7's case.

"So he's," the android rolled in closer, "useless?"

"Yes, and a refit is for the best. Otherwise, our poor Niner would spend the rest of his life . . . as a vegetable."

Millington's Last Game
JJ Toner

About the author

JJ Toner writes short stories and novels. He also edits books for other indie authors. Most of his published books are WW2 spy stories, but his first love has always been science fiction. He is working on a new series called Android Wars. JJ lives in Ireland.

Find out more at www.JJToner.com

* * *

How about a game of chess?

I don't think so.

What's the score so far?

We've played 300 games, give or take.

How many've I won?

None.

Losses?

None.

All draws, huh?

Pretty much.

What about Commander Millington?

Millington beat me in 3,587 games.

Out of how many?

3,613.

Draws?

Twenty-four.

That leaves you with how many wins?

Do the math yourself.

Two?

Two.

You're not counting the last game, are you?

Why shouldn't I? He resigned.

He *died*. That's hardly the same thing.

The game was adjourned. I won by default. He went for a spacewalk and never came back. Those are the rules.

* * *

Open a channel, Sam.

Channel Open. Record On.

This is Gemini Deep Space Mission, day 1,473. Transmitting from 30,778 parsecs. Acting Commander George Dutton. All systems nominal. Acceleration constant at 1.0072 gravities. Velocity 0.0669 light. Estimated time to destination: 707 Gemini days. Nothing exceptional to report. Weather sunny, no cloud cover. Over.

Why do you always say that?

A little humor does no harm.

        Crackle . . . crackle . . . sssssssssssssssssssssssssssssss.

I hear nothing, George.

Quiet!

There's nothing to hear, George.

        sssssssssssssssssssssssssssssssss.

        sssssssssssssssssssssssssssssssss.

Close the channel, Sam.

Record Off. Channel Closed.

I'm scared, Sam.

Why?

What if . . . What if they're all gone?

Mission control, you mean?

Everyone.

What, some global disaster?

Yeah, a nuclear war, an asteroid hit or something.

The roaches will have taken over. Giant roaches everywhere, running everything. King Roach in the White House.

That's not funny, Sam.

Please yourself.

Who decided to give you a sense of humor, anyhow?

* * *

How about a game of chess, Sam? I'll be white. Pawn to king four.

Pawn to king four.

Looks like a draw.

Why do you always do that? We could play the game out.

It was bad enough losing to the commander. How d'you think I'd feel if I lost to a machine?

* * *

Talk to me, George.

What d'you want me to say?

Tell me about Debbie.

I've told you everything about her a thousand times.

Tell me again.

Why?

It's good for your mental health.

She's three years old.

Was.

Don't interrupt. She has blonde curls—

Had.

201

Shut up!

How old would she be now?

In *our* now, she's seven.

And in reality? How old is she in reality?

What does that mean?

If she sent us a message today, how old would she say she was?

Maybe eight, but she'd be nearly nine by the time we got the message.

That's a guess, right?

No. I've done the math. Check it if you like.

What about her mother?

Sylvia must be thirty-seven. A year older than me, now.

✳ ✳ ✳

Play it again, Sam. Play the recording.

We've listened to it a hundred times already.

Just once more, please, Sam.

He's gone, George. He's not coming back.

Computer, reload mission record index 373.

Commander Millington can you hear me?

Yes George, loud and clear. I'm just about to open the outer airlock. All systems are nominal.

Good luck, Commander.

Thanks, George. You're in charge until I get back.

What's it like out there, Commander?

Clear black sky. Lots of stars. No moon.

Any sign of rain?

Sorry, George, I didn't catch that.

Not important, sir. Where are you?

I'm close to the antenna.
How does it look?
It's out of alignment, but it looks undamaged.

. . .

It's fixed. I'm on my way back.
Take your time, Commander.
I'll give you the word when to open the airlock.

. . .

George, my air supply is failing fast (cough). Switching to
backup supply.
Roger that, Commander.

. . .

Commander?
(cough) My backup supply is—
Commander Millington? Come in, Commander!
(wheeze) George, what have you done?

What really happened to the commander, George?

He was unlucky, Sam. A chance event. Nothing I could've done about it.

All the evidence points to murder.

That's crap.

Is it?

Sure. It was an accident. In space, accidents happen all the time.

His suit failed.

Yes. One of the suits was faulty. He chose the wrong one, that's all.

So how come that suit was faulty? I think someone interfered with it.

You mean, you think I interfered with it.

Did you?

What if I did?

You killed him. You murdered the commander.

No, I'm not a killer.

Okay, so explain what you did.

Go to hell.

Tell it like you would to a board of enquiry. George Dutton, Acting Commander of the Gemini Deep Space Mission, please take the stand—

Go to hell!

—and explain to the members of the board what happened to your mission commander, Rijkart Millington. You were beyond mission commit, nearly four years out—close to one light year—when there was an accident.

We lost antenna alignment.

Your antenna was struck by a piece of space debris at high velocity.

Yes, Admiral. We adjourned our game.

Game?

We were playing chess.

I see. Continue.

Commander Millington went out to fix the antenna.

And his suit malfunctioned.

Yes, sir. He had successfully realigned the antenna and started back when—

His air supply ran out.

Yes sir.

How long was he out?

Not long. Maybe twenty minutes.

If memory serves me, these suits hold enough oxygen for a couple of hours.

Yes, sir.

And yet it ran out after twenty minutes.

Roughly, sir, yes.

These suits have an emergency backup supply. Am I right, Acting Commander?

Yes, sir.

And that failed too?

Correct, sir.

And you lost Commander Millington.

He drifted away from the ship. Slowly. I saw him. I watched him drift away. Spinning. It was several hours before I lost sight of him.

You had a second suit.

Yes, sir.

Fully functional.

Yes, sir.

So, you could have gone out after him.

I could have. Yes, sir, but—

But you didn't.

It was my judgment that a rescue attempt would have placed the entire mission in jeopardy. How could I leave the ship unmanned?

Can you offer any explanation for how Commander Millington's spacesuit failed so catastrophically?

It was a chance event, sir.

Explain that.

Just drop it, Sam. I don't want to talk about it anymore.

* * *

You know you're going to turn the ship around.

No way.

You have to abort the mission.

I can't abort.

Why not? You heard the order.

It was garbled.

It told you to abort the mission. You know that's what it said.

Maybe, but the signal was scrambled. It could've been anything.

Like what?

I don't know. Anything.

You're crazy. Mission Control has ordered you to turn around and go home. What's the matter with you? Don't you want to go home?

I'm the mission commander—

Acting.

—and I will carry on to the final destination.

Don't I have a vote?

No, you're a computer.

You're crazy!

I will complete the mission.

For heaven's sake! Why?

What do you think I'll find if I go back?

A hero's welcome. A tickertape parade up Fifth Avenue.

What about my friends and relatives?

They'll be there, waiting.

Most of them'll be dead.

Maybe. You can't know that for sure, George.

Debbie . . .

She'll be grown up. Maybe have children of her own.

Her mother will be dead. Dead and buried.

Everyone dies, George.

If Debbie ever sees me again, she's gonna hate me.

Why?

Because.

Because what?

Just because.

You're being childish.

Because I went away and abandoned her, that's why.

Is that what's bugging you?

Yes, but there's something else.

What is it?

She'll be . . .

What? She'll be what, George? Finish your sentences.

She'll be old.

So what? You'll be old too.

Yes, but she'll be older than me.

That's crazy. It's not possible.

I've done the math. If I turn back today, I'll be in my early fifties by the time I get back. Debbie'll be in her sixties. She'll be older than me, older than her own father!

∗ ∗ ∗

It was a chance event, you say.

Explain.

Only one of the suits was faulty. Commander Millington could have chosen the other one. The two suits were interchangeable. They looked identical. He had a choice.

And that's what you mean by a chance event?

Sure. Also, he could have ordered me to realign the antenna. So he had a three in four chance of living. He was unlucky. He made the wrong choice—twice. Chance killed him.

What would have happened if Millington had sent you out?

I would have died.

Millington would have aborted the mission.

Maybe.

No way he would have continued on his own.

Maybe. We'll never know.

What if you had selected the good suit?

I wouldn't have.

Why not?

I knew which one was faulty.

All right, what if Millington had chosen the good suit?

He would have survived.

Would he?

Probably.

* * *

What are you doing, George?

Remembering.

Debbie on that long sandy beach?

Yes. The sun's warm, the ocean gently lapping. Her mother's lying by my side on the sand, most of her body under an umbrella.

Her legs are getting burned, George. I see a mountain in the distance.

Debbie's in a field, jumping on a haystack. She's laughing. I'm thinking she needs to settle down. She'll burst a blood vessel or something, she's laughing so hard. Sylvia's watching. She's smiling.

She doesn't see the danger. Now Debbie's paddling in the water; wearing a pink hat.

If I use my hands to blank out the scene on both sides, there's just Debbie and the vast ocean.

I see her, George. I see her! Nothing overhead but the blue sky and deep space beyond. Each time she comes down, she topples over into the hay. Her face is red. She's laughing fit to burst.

I bet she'll remember that day until she dies.

Don't you want to go home, George?

More than anything, Sam. I'd give anything to go back, but that's impossible. Don't you see? This is a one-way trip. Always was.

I wish you'd turn the ship around, George.

Why? Why do you care either way?

She's my daughter too, George.

Miranda
By Philip Cahill

About the author

Philip Cahill is a retired accounting academic living in Caen, France. He recently self-published a novel (Noystria) on Amazon. Find out more at
www.amazon.co.uk/Philip-Cahill/e/B0034NBL44

✳ ✳ ✳

The voice was male and spoke with such clarity that I thought for a moment I was speaking to a machine. It was one of those calls that came out of nowhere. One of those that start a sequence of events that ultimately delivers a life-changing shock. He said he wanted to confirm my identity and address. I opened the phone's telepathic channel but the caller was clearly not a telepath because he didn't respond to my request for identification and I couldn't sense my message reaching his mind. I was about to hang up when he mentioned Miranda. This made me pause. I told him he needed to send proof of his identity before I'd talk further.

✳ ✳ ✳

I hadn't seen or thought about her for years. I've been through several regenerations so my memories about Miranda were pretty old. As I waited for the caller to send me his ID file, I tapped into my memory archive and began a search. The first fragment arrived in a few seconds. The last time I saw her, she was singing in a bar no one's ever heard of in a city no one's ever heard of. It was back in the late 27th century, when I lived in France. Before she'd become famous. Before she'd become known from Mercury to the moons of Pluto and beyond.

Some more memory detail arrived.

✳ ✳ ✳

The bar was squeezed between a shop selling overpriced bric-a-brac and a superette, in the warren of medieval streets close to the Place Saint-Sauveur in Caen. In those days, the Bar de la Tour was my last stop on the way home. It was where I would drink a final few whiskies to give me the energy to walk up the hill to my empty bungalow in the Quartier St-Gabriel.

She was close to the end of her set when I arrived. I managed to find a seat at the end of the counter, wedged against the wall. I was lucky because the place was crowded with students that night. They were abnormally quiet, focusing on the small stage at the back of the room. Miranda was accompanied by a keyboard player whose bulk took up most of the stage.

He was fat rather than muscular, with long wiry hair and dark glasses. I didn't like the look of him, but he played as if the notes seeped straight out of his neural substrate. Impossible, of course, because like my caller he was also telepathically blind. I remember the way he caressed the keyboard. It was as if he was frightened it might collapse under the weight of his hands. Miranda stood to the right of the musician, at the edge of the stage.

She didn't move as she sang. She kept her mouth close to the oval disk of the microphone that floated in front of her face, partially obscuring it. She wore a neurotransmission circlet that amplified her telepathy. Beneath it, her long copper-coloured hair cascaded over her shoulders. She wore a silvery dress that

212

clung to her figure and sparkled in the light. She'd changed a lot since the last time I'd seen her.

I found another level of memory detail about that night in the bar.

* * *

I held a banknote between my index and middle fingers and signalled to the barman, Daniel, for a whisky. Sometimes this would work. Sometimes it wouldn't and I'd have to get out of my seat and lean over the bar to bellow out my order. I was in luck that night. He seemed to be in a good mood.

I swallowed a large mouthful of whisky and settled against the wall. Miranda had reached the last song of her set. It was her breakthrough song, "Les Âmes Perdues," "The Lost Souls." A song that spoke of loss, of sorrow, of loneliness that was made only just bearable by memories of a transcendent love. She began to sing so softly that the first few phrases could barely be heard. She didn't look like a telepath at all. None of the glacial expression or the piercing intensity of gaze. Her face and eyes revealed the same kind of warm-heartedness that you can sometimes see in the faces of telepathically blind people. She had an excellent physical voice. It was melodious and powerful, and she enunciated perfectly.

As she sang, she began to build the emotion, using the power of her physical voice with extraordinary dexterity. Behind her appeared an image of two classically beautiful lovers floating toward each other against a celestial backdrop. She went into telepath and augmented the vocal line, making it more musical and profound. When the lover's bodies briefly touched, then parted, she added an emotional chord structure and poured more power into the components of her singing voice. She uttered a plaintive call as the space between the lovers increased.

I knew the song, of course, so I responded to the call, in telepath. I, the object of her love, struggling to get back to her, clawing at the emptiness of interstellar space. I had no amplification, but Miranda sensed me. I couldn't tell if she had recognized me or not. She began to extemporize around my response, flashing a few micro-seconds of gentle mockery at me alone, before dissolving her derision into a sincere, enveloping warmth that she shared with the crowd.

I responded to her warmth with a gesture of respectful and humble admiration and continued the lyrics as best I could.

She began adding layer upon layer of additional embellishments. She seemed to be herself, her lover, and the passion of love itself. At the same time, she augmented the power of the vocal line again. I carried on for as long as I could, but I was exhausted. She sent me a personal message of thanks as I lapsed into telepathic silence. But there was still no hint of recognition. I felt the attention of her mind moving away from me as she prepared for the climax of the song.

She took her time, gestured to the musician to subdue his keyboard, and focused on her extraordinary vocal and telepathic voices. When she reached the first notes of the finale, I sensed that she'd decided to hold back from unleashing the full power of the emotion that she was capable of expressing, as if she didn't want to cross a threshold of intensity that could cause fear and pain.

In the final minutes of the song, the keyboard player stopped playing and Miranda concentrated on her physical voice. She eased off on the telepathic augmentation and poured out the final phrases into the souls of the audience.

Then, blackness. In the darkness Miranda was invisible. The keyboard player started playing again as the lights came up, but she was gone. I signalled to the barman for another drink, but he shook his head. The applause thundered off the ceiling.

I wanted to run from the bar, to the street door at the back of the building. I wanted to thank her for singing my song like that, but I knew she wouldn't want to speak to me. Part of the reason she could sing so powerfully about emotional pain was me. I should never have left her the way I did. As I said, I never saw her again. I think the guilt kept me away. Guilt at what I'd done, compounded with remorse at the way she publicized my song and earned me money that I wasted. Never enjoyed.

The royalties had dried up after fifty years when the rights to the song had entered the public domain. I was not completely broke. I could still afford whisky, but only just.

* * *

The identity file arrived so I resumed the call. He was a researcher from a law firm. Lawyers often use non-telepaths as investigators because they're cheaper and they tend to be very good at processing physical evidence. Miranda had gone missing on one of the Saturnian moons five years ago. They'd found the body only a month ago. He wouldn't commit himself. Said only that he'd called to confirm my identity and my whereabouts. But I wondered why he'd contacted me. Had Miranda left me the bulk of her estate?

Subspecies
By John Bowers

About the author

John Bowers began writing in 1961 and completed six novels by the time he graduated high school. Now a retired computer programmer, he is the author of the *Fighter Queen* series; the *Nick Walker, U.F. Marshal* series; and the *Starport* series. All are available on Amazon. Bowers lives in California.

Find out more at
www.amazon.com/John-Bowers/e/B004UFOT3U

* * *

Xirtam gazed out the viewport at the majestic blue planet spinning below. It was a stunning world, one of the most beautiful he'd seen, but his immediate attention was focused on a transfer shuttle approaching from the ship that had just arrived in orbit.

His principal eye narrowed as the shuttle drew near. He felt a stir of unease as it docked—it was the first contact from the Husk in over a decade, and completely unexpected. Something must be up.

As the airlock opened, his emote-eye flashed in surprise, rippling yellow and orange, as Martam emerged from the airlock. He hadn't seen his old friend in over a hundred galactic seasons. As Martam slithered up to him, he leaned forward until their cylindrical foreheads touched.

"Old friend. I was not expecting you. Welcome to the Spiral."

Martam's emote-eye glowed a warm green. "I requested it. After my cell-mate withered, I had no reason to stay at home."

"Wirtam has withered? I had not heard. My condolences."

Martam's emote-eye flickered in a shrug. "He was much older than I. It was inevitable."

"Even so . . ."

"Tell me about the project. How does it go?"

Xirtam felt a flush of satisfaction. Martam had always been a pragmatist, preferring duty over emotion. He took Martam's arm and led him toward the laboratory.

"Actually, the project is almost complete. But you are in time to assist in the final evaluation."

"You've been out here for nearly a century. Exactly what is it that you're doing?"

"It has been very frustrating." Xirtam's emote-eye rolled in a sigh. "Early indications were mixed, so it has taken much longer than usual to monitor this planet and determine if it is a threat to the stellar society."

"Doctrine dictates that, if there is any question, the planet must be sterilized."

"Yes, I know, but this world is so . . . complex."

"Complex? How?"

"The sheer abundance of life is beyond anything we have ever seen. There isn't just one species here, or a hundred, but millions. Perhaps billions—we still don't have an accurate count."

"Sentient?"

"No. So far we have only found one sentient species, but the variety is astonishing. Plant, animal, fungal, insect, microbial —the oceans are teeming with life, and the planet even has species that soar through the atmosphere."

"*Flying* species? That is unusual. Normally we don't see more than two or three major species on a single world."

"Precisely. Indications are that evolution here has been in progress for billions of galactic cycles; we see evidence that more species have gone extinct than are currently extant."

Martam's emote-eye widened. "Unbelievable!"

"From a purely scientific perspective, I hesitate to sterilize this planet. Threat or no threat."

"I understand." Martam's emote-eye closed in thought. "Unfortunately, if it is determined the threat is real, the Husk will not share your reluctance. It will be the end of the road for this world."

"I know. It would simply be a shame to extinguish it. That is why I've taken so long to make a determination. I'm looking for any possible reason to save this planet."

"What have you found so far? What are the indicators?"

Xirtam's emote-eye sagged. "Not good."

"Tell me about the dominant species. What is it called?"

"It calls itself Human."

"You said it is sentient?"

"Yes. Come, let me show you."

* * *

Xirtam led his old friend into the belly of the ship where specimens were on display. Martam was amazed at the hundreds of exhibits, each one perfectly preserved. Animals, birds, insects, aquatics—thousands of them filling a cavernous hold. Martam's emote-eye expanded and contracted again and again, betraying his absolute astonishment at what he was seeing.

Finally, they passed into another section, this one containing holding cells. For the first time, Martam gazed upon the naked, virtually hairless specimen that so attracted Xirtam.

The subject sat in a chair with its eyes closed. To Martam's amazement, the eyes in the specimen's head were set on a parallel plane, and not vertically, as was common throughout the galaxy. The eyes were closed, the specimen calm. The only sign of life was a slow rising and falling of the upper torso region.

"This is the sentient?" Martam asked.

"Yes." Xirtam's emote-eye blinked rapidly, revealing his anxiety. "This is the one that determines whether the planet below has reached the end of the road."

"What is the problem? You said the outlook is not good."

"It is difficult to know where to begin. For one thing, this species is reproducing at a staggering rate. When we began our observations, it had about two billion units scattered all over the planet. In less than one hundred galactic cycles, the number has more than tripled. This increase has threatened many other species with extinction, and there is a question whether the food supply can sustain a continued increase at the same rate."

"That hardly seems to be cause for sterilization."

"No, it is just a curiosity. The problem is much greater than that. This species periodically makes war upon itself. It appears peaceful most of the time but is actually a violent, terrifying life form."

"War upon itself?" Martam was shocked. "For what purpose?"

"It could be an evolutionary device for population control, but we have never seen this before. What is striking is that it isn't uniform. Each individual unit looks different than all the others, everything from eye and skin color to hair density to mental capacity. It comes in a variety of shapes, all with the same body parts, but some are tall, others short; some are heavy and others light. It speaks a multitude of languages, each one specific to a region or sub-group."

"They are all dangerous?"

"Potentially, yes. It discovered space travel a few decades ago but fortunately has not yet ventured out beyond the first couple of planets. If it ever attains interstellar capability, the threat could be monumental."

"How long until that happens?"

"Difficult to say but probably not more than one or two centuries. We need to make a judgment before then."

"How many have you examined?"

"Almost a million."

"And the results?"

"Uniformly negative."

Martam gazed at his friend a moment.

"You seem to indicate that this species is beyond hope. Yet I sense that you haven't quite given up on it."

"You know me too well, old friend." Xirtam's emote-eye watered in self-deprecation. "Yes, that is correct—despite the horrible implications, I still have hopes for this species." His head inclined to indicate the life form in the chair. "This unit seems to be different from the others we have studied. If I can confirm this distinction, I can make a case for further study, which will at least offer a delay in final judgment, and might reveal evidence that the species can be salvaged."

Martam's emote-eye narrowed. "Why is this one different? *How* is it different?"

Xirtam's emote-eye glowed green.

"I was hoping you would ask."

* * *

Xirtam fiddled with a knob on the control panel for the holding cell. The light inside the cell brightened and cool air flowed across the subject in the chair, riffling its hair. The subject opened its eyes. Martam gazed at it for a moment.

"Why are its eyes parallel? What is the purpose of that?"

"It appears to provide three-dimensional depth perception. There is no other purpose that we can determine."

"The individual eyes should provide that!"

"They should, but they do not. It is an inferior design, but it seems to work well for them."

"Can it commune with us?"

"No. It needs sound waves to express its thoughts."

"Let me hear it. Speak to it."

Xirtam's thoughts activated a translator that converted his mental waves into sound. The sound was emitted into the holding cell via an electronic device. Xirtam and Martam could hear the words, but they were mere noises.

"Hello. Can you hear me?"

The subject's eyes narrowed and its forehead wrinkled. Martam wondered what that meant.

"Yes. I hear you. How are you today?"

"I am well. I have a friend who wants to observe you. Is that all right?"

"Yes, of course." The subject's lips pulled back, revealing white teeth. "The more the merrier."

"Thank you. My friend would like to know your name. Could you speak it for him?"

"My name is Adam."

"Is Adam your real name?"

"No. It is the name you gave me."

"Do you know why I gave you that name?"

"Not really . . . unless I am to be the first."

"The first of what?"

"I'm not sure. Maybe you're going to use me to create a new society."

"Why would you think I was going to do that?"

"Because Adam was the name of the first man. Of course, I'm only speculating. I don't know the real reason that I'm here."

Xirtam deactivated the translator. He turned to Martam. "You can see that it is intelligent."

"Yes. It also seems very peaceful."

"Many of them do. Some are very hostile, even aggressive, and others seem terrified. This one is the calmest one I've ever studied." He turned the translator on again.

"Adam, are you hungry?"

"A little. But I can wait a while longer."

"Very well. Adam, are you afraid?"

"No."

"Surely this experience must be new to you, and frightening."

"I can see why you would think that. I'm sure most people like me would be scared, but I'm not."

"And why not?"

"Because I have faith."

"Faith in what? Why does this faith make you not afraid?"

"I have faith in God. I believe God has a plan for me, and this may be part of it."

Xirtam glanced at Martam, then pressed his head against the glass.

"Thank you, Adam. We will talk more in a few minutes."

"I'll be here."

Xirtam deactivated the translator. Martam's emote-eye expanded and contracted rapidly. He was confused. "What is this 'god' that it speaks of?"

Xirtam's emote-eye rolled.

"I forgot, you haven't been exposed to this yet. Of all the thousands of worlds we have evaluated, this one is unique in that respect. Since the dawn of its evolution, this species has worshiped a variety of deities, many of them natural, others manufactured. The god this one worships appears to be invisible, which makes its devotion all the more puzzling."

"I still don't understand. Worship?"

"Ah, how to explain. We have nothing like it in the Husk, nor anywhere else in the galaxy. It is a devotion, apparently—a high reverence for some object or being. We haven't discovered the cause of this phenomenon, but it seems to be a pathological need in many of this species."

"I see. And they have more than one such . . . *deity?*"

"Indeed. We have identified a dozen major objects of this kind of devotion, and hundreds of minor ones; they seem to be regional in nature. What is truly disturbing is that adherents to these philosophies tend to be militaristic. Most of them are willing to kill each other simply for adhering to the wrong deity. Many such wars have already been fought and we can safely assume that many more will be fought in the future."

Martam's emote-eye bleached white in a shudder.

"Imagine! If they will war against their own kind for merely thinking something different, how willing would they be to war against races they have not yet encountered?"

Xirtam lowered his head in sadness.

"You are a quick study, Martam. These are my fears exactly."

"And yet you hold out hope?"

"Very little, actually, but . . . well, I need to finish my evaluation of this Adam. So far, it has not reacted with the same hostility as previous subjects. It is my hope that it may have evolved beyond them, and if that is the case, we might be prudent to give them a little more time."

"How is it possible that one individual can evolve without the entire species evolving?"

"I'm not certain that it is, but this Adam may represent a new subspecies that is more enlightened—or at least more open-minded—than the others. If this proves to be the case, we may be able to nudge that evolution along and pull this civilization out of its self-imposed darkness."

"A subspecies?"

"Yes."

"What is it called?"

"The only name I know is the one Adam supplied: Christian."

* * *

"I should feed it. Other subjects, including the hostile ones, have become more communicative after taking sustenance."

"What is the source of its nutrition? Organic? Mineral?"

"Organic. It consumes a variety of vegetation and animal materials."

"Animal? You mean they are flesh-eaters?" Martam's emote-eye bleached white again.

"Yes. They have been observed to eat almost every other type of animated species on the planet, though most of them favor just a few dozen, which they raise on farms for the purpose."

"Disgusting!"

225

"Yes, quite."

Xirtam touched another button and a wall panel opened inside the cell. A tray extended with a colorful, steaming mix of unrecognizable substances. Adam rose from its chair and approached the tray. It began putting materials into its mouth with its fingers and chewed them with its teeth. It seemed to relish the meal.

Martam watched in awe. "The nutrients are hot! Is it always so?"

"No. Adam and the others we have studied will eat the nutrients cold as well but seem to prefer them heated."

"Fascinating."

Adam ate for several minutes, then wiped its hands and returned to its chair. As it sat down, it bowed its head momentarily, murmured something, then made a brief, perpendicular motion with its hand across its torso region.

"What was that about?" Martam asked.

"It appears to be a gesture of appreciation to its deity. We still don't fully understand it."

"Why would it offer appreciation to its deity? *You* are the one who supplied the nutrients. It should be thanking you!"

Xirtam's emote-eye flickered. "Just one more curiosity."

Martam's emote-eye rolled in a sigh.

"Well, my friend, I hesitate to rush you, but I have been instructed to urge that you wrap this up. The Husk wants a judgment on this planet and—I'm sorry to tell you—they are annoyed at the delay. You really must make a determination."

"Right now?"

"As quickly as possible. What else do you need to make a decision?"

Xirtam's emote-eye closed as he considered.

"I was hoping to establish a closer rapport with the subject before pressing it too hard. I need to understand what it would take to provoke it."

"Go ahead, then. I hate to rush you, but you must get on with it."

Xirtam's emote-eye sagged. He nodded.

"Very well. I understand."

$$* \quad * \quad *$$

"Adam, can you hear me?"

"Yes."

"I hope the meal was satisfactory?"

"It was wonderful. Thank you."

"I have some questions for you, if you don't mind."

"No problem. Fire away."

Xirtam's emote-eye narrowed. He didn't understand the reference to fire, but perhaps it wasn't important.

"Have you ever terminated another of your own species?"

Adam frowned. "Terminated? Do you mean, killed?"

"Yes, that is correct. Have you ever killed one of your own kind?"

"No."

"May I ask why not?"

"It would be immoral, not to mention illegal."

"I see. Can you think of any circumstances or situations in which you would feel justified in killing one of your own kind?"

Adam didn't answer immediately. Its forehead wrinkled again.

"I suppose so."

"Can you tell me what such a circumstance or situation might be?"

"Well—maybe to save someone else."

"Please elaborate."

"If I saw someone about to kill an innocent person, I might be tempted to intervene."

"Very well. What about yourself? Would you kill to protect your own existence?"

"That's also possible. I would like to think there was a better solution, but we are programmed with a very strong sense of self-preservation."

"So, to be clear, you cannot say that you definitely would *not* kill to save yourself?"

"I can't say that, no."

"Very well. You are aware that your species—you Humans —frequently make war upon each other?"

"Yes, of course. Everyone knows that."

"How do you feel about that?"

"I think it's terrible. God clearly commands us not to kill one another, and yet we do."

"How can you explain that?"

"Not everyone believes in God. If everyone believed and obeyed, we would have no more wars."

Xirtam and Martam made emote-eye contact. Xirtam continued.

"When you speak of this God that you worship, you say that not everyone believes in it."

"Correct."

"Yet almost everyone on your planet—almost every Human—believes in some sort of deity."

"Except for the atheists, I suppose that's true."

"Who are the atheists?"

"Weirdos. They don't believe in God or creation or any of the religious teachings."

"Have these atheists ever started a war?"

"I—uh . . . hmm. You know, I'm not sure."

"Yet many wars have been started and fought by those who believe in a deity?"

"Unfortunately, yes."

"What would it take to persuade them to stop doing this?"

"Persuade them? You've got to be kidding. You can't persuade them. Nobody can. As long as people ignore the True God and disobey Him, wars will never end."

"You indicated that these atheists don't believe in your True God, correct?"

"Yes, that's right."

"Yet they have never, to your knowledge, started a war."

"As far as I know, that's true. But I could be wrong about that." Adam shifted in its chair. "In any case, there aren't all that many atheists. They are in the minority compared to the rest of the world."

"I see. Tell me, Adam, these religious wars . . . are they always between followers of your True God and other deities?"

"No, not always. We've had wars between Christian factions, but those were centuries ago. I think we've outgrown most of that. At least I hope so."

"I hope so, too. Adam, if your God—or those who believe in your God—started a war, would you fight?"

For the first time, Xirtam sensed that Adam was uncomfortable. It shifted in its chair and folded its upper appendages across its torso.

"I wouldn't want to. But if it was necessary, then I might."

"What would make it necessary?"

"That's a big question. If my home were threatened, for example."

"Any other reason?"

"I can't say. It would depend on a lot of factors."

"Give me another example."

Adam was silent for a long moment. Finally, it spoke.

"Fear, I guess."

"Fear?"

"Yes. When you corner an animal, even a peaceful animal, it will fight for its life. Humans are no different."

"Very well."

Xirtam stood in thought for a moment, his emote-eye flickering.

"Adam, do you believe your species is superior to all others?"

Adam's mouth opened and a harsh, staccato sound emitted. After a moment it became quiet.

"I used to think that, but after coming here, I was obviously wrong. You have technology far superior to anything we've developed."

"What if I told you that the galaxy contains thousands of civilizations, all of them different? How would that make you feel?"

Adam's face swelled as air was expelled from its orifice.

"Wow, that's a big one. Intimidated, I guess."

"Intimidated?"

"No. Terrified."

"If you were to encounter some of these civilizations, what would your reaction be?"

"Fear."

"Would you try to kill them?"

"Not . . . not if they were peaceful."

"Are you sure about that?"

"Yes. As sure as I can be."

"What does that mean?"

"I mean, nobody really knows what they will do in a situation like that until it happens."

"I see."

"Why are you asking me all these questions about war and killing? Are you planning an invasion?"

Water gushed from the emote-eyes of both Xirtam and Martam as they laughed.

"No," Xirtam said. "We aren't going to invade you. But for the sake of discussion, let's assume that we were. You would fight us then, would you not?"

"That wouldn't be my call. My leaders would decide that."

"Suppose *you* were the leader? If you had the final decision, what would it be?"

"If you brought people here who were looking for a home and were willing to coexist, I would try to accommodate that."

"Even if we didn't worship your True God?"

"Yes, even then."

"Very well. Suppose, then, that we came with peaceful intentions but asked you to abandon your God. What would you do then?"

"I would say no."

"And if we insisted? If we can offer something better?"

Adam's face flushed bright red and it leaped to its feet. The knobs at the end of its appendages clenched into clubs. Its breathing became irregular.

"I WOULD SLAUGHTER EVERY LAST ONE OF YOU!"

Xirtam's emote-eye rolled in a sigh. He turned off the translator and faced Martam.

"I am sorry, old friend," Martam said. "Are the missile tubes loaded?"

"Yes."

"Would you like me to give the order?"

231

"No. I'll do it."

Survivor Log
Those left behind
By Caleb Fast

About the author

Caleb Fast is a twenty-two-year-old science fiction author from the Pacific Northwest. He's a lifelong fan of all things sci-fi, especially military sci-fi and space operas. He's the author of over a dozen books and is showing no signs of slowing down! Find out more at www.amazon.com/Caleb-Fast/e/B07R6NZXBY

✳ ✳ ✳

Dianna Wrigley
Sector Eleven, Galatia

"Keep your eyes on the tree line!" Carver cries out as he lets off a few rounds into some of the underbrush.

Dianna is about to tell Carver that they're low on ammo when one of the ghastly monsters tumbles out of the brush and collapses. This particular beast looked like a cross between a srin and some sort of bird-like creature. Dianna looks a little closer at the beast and she notes that its claws are drenched with the blood of at least one person that it must have killed recently. There are several scraps of clothing peeking out of the monster's srin-like mouth and Dianna nearly gags as she sees a partially chewed up human hand hanging down the side of its powerful jaw.

"They're waiting for us to let our guard down," Dianna points out hopelessly as she shrinks back against one of the four large trucks that make up their modest convoy. Three are armored; the lone unarmored vehicle is bathed in blood, from when its occupants had been slaughtered the night before.

The others had warned against splitting up the main group, but Dianna and the rest of her group want nothing to do with the Resistance. After all, it was the Resistance that, in one way or another, landed them in Paradise prison. Dianna and everyone else in her modest group of a hundred or so survivors had wanted to build something to last on this beautiful, forested world.

But that was before the first of the monsters showed their ugly heads.

The monsters, or hybrids, or beasts, or whatever they were actually called, have a startling propensity to kill. They chalked up their first kill yesterday, just a few hours after Dianna and the others split off from the main group. Since then, another seventy or so people have been slain. Some of those killed are fed upon while others are seemingly killed for sport.

Most everyone who died was killed during a night that felt like it would never end. Dianna didn't sleep a wink, and she is certain no one else has either. Throughout the night, bloodcurdling cries sounded from all across the small campsite as people either ventured too far away from the fire or when the monsters snuck into camp.

"I see one!" someone shouts. They blindly open fire into the trees.

Carver rips the rifle out of the man's hand and smacks him across the head before reminding him, "We're already low on ammo, don't waste what we have left!"

Despite their best efforts, Dianna and the remaining thirty-four survivors are running desperately low on munitions. They pick up every bit of ammo and all the firearms and gear they can from the dead, no matter how much blood is on it. The dead won't be needing it anymore. Often, there isn't enough of a body left to loot.

Her lip quivering at the thought of the torn apart bodies, Dianna instinctively reaches down to her hip. She runs her fingers across the three magazines she has remaining. Knowing that she still has ammo brings her a sense of security that she knows won't last too much longer. She glances down at her feet and sees dozens of spent rounds. Frowning, she also notes the fifteen or so bullets that turned out to be duds and nearly cost her her life.

Carver returns the old rifle to the man who had momentarily lost his cool. He casts his attention to the trees. After several still seconds, he calls out for everyone to hear, "We all know that there's only one thing we can do right now!"

"How do we know that they'll take us back?" Dianna asks weakly.

"We don't, but I think it's our best chance," Carver replies with the same response he had the night before. Last night, Dianna had been reluctant to give in. But that felt like an eternity ago.

"All in favor?" Dianna prompts. She continues scanning the foliage.

"I'm in," someone says.

"Me too," another whimpers.

Everyone in the group quickly agrees to the last-ditch effort of survival. Dianna lets a few tears stream down her cheeks as she mourns the needless loss of so many people. If they had all simply stuck with the main group, more of them might still be alive.

"All right." Dianna quickly wipes the tears from her eyes. She musters the strongest voice she can. "Everyone pile into the trucks. We should be safer in them than we are out there."

"But last night that didn't work very well," someone whines. He's cut off by the sound of several armored trucks' doors opening and closing and the group mounts up. Despite the man's misgivings, everyone else is ready to get a move on.

"We can leave that one, then." Dianna nods to the complainer. Her eyes linger on the blood-soaked unarmored truck. The vehicle doesn't have a roof and Dianna can't help but stare at the blood-stained seats. Nearly the entire vehicle is covered in blood and Dianna shudders in terror as even more images of the gruesome night flash before her eyes.

"Get in!" Carver takes a hold of her shirt and yanks her into the truck. He plops her as carefully as he can into the passenger seat before he reaches over her to close the heavy door. Firing up the truck's engine, Carver kicks it into reverse. "We have to go backward until we find a place to spin around."

Without waiting for a response, Carver floors it and the truck lurches. Dianna stares ahead blankly as the other two trucks clumsily follow Carver's lead backward.

After a minute or so, Dianna finally blinks, realizing tears are flowing down her cheeks once more. She quickly turns away from Carver and looks outside through the bulletproof window. She finally allows them to flow freely.

Outside, Dianna can see dark splotches on the ground where people have been cut down by the monsters and fed upon. In the handful of places where they left the bodies, Dianna's greeted with sights that she knows she'll never forget —at least, if she survives the day.

In such a short amount of time, so many have been killed and here Dianna is: still alive. Still in one piece.

"On your left!" Dianna hears a voice cry out from somewhere outside their truck.

Dianna looks out the windscreen at the truck in front of them just in time to see one of the largest of the monsters plow into its left side. This monster looks like a supersized reptilian rhinoceros and it quickly pushes the armored truck off the small path that they carved through the forest the day before. Once the truck is a short way off the path, the monster starts ripping it apart like a child rips into a birthday gift. Pieces of metal and flesh fly in all directions as the beast feeds.

"Drive!" Dianna cries out.

Carver wordlessly does his best to accelerate. The engine roars as it struggles to propel the hulking overladen truck over rough terrain. Several people in the seats behind Dianna start shouting, but Dianna can't make out any of the words.

The third armored truck also picks up its pace. In response to their quickened speed, Carver abruptly drives off the path slightly. He spins their vehicle around. It's the best three-point-turn Dianna's ever witnessed. Now facing the right way, Carver slams his foot down on the accelerator. The truck surges forward and away from the killings.

Behind them, several loud crashes sound. She can hear the tires on the other truck squealing. A moment later, several screams reach Dianna's ears, but she doesn't dare turn around to see anyone else die.

For the moment, they are alive.

The Hunt
By JJ Porter

About the author

JJ has lived in Santa Cruz, California for 52 years. He spends much of his time acting. He has been in fourteen plays, one of which he wrote, produced, and directed. JJ likes to ride his bike, garden and people watch. He started writing late in life and has published one book, finished his second which is now being edited, and has developed some ideas on the third book of the trilogy. Find out more at www.jjbooks.space.

✳ ✳ ✳

Batu gazed into the fire. He felt Dream Smoke starting to take its affect. His whole body seemed to be falling under the powerful vapor's spell. Light was coming into Our Place. Soon, Sun would appear again and begin to float into Sky. Our Place would be awakening to the sounds of another day. As Sun started to appear, the winged ones would start to tell their story. Aguagus would squawk and talk of going to Big River to dive for the swimming ones. Hatua would let out his long cry as he swooped from tree to tree searching for small ones to eat. When the Magutes found their first nest of Begeeli bugs, the Magutes would chatter like excited women.

Batu's brother, Blegwa, nudged him. Batu's gaze moved to the pipe in Blegwa's hand, the pipe with Dream Smoke. Batu took the pipe from Blegwa, slowly put it to his lips, and inhaled deeply. He would soon be ready for the Big Hunt. He would not be hunting Buru or Makira or Latrumba for their meat. He would not be hunting Mirika, a powerful and crafty cat. Possession of Mirika skulls gave the Hunter great powers. Batu already had three Mirika skulls on his waist. Some excellent Hunters had one or two Mirika skulls, but most had none. Batu, with three, was hailed by Story Tellers as one of Our Place's greatest Hunters.

Today he was preparing for the greatest hunt of his life—not for meat, not for skulls, but for the Invader who had been trespassing on Our Place. Batu knew that if he and his brothers could capture the Invader, its spirit would bring great power to Our Place. The wise one, Sanisi, began the dance of Grugru the Worm. Grugru would hide under the leaves of Kintura and become invisible to its prey. She would then wait for some unsuspecting small one to wander into her trap. Grugru was very patient.

The wise one fell to his knees, and then he lay face down on the ground. He began to undulate, mimicking Grugru. He moved around the fire, half crawling and half moving, worm-like. Then Sanisi began to chant. His words told the story of Mataku, the first Hunter to feel the presence of the Invader. Mataku, who had walked with Batu's grandfather, had been many days with Dream Smoke. He became one with Grugru, crawled to Kintura and covered himself with her leaves. He lay still beneath the leaves of Kintura for many days. Then one night, after Sun had left Our Place, Mataku felt the presence of the Invader.

"Invader is like a cat," said Sanisi. "He can see at night and can hear like Blind Flyer. He leaves no scent, can see through trees, and lives in Big River. He is very clumsy. His feet step heavily on the paths. However, he cannot see through the leaves of Kintura."

Then Sanisi said that to capture the Invader, the Hunters must be like Grugru. They must crawl like a worm, bury themselves under the leaves of Kintura and lie in wait for many days without food or drink. They must not move, not even their lips or eyelids. Even breathing must come close to stopping. When the time comes, Hunters must come to life and immediately pursue the Invader with the passion of a young Hunter on his first Chase.

Batu became aware of Sanisi gazing at him across the smoldering fire. The wise one cocked his head to one side, and he stared at Batu with steady, piercing eyes. A band of white circled each one of Sanisi's eyes. Red bordered Sanisi's black stained teeth from under his nose to halfway between his lower lip and his chin. His bare torso and chest had six black stripes on either side. His arms and legs were painted black. Sanisi was Grugru.

Sanisi began to chant the praises of Hunters. "They will bring great power to the village," he declared. "The Invader, who violates Our Place, will be captured. The great Hunters of Our Place will lay in wait like Grugru until the clumsy-footed Invader comes near. Then a Hunter will leap from his hiding place beneath Kintura's leaves and pierce the Invader's scale-like skin with a dart tipped with the body-numbing Anuu juice."

The seven Hunters could feel themselves changing into Grugru. Batu began crawling like Grugru. One by one the other Hunters followed suit until they were all mimicking Sanisi's Grugru Dance. Batu, the leader, stopped at River Path. He knew that the Invader lived in Big River. Batu began crawling down River Path.

Sanisi was the last to leave the campfire. He was no longer crawling. Instead, he ran low to the ground, monkey style—legs bent, back bent, hands on the ground. He approached each of the Hunters and put his head close to theirs. Then he slipped something into each one's hand. Batu was last.

"Batu, you are the great Hunter," Sanisi murmured, "This is your hunt. You are Grugru, quiet and patient while you wait, quick and powerful when you attack." Sanisi put Life Seed into Batu's hand. "When you hear the clumsy-footed Invader and rise up to capture him, eat Life Seed immediately. It will give you great strength."

Batu took Life Seed in his hand and continued to crawl. He was scanning the horizon when he saw, to his left and many steps from River Path, an opening between two giant Bakuyus. Some force drew him toward the opening between the trees. He knew that he must go in that direction to find his spot. Some Hunters had already left River Path to look for their spot while others continued. Soon all Hunters would be in various spots between Big River and Home Circle . . . waiting.

Then Batu saw Kintura. He knew that was his spot. When he reached Kintura, he began digging away layers of leaves. He dug out an area large enough for him to lie in, lay on his back and covered himself with the Kintura leaves. After Batu had covered himself, he became very still. He relaxed and let Dream Smoke take him. His breathing slowed to imperceptibility. Then Batu waited.

∗ ∗ ∗

VI Charles Jenkins sat in the submerged two-person underwater craft. KC and Jenkins were both VIs. The only qualification for becoming a VI, or Venuvian Integrate—besides the dreaded Monthly Full Body Inventory, otherwise known as the Monthly —was to hold a Venuvian position. The Venuvian aliens had arrived in Earth's solar system over 200 years ago. KC was officially an Advanced VI. To become an Advanced VI, in addition to taking the Monthlies, one had to complete a 4-year course at a Venuvian Academy and pass a vigorous physical requirement every year. The great majority of those seeking to enter the space travel program accepted low-level positions just to qualify. They were looking for adventure or, for some reason, they wanted to escape from Earth.

Jenkins scanned the control panel studying three monitors. One monitor displayed the satellite's view of KC—whatever it could pick up through the thick vegetation. KC, who was the VI on the ground, had to find the unit that recorded and transmitted native activity and replace its power supply. It was difficult to get decent video images, but with the help of the transmitters in KC's suit and some computer enhancement, Jenkins could follow his reddish-yellow shape as it moved through the tropical rainforest. The second monitor displayed what KC saw through his night-apparatus. The third monitor showed a 360-degree picture of what surrounded KC. During these retrieval missions, one fear was that a VI would get a surprise visit by a big cat. Even with the 360-degree scanning device mounted on KC's headgear, Jenkins might not detect a big cat until it was dangerously close. However, the biggest concern during a retrieval mission came from humans. The Adabuma, the tribe that inhabited this area, were fiercely territorial and would not hesitate to kill and devour anyone caught trespassing on their territory.

Two Venuvian academies offered programs that studied every detail of the Adabuma in the Amazon Basin. The Adabuma had somehow remained isolated from the rest of the world. There were only two other isolated groups on Earth that had managed to avoid the encroachment of the more technically advanced societies—both were located in Central Africa. The academies stressed that, although as much information as possible should be gathered, detection must be avoided.

Even though there had been one near detection here a hundred and fifty years ago, Jenkins felt that the chance of KC running into any of the local inhabitants was slight. Forty-eight hours prior to KC's arrival, the area had been totally scanned by satellite. The Environmental Data Collection Module had monitored the Adabuma. There were no traces of any unusual movements. In fact, the Adabuma had been unusually quiet for the past four days.

KC peered through his night-vision apparatus. He had trained six years for this assignment—three at the academy and three in a rainforest. There had even been simulated attacks by big cats, but this was different. Training was like a game. This was the real thing, and KC knew that reality had a way of being unpredictable.

This recovery mission required replacing the power module in the Environment Observation Unit. Few of the VIs who had studied isolated cultures actually got a chance to walk on a path, or see the trees, or feel and smell the thick jungle of the people they studied. KC knew as much as a VI could know about the Adabuma, and now he was actually there, walking, breathing, and seeing.

"Jenkins, you see anything I don't see?"

"All clear."

"It was more fun at VI School. Then at least I'd get jumped by a big cat or fall into a pit or even get attacked by a night-walking Adabuma."

"All clear," Jenkins repeated dryly. "Just get in, exchange the power supply, and get out."

"I just wish something would happen." KC would never forget that wish.

* * *

Batu felt it. It was not the small insects crawling over his body, sometimes stopping to rest and accepting his subdued warmth, sometimes burrowing under him, sometimes biting. It was not the dryness in his mouth, the gnawing hunger pangs in his stomach, the aches in his muscles, or the stiffness in his bones that awakened Batu's senses. He felt movement, soundless vibrations. It was not a movement of Our Place. Batu did not know how long he had been lying under Kintura's leaves, not moving, willing his senses and bodily functions to slow, almost stop. But there was still that inner spot that was awake, wound like a tightly coiled spring, ready to explode and bring his near comatose body to life. The movement was coming closer. Each vibration was like a silent scream. Then it happened. Like an uncontrolled eruption inside Batu's entire body. In one motion, Batu rolled to his stomach, sprang to his feet, and let out a blood-chilling scream.

* * *

Jenkins nervously watched the monitors. Jenkins was a worrier. Nothing had gone wrong, nothing should go wrong, but he still worried that something would go wrong. He worried that a cat would charge KC so suddenly that Jenkins would not have time to warn him. He worried that KC would trip over an unseen branch and would need Jenkins to exit the underwater craft and come to his aid. He worried he would make a mistake, the mission would fail and it would be his fault. He worried an uncharted meteor would crash through the jungle canopy and the whole area would explode.

Now, as he studied the monitors, he didn't worry about the local tribe. The monitors were mostly pale green with light and dark outlines. Jenkins carefully studied his monitors looking for any sign of change. Then he heard it. It was somewhere near KC but barely audible. The sound sent a chill through Jenkins. It could have been a weird audio feedback, but Jenkins knew instinctively that it was not.

The Venuvians had trained him to recognize every known jungle sound. This sound was human. "KC, I have detected human activity."

"Human?"

"Yes."

"The only humans around here are Adabuma."

"Be advised that there is a human in the vicinity."

"What's the location?"

"It's in front of you somewhere; I haven't picked up a visual yet."

At that moment, there was another yell, this time much closer. Jenkins saw the figure before KC did. Definitely human. It suddenly appeared out of the ground, sprang to its feet, stumbled, regained its footing, yelled, and then began running toward KC. Then another figure appeared, already running, and then another.

"Abort," ordered Jenkins. Jenkins's adrenaline was flowing. There was a definite edge to his voice.

"Abort?"

"Abort!" This time Jenkins yelled.

"What about—" Fifty meters in front of KC, something or someone appeared. The figure had suddenly stood up, stumbled, hesitated for a few seconds, and then let out a fierce cry. KC knew that the cry signaled the beginning of a hunt. He saw the figure put a hand to its mouth and begin to run in KC's direction but not directly toward him. KC realized the figure had not yet seen him. "How many?" asked KC.

"Seven so far, but scans weren't detecting them until they stood."

"Where are they?"

"All in front of you, so far."

"How far to the module?"

"Get the hell out of there, KC. Abort! Abort!"

"How far to the module?" KC's voice seemed calm and hard.

Jenkins knew KC was not yet ready to abort, and to try to convince him to abort would be a time waster. "You've got 614 meters—your best time for changing and resetting a module is 6.3 minutes. Then 1,500 meters back to the craft. If you can get past the Adabuma."

KC slowly crouched. He had a better chance of going undetected if he remained motionless. At the academy, KC had prepared for what the Venuvians had considered every possible emergency. None of the possibilities had included an encounter with seven undetected Adabuma. Now, as KC crouched near a bush, an Adabuman hunter passed within twenty meters, and at least six others were in the vicinity.

The Venuvians, supposedly the bearers of a scientifically advanced civilization, had miscalculated. A group of Hunters was closing in with the intent of capturing him—or worse. KC had a few seconds to decide: abort or complete a mission he'd trained the last six years for. His first job was to survive.

* * *

Pain shot through Batu's body. His mind ignored it. The Hunt— that was his focus. He began running. The Chase had begun, and knowledge of the Hunt would come. He was chewing on a Life Seed and soon the pain would fade from his arms, legs, and chest. The Spirit would return. The Chase would not wait. Batu heard the cry of another Hunter, and then another. Batu let out another yell, one that was slightly different from his first. A chorus of yells responded.

The Net was complete and all the Hunters were running. The Chase was on. Batu cried out again and all the Hunters came to a complete stop.

Every Hunter listened for the slightest movement, hoping to hear a sound from their prey. No one breathed. Batu's trained ear heard nothing, not a twig snapping, not the swish of a bush swinging back into place—nothing. Batu's mind had a flash of clarity. It was his ability to clear his mind that had made Batu the great Hunter.

The Prey—what was the Prey? How did the Prey think? What would the Prey do? Batu realized that he had made a mistake.

* * *

KC broke into a fast jog, hoping that all the hunters had joined the chase.

"Jenkins."

"Here," replied Jenkins.

"In about one or two minutes, one of the hunters will yell. I want you to track his every movement and sound. If there is a second yell, track him too, and tie their sound into my audio." KC accelerated into a full sprint, thankful for the rigorous training he had gone through after accepting this assignment. He knew he could keep up this grueling pace for at least ten minutes but certainly no more than fifteen. Plenty of time to get to the module, change and reset the pod, and get back to the craft. That is, if there were no obstacles. But there were obstacles, seven of them—seven strong and swift hunters—and KC was their prey.

KC knew that with his equipment, he could not outrun an Adabuman hunter. But his equipment was the only edge he had. If he could not outrun the Adabuma, he would have to outsmart them. KC heard the yell that meant that all the hunters would stop and listen for any sound. KC stopped and tried not to make any sound. Even his heavy breathing became controlled.

If a hunter heard anything, he'd signal the leader and the chase would continue; if not, the hunters would wait for a signal from the leader. KC hoped the hunters would keep running toward the river. Still, he suspected their paths would likely cross.

* * *

Batu stood erect. He sniffed the air. Listened for the slightest sound that might indicate the whereabouts of the Prey. Batu could feel it. He knew that the Invader was no longer in front of him. He was too clumsy to outrun the Hunters. He could not feel Our Place. But he was clever. He would not try to outrun the Hunters: he would try to outmaneuver them or try to trick them. Batu must retrace his steps. What should his next command be? If the Hunters reversed the Chase, they might pass the undetected Invader again.

Batu thought about Fake Bush, the small animal that boys chased before they were Hunters. Fake Bush, when pursued, often would curl into a ball, disguising itself as a bush. The boys would usually run past it before they discovered Fake Bush's trick. As a boy, Batu had always been the first to discover Fake Bush's deception and call for the others to retrace their steps. It had been an early sign that Batu would be a great Hunter. Batu now gave the only command that might catch the Invader. He cried out for his men to retrace their steps and search for Fake Bush.

* * *

Jenkins heard the command. Although he was familiar with the Adabuma language, he only caught a few words. His immediate focus turned to tracking the lead hunter. The monitors picked up the sound, and within seconds his bead was on the leader.

"They're heading back in your direction. The leader said something about 'bush.' I've got you tied into his audio. Now let me get you a visual."

Immediately KC could see the hunters' figures moving toward him in a zigzag fashion. This time they were looking more closely. The net was growing tighter. KC began to run toward the module again—running, thinking, calculating. How could he get past the net?

"Jenkins, we have to create a distraction."

"What do you mean 'we'? There's not much I can do from here."

"Think of something." KC was talking more to himself than to Jenkins. "An explosion, a flash of light—do you think Central could provide us with fireworks?"

A loud beeping indicated he was approaching the buried module just fifteen meters in front of him. At the same time, the Environmental Data Collection Module pushed its way out of the ground with one meter of soil above it.

"I have module contact. Power supply exchange procedure in progress." KC fell to one knee, and within minutes he had opened the access hatch and removed the old power supply. He inserted the new power supply into the module, made the connection, rechecked the connections, checked all the readouts, rechecked the readouts, closed the access panel, then hit his utility belt. The module sank back into the ground.

"Power supply exchange complete." KC expertly rearranged the ground coverings so the area looked undisturbed, removed a small spray canister from another pocket, and sprayed the area with an odor neutralizer. The whole procedure had taken 5.9 minutes, a record for KC. He was about to replace the spray canister when he stopped.

"Time before the Adabuma arrive?"

"At current speed, between five and seven minutes."

"Is this spray neutralizer flammable?"

"Slightly," said Jenkins without enthusiasm.

"Pressure?"

"Five hundred bars," said Jenkins. "Don't forget, the Venuvians want us to leave no evidence of our visit."

"Would they consider a captured VI evidence of our visit?"

"Yes."

"This old power supply must still have enough energy to create a spark."

"More than enough. I don't know what's on your mind, but it sounds dangerous."

"Just a diversion," KC said casually. "How do I get this power supply open without totally destroying it?"

"I don't know."

"If I could create a spark, I could start a fire with the odor-neutralizing spray."

"You could."

"How about I use the fire to burn through the hose on my emergency breathing apparatus?"

Jenkins saw immediately where KC was going. Once the fire had burned through the hose, the escaping oxygen mixture, which was under 500 bars of pressure, would turn the oxygen tank into a projectile. KC removed the oxygen tank from a side pocket. He began using it like a hammer, trying to break open the power supply.

"Any chance of this exploding?" KC asked.

"Slight, very slight."

He cracked the power supply. *Now to just open it.* Then KC heard another hoot.

* * *

Batu was beginning to fear that he had somehow let the Invader escape when he heard it. The sound of the Hunters jostling the bushes almost drowned it out, but Batu's finely tuned ears detected something that was not of Our Place. With one soft command cry, Batu ordered the Hunters to stop and listen. Silence. With a series of bird-like cries, Batu told the Hunters to run twenty paces, then stop and listen. Batu did not move. He heard the unfamiliar sound again. This time, he got a better sense of what direction it had come from. The Hunters had stopped and were listening. Batu began to sprint toward the sound while giving another series of cries telling the Hunters to follow him and tighten the Net. The Chase had resumed.

* * *

"I think they've spotted you," said Jenkins. "They'll engage in about two minutes."

KC began to work feverishly. "I'm going to light up when I get a spark," he said.

"Judging from their direction and speed, I think they already know where you are."

One more smash with the oxygen tank and the power supply opened. KC's night-vision apparatus did not work on cold objects so he had to flip up his night-vision apparatus. He ripped out two wires and connected them. He jumped as a larger than expected spark leaped from the wires. "Still plenty of spark." KC pulled out the odor neutralizer.

"One minute, max," Jenkins reminded.

KC saw a green mist escaping from the odor-neutralizing dispenser. He touched the two wires together again—another flash. KC cursed under his breath.

"What?" Jenkins asked, with obvious concern in his voice.

"Flame but no fire," answered KC.

"You'll have to completely saturate the hose to get it to burn," Jenkins said firmly. "Thirty seconds."

KC watched as the green mist began to form a film on the hose. He had only one more chance. If he didn't wait for enough mist to escape, there might not be a fire. If he waited too long, the Adabuma hunters would be joining him. KC touched the wires. The hose ignited.

"We have ignition," KC said. He lowered his night-vision apparatus. "Help me get around these guys before the tank launches." He took off in a sprint.

"Fifteen degrees right, quick!" said Jenkins. There was some relief in his voice, but it still sounded tense. There was a small explosion. KC could hear the oxygen canister shooting through the brush. It was getting louder.

"Reverse direction," Jenkins ordered. "Now!"

KC heard the canister pass, followed by the hunters.

"It looks like the hunters have taken the bait," said KC.

"All but one," said Jenkins.

"What?"

"The leader's still between you and the river."

* * *

Batu saw the light. It was not of Our Place. He heard the strange explosion and the snakelike hissing. He also heard the bushes being smashed by . . . by what? It was a different sound than the Invader made. The Invader was clever—too clever to make such a light, too clever to cause such noises. It was a trick. Batu stood his ground while the other Hunters continued their Chase. The sounds of Hunters faded—and then cries of victory. Batu still did not move. Then he heard it. The sound of someone running! Hunters did not make such noise. Batu knew it had to be the Invader. He assumed a crouching position close to the ground and waited.

* * *

"You're heading straight for him," said Jenkins. "He's about fifty meters ahead. Turn right."

KC made a sharp right. He heard a cry from the leader.

"The leaders is on the move again," said Jenkins. "He's on a course to intercept you before you reach the river. Looks like he's locked in on you. Be careful, those guys carry poison."

"Yeah." KC was conserving his strength.

"Maybe you should get your stun gun ready," said Jenkins.

"Deadly," said KC.

The stun gun was set with a charge strong enough to put down a big cat. It could kill a man.

"You're on a collision course," said Jenkins.

KC saw a figure approaching on his right. KC knew he

254

could not win a footrace. He stopped abruptly and watched the leader run a few steps and stop as well. The figure began moving slowly toward KC.

"Damn, he's good," muttered KC.

"You can't hang out too long," said Jenkins. "The rest of the gang is heading straight for you."

KC waited. He could hear the others coming.

"Move KC!" yelled Jenkins.

Hoping the sound of the approaching hunters would cover his movement, KC sprinted a few meters to his left, then stopped again. The leader kept going in the same direction. KC made another dash straight toward the river. The leader stopped to listen. The other hunters were nearby. The leader turned and headed straight for the river.

* * *

Batu had made another mistake. He knew the Invader was heading toward Big River, but instead of heading for Big River himself, he had tried to cut off the Invader. Now Batu headed for Big River, ignoring the noise made by the Invader. He hoped to catch the Invader before he could escape into Big River. The Hunters' Net should keep the Invader from retracing his steps, so he would have to go to Big River. Batu reached the Big River, crouched low to the ground, prepared his poison dart, and waited.

* * *

"You've got six hunters behind, and the leader is between you and the vehicle," said Jenkins.

"I've got a visual," whispered KC. "I'm going to take out

255

the leader." KC headed straight for him.

* * *

Batu heard it. The Invader approaching. Batu leaped up, numbing poison dart in hand, ready to drive it into the Invader. For a fraction of a second, he could see the Invader's silhouette. That was the last thing he remembered before he was blinded by a flash of light.

* * *

KC raised his night-vision apparatus and activated his emergency torchlight. He stopped face-to-face with the leader. KC had seen visuals of the Adabuma hunters, but none compared to the real thing. The hunter was momentarily frozen by KC's light. The leader's eyes were strong, steady, wise. There was no hatred, no fear, just a hunter seeking prey. KC immediately delivered a blow to Batu's chest. The blow, delivered with expert accuracy, was enough to knock the hunter to the ground and render him temporarily unconscious.

"Ready to come aboard," said KC.

He jumped into the river just as the craft pushed its way above the water. On shore, the other hunters arrived and surrounded Batu just as the craft submerged with KC on board. KC stepped into the main compartment dripping wet.

"Okay Jenkins, let's go home."

Nate's Place
By Mike Clarke

About the author

Michael started writing fiction in 2014 when a story wouldn't let go of his brain. Hand-written notes, scribbled in the dark, snowballed into carpal tunnel syndrome, editing, and revisions. He's published two novels in the *Ascension* series, *MetaSentient* and *Numen Hunting*. His science fiction is speculative, including many post-human themes such as the artificial intelligence singularity, mind uploads, robots, and virtual worlds. To keep things interesting, he sprinkles in space-time theories as well as metaphysical concepts, such as sentient universe and aliens tinkering with human DNA over millennia. Michael lives and roams the countryside with his vagabond wife, Susan, in Burnaby, B.C., Canada.

Find out more at https://ascendpublishing.home.blog.

* * *

The hot exhaust pipes ping as I step down out of the ancient SUV, the smell of hot metal and cooking beach grass wafting up as I listen for the sound of surf. While senses trigger vivid flashes of exploring the dunes as a child, they unbalance the numb grey of my emotions.

Approaching the only potential structure, my retro sneakers lose grip in the white sand blown across the walkway. The ocean wind has blown tendrils of sand across the yard, but this beautiful isolation might help to fill the hole in my heart, one tiny grain of sand at a time.

As my glasses turn a dark shade of blue, the rounded granite outcrop reveals no discernible handles or hinges, just a smooth, black door. I guess it's inevitable I would end up here. No place left to go. I have to lift my glasses to see a small panel. I rasp, "Nate here. Open sesame," and cough.

A green light flickers as the door opens with a pleasant sigh.

I can't recall the last time I spoke out loud.

Stepping into a cave, I remove my sunglasses and blink as my eyes adjust to the darkness. A fleeting presence flickers in my mind, but I shake my head slightly.

"Hello, anyone here?"

Echoes and silence, but not complete silence. The longer I stand, the more small noises stand out above the ringing in my ears, the breath of air circulating and faint skittish sounds of metal on stone echoing in distant rooms.

Did my eyes adjust or has the lighting come up? Not sure. A glass ring encircles the domed foyer, dispersing sunlight as I move through the rooms. Looking up pierces my brain fog. Even the ceiling stones are granite beams joining each other at the top of the dome. Who built this place?

I start as my sneaker squeaks on the polished granite.

"Jeez, chill Nate." My voice echoes down the hall, leading my eyes to peer deeper. Might as well take the tour.

In the largest hallway, where I've strolled, the three-meter arched ceiling sparkles from a strip of dispersed sunlight. The cave opens into a circular room, with a two-meter-high swath of blue-tinted windows facing south, toward the mouth of the harbor. "Ooh, nice."

I jump as I catch sight of what looks like another person in the corner of my eye. A life-sized portrait of a woman with wavy brown hair gazes into my eyes with a smile. Is my mind playing tricks on me or did she change her expression? Just in case, I wave, saying, "Hi, I'm Nate."

No answer, sanity restored. I step up to examine the image. It seems to be static, but you never know these days. With the tip of my finger, I touch its smooth glass. Turning my fingertip to check, yes, no dust.

I move to a large captain's chair in front of the window. It's hard, smooth, and black. Carbon, I'm guessing, and strangely springy and comfortable. "Ahh. Not so bad."

It has been a long couple of days. What would've normally taken hours by car two decades ago now takes days. I've had to ford streams, pulling the three-ton beast by winch across slimy boulders in fast moving water, blasting my way across bogs, engine roaring and black mud kicking up in a rooster tail. Nature is reclaiming the place, so I slept in the truck, back seats folded down, listening to wolf-coyotes crying and chuffing in the distance. Coyotes wouldn't be problem but these were apex predators.

Getting away and healing seemed like the right thing to do. At least, that's what the doctors said. All these years of clawing my way up, controlling my world, and creating a family should come to this, letting it all go. Sleep calls my exhausted body back into the chair.

$$* \quad * \quad *$$

"Morning already?"

I swear I can hear a woman's voice humming in another room as I open my eyes and watch a gentle surf rolling onto the beach. The chair seems to lift me to standing, as I shuffle off to the bathroom I'd seen off the main hallway. On the way, I peek into the kitchen to check the voice. Nothing. In the bathroom, the taps work, and there's hot water and a shower. No soap, but who cares after slogging it out for two days? My clothes smell like I've just cleaned a sewer. "Oh, gross. Any towels?" Yep, fluffy white ones. "What is up with this place?"

I step back out into the room with a view, tying a towel around my waist.

"Nate, you're going nuts. She didn't just wink at you. It's all in your head." My feet slap against the floor as I pad further down the hall toward the kitchen. "What the . . ." There's a fresh pot of coffee steaming on the stone counter.

$$* \quad * \quad *$$

I'm sitting here sipping coffee and what skitters across the counter and into the sink? It's a big freaking metallic spider, copper colored, with fine little legs and joints. It's cleaning dishes! Oh, so that's what keeps this place clean. "So you're what I heard yesterday when I got in."

It stops and two crab-like eyes swivel around to scan me. The sharp knife-like scraping tools on its front pinchers could do some damage. I'm tensing up, but it goes back to its work and ignores me.

I hear more skittering in the hallway.

Doing laundry, maybe? And it is. A small bot works, picking through my other clothes that are just as filthy as the ones I've taken off, or worse. Nice breeze.

It's creepy. Her eyes follow me whenever I walk through the main living room. Finding the bedroom space with another wrap-around window facing south, I toss my bag in the corner. The bed's even turned down like a five-star hotel, and through the window, I watch the wind whip the tops off the gentle surf. Nice.

There's a cotton robe hanging on the door. Perfect. My mind starts nagging. This is too good to be true.

A wave of grief washes over me. I catch my breath and sit on the bed, gasping, as my knees wobble. The vision of nano turning my wife and daughter into pink goo flashes in my mind's eye. I gasp as my knees wobble.

"It should have been me, not them, damn it!" I pound my fist into the comfy bed with a soft, plomp sound. There's a skittering outside my door. Little crab eyes swivel around its edge. "I'm okay."

It skitters away to return with a carefully folded stack of laundry on its head. Despite the grey veil in my mind, I can't help myself and laugh. "Ha, you're a cute little bugger." I automatically play a dialog in my mind describing the cute little robot to my daughter, Violet, causing a stab to my heart. I'll never get to tell her. Not one for uncontrolled sobbing, I shock myself at how easily it flows.

Forcing myself to get dressed, I stretch and see what looks like a boathouse on the far side of the beach, among some rounded outcrops. "Get out for a walk every day," they said. "Don't just sit around and feel sorry for yourself." Yeah, some exploring's in order. Shake this off. I throw on a white t-shirt and shorts from the clean laundry pile and grab a pair of flip-flops from my bag. My glasses turn a dark shade as the door opens and I emerge into the sultry heat.

I slip on the flip-flops; the sand burns my feet. "Oh, this takes me back." I walk to the edge of the small grass-covered dunes. Inhaling the combination of cooking beach grass, ocean spray and washed-up seaweed is re-firing childhood memories. "My family won't experience this. They're gone." My mind swirls back into the grey fog.

The hair stands up on the back of my neck as I hear dry grass crunching underfoot. That's not me! I turn around slowly, feeling the energy flow out of my fingertips. A doe is chewing on the sweet peas growing wild along the dunes. She blinks her brown eyes and keeps on munching.

"No fear. How long since you've seen a human?"

She just flinches her tail and ignores me, so I turn and keep on walking to the beach, crunching over the dried tangle of eelgrass and seaweed. The water's warm and reflects the red roof of a boathouse.

The door swings open, grinding sand underneath. I've placed my hand on a black glass pad. Lights flicker. They come to life, illuminating a small dingy leaning on the wall in front of a larger, upside-down boat. An electric motor is clamped to a bench nearby and plugged into a charging station, the far wall lined with lobster traps.

"Lobster! Dang!" I do a little dance over to the bench to examine the tools. "Yep, everything is here. Tomorrow morning we'll set a few traps, skipper." I explore the traps to check their state of repair. They seem to be freshly printed. At the end of the bench sits a pile of mangled pots. Weird.

Walking back to the house, I notice the glint of brass on the beach. There's a large crab-shaped bot laying there, as I approach, half covered in sand and seaweed. I pull it up and untangle a long piece of yellow rope twisted around its legs. It doesn't move, I carry it back to the house, recovering a lost soldier. I approach and the door opens quickly, three smaller brass and copper bots scrambling out. I set the one I found down and they clean the sand off its listless body, then carry it away toward the inner recesses. The wheels of my analytical mind spin. These crab-bots are either autonomous with social capabilities or centrally controlled.

Not sure I trust them, I look back at the muddy truck at the edge of the trees, my mind plunging back into the grey abyss.

They could have said thanks. Numbed, I shrug, toss off my flip-flops and shuffle off to the kitchen.

"Okay, what's going on here?" The fridge contains water, and what seems to be hamburger and pasta. I take a deep breath. It doesn't make sense. I'm supposed to buy a getaway cottage on a remote beach and I get a spooky robotic cave, carved in stone?

A female voice from the living room calls, "Nate, please come in. I've some explaining to do." The woman in the portrait is now sitting in the chair she'd been leaning on, waving me to the captain's chair.

"I'm Angela. Please come sit down."

I do sit, but gingerly, half expecting the arms of the chair to grab me. "Are you in this house?"

"Yes, as a matter of speaking. I am this house."

"So, you live here?"

"Yes. It's a long story. Are you comfortable?"

"Yes, well, physically, anyway."

"You realize anything this nice should have cost more on the market."

I nod. "A lot more."

"When I saw that you were looking for a getaway, I couldn't resist. Our personalities match up perfectly."

"Our personalities? Wait a sec, Angela Smith? You built this place? You passed away almost twenty years ago."

"Yes, that's me, and yes, I did. My body did. The gravestone's out there in the dunes."

I lean back in the chair, soaking in the strange news. "So, I'm speaking to a copy of Angela's mind?"

"My mind, me."

Of course. I must be sitting there, gape-faced, because she smiles and continues. "I presented you with an opportunity perfect for your budget."

"How do you know my budget?"

"Come on Nate, we both know you're careless with passwords. I took a peek at your balances and saw that you cashed out nicely from your AI services company. I can tell you more later but, the accident. It didn't happen because of anything you did."

My face flushes with rage. "What the hell do you know about the accident?" I stand then, my knees buckling.

"I know that it's why you're here, and why you got out of your company. I also know how it came about. Yours isn't the only company I can get into."

"You're a hacker?"

"Not a black hat, but it keeps me in the loop these days."

"There's lots of news out there. You needn't hack for it."

"Oh, that," she says, waving her hand dismissively. "That's all bullshit. Hardly any of it resembles the truth."

"Back to the house. How did you make an offer only to me?"

She lowers her glance, looks up with her eyes and smiles. "The realty company is loose with their passwords too, so I made an individual proposal that only you would see and did the paperwork behind the scenes."

The hackles are up on my neck. "So, I really own you?"

"Ha, don't let that get to your head, young man. You own this house and the property it sits on. I live here too."

I've had enough of this dance. "In a computer system that I own."

"Technically, yes but we need to come to an agreement, and that needs to happen before the seller's remorse clause expires."

"Aha, I'm getting this then. You need me and I get to live here," I say flatly. "And if I don't agree, your estate rips up the contract and throws me out."

"Essentially." Her eyes soften as she tilts her head, giving her long hair a shake.

"We don't seem to trust each other, but I admit you've been very kind and hospitable, so far. How long before the clause expires?"

"Ten days. I know all about you and I like what I see so far, Nate. So, this is about you trusting me. Let's give it a few days and see how it works out, OK?"

"Agreed. It's weird, but let's sleep on this and see what it looks like in the morning."

"There's one favor I'd like to ask. There was a previous owner, and I need your help with something."

"I don't mean to prod but did he enter into a similar agreement with you?"

She crosses her arms and quickly reverses it, changing seating position, clearly uncomfortable with my line of questioning. "Yes, he did, and we lived together for ten years. He rebuilt the boat house out there. It was a kind of obsession with him, really. He said it gave him reason to live."

"*Old Man and the Sea?*"

"No, more like *Moby Dick.*"

"A whale?"

"Well, a whale of a lobster."

"Seriously?" I fight back a smile, the absurdity of the situation drawing me out of the brain fog. "He drowned out there chasing lobster?"

"He was testing a fishing bot one day and didn't return. We never found the body, although his jacket washed up on the beach. Here's the thing. I uploaded my mind into this house when I died of cancer. He was going to join me eventually, but he uploaded his mind into that fishing bot first. Wanted to explore the ocean."

"You're computer folks, and have a backup, right? For him?"

"No, only what we uploaded into the bot. He only backed up his work when he'd tested things eight times. That was number seven."

"Sorry to hear that."

"I'd like you to retrieve the bot."

"Whoa, for you two to live happily ever after? This is heavy stuff. What if I can't find it?"

"I'll help you. I have access to detailed sat imagery and I know where it isn't, so I can guide you to the spots where it may be."

My eyes betray me at this point. I figure that the trapped animal look is easy to spot and detect a twitch of satisfaction on her face. I sigh with resignation. "I guess that's it, then. I'm going out to check the gear and get the boat ready for tomorrow morning."

✳ ✳ ✳

I throw on some jeans, sneakers and a t-shirt and stroll to the boathouse. It is cool inside the brick building. A guy with a green flannel work shirt and rubber boots stares back at me from a faded photo pinned to the roughed in wall. "So, I'm picking up where you left off, huh?"

Using rope and pulley, I lift the boat, turning it over and pulling it onto the skids. Through the open the doors I can't see much. Better safe than sorry, so I decide to scope things out.

I ship the oars and drag the smaller dinghy out onto the skids, nearly falling on the slippery beams. I then pull the dinghy around and head out to deeper water, hearing the small waves slapping against the flat of the bow. It doesn't take long to lose sight of the bottom. Looking down, it's jet black. No telling what's down there or how deep it is.

I realize that I don't have an indefinite amount of rope, or arms to pull the traps from any significant depth. I need to do my homework, get a chart of the harbor, and some diving gear.

* * *

Back in the boat house, I open drawers and boxes and find a set of rolled up, plastic-coated charts. As I flatten them out, there's a red circle drawn around a set of shoals not far offshore. That's the most likely spot for testing, and not too deep.

Three traps are already weighted with flat rocks so I'll just use those. I lift the traps into the boat and carefully coil up the ropes, then tie the buoys. That should be enough until I get the hang of it.

Time for dinner. As I enter the house and remove my flip-flops, the fragrance of tomato sauce and pasta embraces me. I half expect to see my wife, Becky, standing there in the kitchen, but there are two copper and brass bots on the counter, one stirring the sauce with a black spoon, the other peering into a boiling pot of water. Who is cooking me dinner—Angela or the bots?

I look back to Angela's portrait and just see her static image as I walk into the bedroom to freshen up. When I walk back into the living room, Angela waves.

"Hi Nate. How was your afternoon?"

"Nice, I got a good hike and swim in, prepped the pots and boat. I see we have some helpers."

"Dinner is served."

"I'm starving, haven't eaten a whole meal in days."

A bot swivels its eyes to me and buzzes, "Bon appetit."

The salt air and hard work knock me out.

✳ ✳ ✳

I wake to the distant sound of seagulls and surf. In the kitchen, my breakfast burrito is hot in the microwave as the coffee machine beeps its completion.

"Ahh, life is good. Thanks!" I say to the walls.

Twin mechanical eyes pop from behind the microwave. "De nada."

✳ ✳ ✳

A light breeze off the land brings the complex aroma of beach and forest as I walk across the dew-dampened grass. A tap on the wrist compass to check its function. It buzzes. Check.

Then my own list. Traps, floats, rope, pulleys, cutting tools, clamps. Check.

"Rock 'n' roll."

Scrambling down to the boat's bow, I push off, backward. As I twist the handle and steer to the south, the spray refreshes my senses. Clouds streak the sky and gusts stir up chop on the surface, but it only shudders the frame on this boat. We just bounce along and wallow between the swells. This reminds me of an afternoon thunderstorm blowing in.

There are a few clouds overhead but I see a dark grey smudge on the western horizon, so I'll make just an exploratory dive, and cut it short. All I could find was snorkel gear, so it has to be a shallow survey anyway.

The water is clear and warm, but after thirty minutes of swimming grid lines, I have nothing to show. If I was a lobster, where would I be?

I spy a darker segment of drop-off on the eastern end of the shoal. That will be where the cooler water is. The surf would knock more food into the deep, so off I go. No sooner than I start the grid, I see a yellow rope coated with slime, with a floater that doesn't quite reach the surface, even at low tide. This could be it. I adjust the light strap on my head and do my free-dive breathing prep. Finally, some adventure. Deep down, it's really an escape from the stone around my neck, and the doubts about who I was: a loner who killed the ones he loved. The adrenaline and salt spray of treasure hunting call, and my mind answers. I've got two minutes to get down there and back.

Taking a few deep breaths, I dive, reaching the float and the rope. It's heavy enough that I can pull myself down. Tying a piece of rope to the float, I let it drift upward to the surface with its own white buoy.

I descend, hand-over-hand, into the darkening water, feeling the pressure increase on my mask. My hand hits something solid and slippery. When I swing the thin stream of light, it illuminates the remains of a human leg, tangled in the rope and with large saw-tooth marks on the bone.

Survive! My lungs burn, and my mind screams for breath, so I kick hard. I surface to the sight of low, circling clouds. "Oh crap, that was fast." No time to think.

Back in the boat, I weigh anchor and buzz over to the white buoy. Hooking it toward the wooden roller on the side, I pull. This thing is heavier than I am.

I heave the rope and its grizzly entrapment up and, just as my arms seem they'll give out, I see metal reflecting in the water. It's too heavy for me to lift, so I tie it off to dangle below the boat.

A grey curtain of heavy rain approaches but the boat's slowed by the heavy load it's dragging behind. It churns its way across the harbor while I hold the motor wide open. Hope we have enough juice to make it.

Wet gusts blow the chop-spray back over the boat. This could be a rough landing. Riding a swell up the ramp, I jump out, grab the bow, and struggle up the slimy logs as the rain gusts in. Looking down at the angry chop, I realize I'm lucky not to fall in. The winch whines as it slowly drags the boat and trailing cargo up the ramp. After a struggle, both are inside the boathouse, sand and sea water escaping every crack and opening of the bot.

I give it a tap. No wonder it's so heavy. Hope you're still in there, buddy.

* * *

Inside the house, exhausted, my body falls into the chair. Outside the window, the wind whips the grass as sheets of downpour drench the sand. I sense movement behind me, so I spin the chair around to face Angela. She sits forward on the edge of a chair.

"You found it?"

"Yes, that and something else. His leg was still tangled in the rope. It must have pulled him overboard. A sad way to go."

"Yes, very sad, but I suspected as much when I found his jacket washed up on the beach. I expect the bull sharks took the rest."

"Yeah, most likely since the Gulf Stream came north. How do you want to handle it, the bot and his remains?"

"I'd like to you to bury his remains next to my grave, please. Bring the bot into the house and leave it in the entryway."

I suppress an image of a deformed servant muttering "Yes, Master." So now I'm digging graves. What next? The prospect of driving that beast of a truck to the city brings me back to my new reality. "No time like the present."

∗ ∗ ∗

Dripping with rain, a rusty hand cart with fat tires leans against the boathouse. I wedge the bot up into the cart and drag it to the house. It's met by three smaller bots. I step back as they drag it down the hall and through a black doorway, scurrying away with their prize. Soaked and exhausted, I turn away.

I've never buried anyone before. I wrap this part of my predecessor respectfully in a clean white sheet, much cleaner than my own shirt. After the last shovel of sand, the sun breaks through the clouds and the gentle surf and birdsong fill my empty mind. I sit for a while, catching my breath.

Back at the house, I kick my boots off and pad wet sock footprints toward the bedroom. But I stop and stare at Angela's picture, she and her man standing side by side. Holding hands and smiling.

Printed in Great Britain
by Amazon